Deathless

Deathless

*The Complete, Uncensored, Heartbreaking,
and Amazing Autobiography of Serach bat Asher,
the Oldest Woman in the World*

By Andrew Ramer

Foreword by
Rabbi Amichai Lau-Lavie

RESOURCE *Publications* · Eugene, Oregon

DEATHLESS
The Complete, Uncensored, Heartbreaking,
and Amazing Autobiography of Serach bat Asher,
the Oldest Woman in the World

Resource Publications
An Imprint of Wipf and Stock Publishers
199 W. 8th Ave., Suite 3
Eugene, OR 97401

www.wipfandstock.com

PAPERBACK ISBN: 978-1-5326-1202-2
HARDCOVER ISBN: 978-1-5326-1204-6
EBOOK ISBN: 978-1-5326-1203-9
Manufactured in the U.S.A.

For Constance Tomestic

1929—2017

With love and gratitude.

Your heart and home were a haven

when one was needed more than fifty years ago.

Contents

Foreword

THIS STORY STARTS WITH a little girl, singing to herself behind the tents, not knowing just how deeply soothing her songs are to her grandpa, the patriarch Jacob, shrouded in his grief. As a reward for his healing, Serach bat Asher will become the oldest woman to live within the pages of the Bible, perhaps beyond, and the story, her story, never quite seems to end either. Some stories are worth infinity.

Known to us through a narrative that is part myth, part midrash, part mystery, this lesser-known heroine from the margins of Jewish folklore is enjoying a comeback. After thousands of years in footnotes, Serach's story once again pops up in children's books, feminist anthologies, and in this astounding work of fiction. It's not just a story about the power of song that Serach brings to us, but also a critical message for humanity's progress and for what it means to persist, to resist, to be other, and to belong.

Like other mythic muses, Serach is the one who chooses when to show up and with whom to chat. One hot summer afternoon in the last year of the 20th century I was hanging out on Venice Beach in California when I caught a glimpse of an older woman with white hair and a bikini, rollerblading down the boardwalk, headphones on, and singing loudly. Possibly in Yiddish. That night I started writing about Auntie Mem, a tough old Holocaust survivor who chose to live in California and chose to live, live, live. Some of what she had to say was published and even made it to the stage, her essence living on—always surprising, bitter, not sweet, but funny, loving, and in-your-face real. Whoever that rollerblading woman was, and no matter where the story came from—she profoundly changed my life.

Many years later my dear friend and revered teacher Andrew showed me the outline of a project he'd been working on: the story of the 3,000 years of Serach, including the part where she's living—on Venice Beach. "We've already met, right on the beach," I told him, with amazement. And now I know I'm not the only lucky one. Serach, a heroine with many faces, has a lot to say and she knows how to find the proper channels. That's how she met Andrew.

Andrew Ramer is a brilliant bard who knows how to spin sacred texts and how to queer the very myths we're living. His Serach is a crone with an eye on the big picture and the long arc, a brittle laugh and the wizened wisdom of longevity that has a lot say to our impatient digital days of instant gratification. This is a prophetic work of protest, only somewhat shrouded in the veils of satire and imagined meanderings through time and space, the tale of a survivor, of an often-bitter old woman whose story isn't always easy to read. Through his telling of her travels he is not just telling us her story but is also offering a radical way to reread the original biblical stories themselves, now more queer, more nuanced, and even more interesting.

A longtime scholar and author of midrash, Andrew wrote about this delicate process of retelling in his book Queering the Text: "The text itself changes, and we do as a result. While this may seem radical, it is, in fact, a part of a longstanding anti-fundamentalist strand of the Jewish tradition, which sees the Bible not as a quasi-historical record. . . but as a font of multiple interpretations."

So here she is. Put on your seat belts, and enjoy the ride. And if and when you meet her, on the beach at dusk, in the margins of this book, or in your dreaming, please send regards and pause to listen with attention. This story begins with a girl who is singing, and if you are reading this—she'll be singing her songs for you.

Rabbi Amichai Lau-Lavie

Creator of Storahtelling and the
founding spiritual leader of Lab/Shul NYC

Ours is not a bloodline but a textline.

Amos Oz &
Fania Oz-Salzberger

I want an invented truth.

Clarice Lispector

The Family Tree of Serach bat Asher

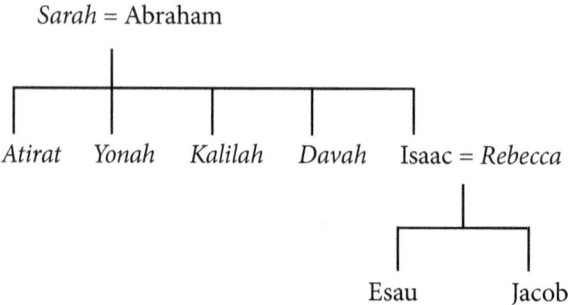

Sarah = Abraham

Atirat   *Yonah*   *Kalilah*   *Davah*   Isaac = *Rebecca*

Esau   Jacob

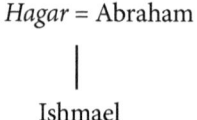

Hagar = Abraham

Ishmael

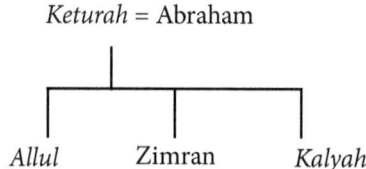

Keturah = Abraham

Allul   Zimran   *Kalyah*

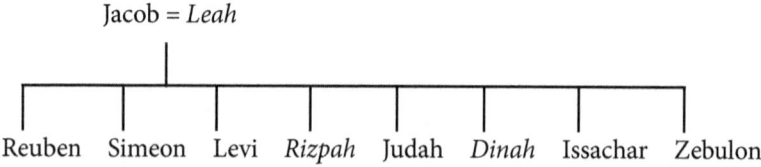

Jacob = *Leah*

Reuben   Simeon   Levi   *Rizpah*   Judah   *Dinah*   Issachar   Zebulon

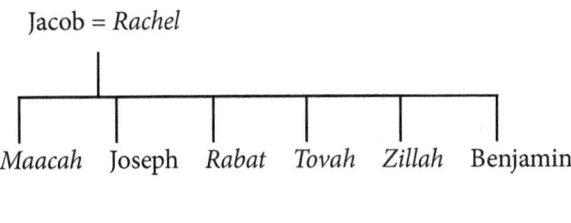

Jacob = *Rachel*

Maacah Joseph *Rabat* *Tovah* *Zillah* Benjamin

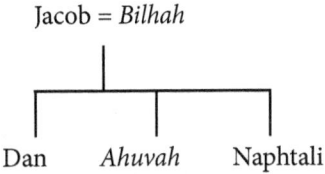

Jacob = *Bilhah*

Dan *Ahuvah* Naphtali

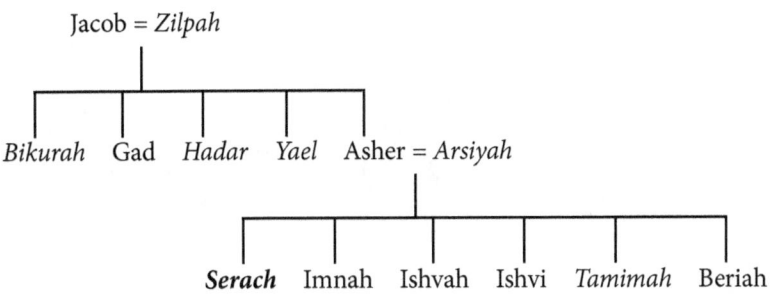

Jacob = *Zilpah*

Bikurah Gad *Hadar* *Yael* Asher = *Arsiyah*

Serach Imnah Ishvah Ishvi *Tamimah* Beriah

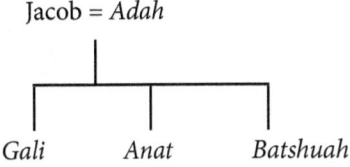

Jacob = *Adah*

Gali *Anat* *Batshuah*

Chapter One

In which I introduce myself
and begin my ancient story

PEOPLE SAY WE HEBREWS are a talkative nation. This is true. It's also true that our contribution to world literature is far greater than our small numbers would indicate. How could this not be the case when the god of our national epic is said to have brought the entire universe into being with words? We are a people of words, a people of the book, as our Muslim cousins call us. In fact we are a people with lots and lots of books. And yet, for every story that we've written or told there are as many that have not been told. Take my own case, for example.

You may have heard of me, as I am mentioned—by name only—three times in the Hebrew Bible. I make my first brief appearance in chapter 46, verse 17 of the book of *Genesis,* in a list of the family members who went down to Egypt with my beloved grandfather, the patriarch Jacob, where I appear among my father's children:

> *Asher's sons: Imnah, Ishvah, Ishvi, and Beriah, and their sister*
> *Serach. Beriah's sons: Heber and Malchiel.*

If you take a look at the full text you will see that almost everyone in the list is male. The few women named, and one unnamed, seem to be asides—but please pay attention to the other female descendant who is named, my aunt Dinah. Later you will understand why.

There's a nearly identical list in the last book of the Hebrew Bible, *Chronicles,* which is very tidy, showing up at the beginning and the end of the book—but my name in those lists won't tell you anything about me, because everything about me was either left out—or cut out—by several sets of ancient editors.

The text of the Torah as it exists today says that I was the only daughter of Asher the son of Jacob, the son of Isaac, the son of Abraham, all of which is true. I *am* the daughter of Asher, but your Torah says nothing else about me, and doesn't mention my mother Arsiyah or my full sister Tamimah at all. In fact, the Bible says almost nothing about most of the women in my family. For instance, the Torah tells us that my Grandfather Jacob had four wives, twelve sons, and just one daughter, Dinah, when in fact he had five wives and thirteen daughters. But where are their stories? Forgotten, never written down, or deliberately edited out of the book, for a variety of reasons that you will come to understand in due course.

In this memoir I promise to tell you the truth just as I observed it— but the truth often contradicts recorded history, as you may have noticed yourself. And while History is a subject that is taught in schools all over the planet, Truth has not been a required subject anywhere that I've ever heard about since the time of the ancient Greek philosophers. But let me get back to my story.

I make my second named appearance in the Bible in the book of *Numbers,* in chapter 26, verse 46, where you will find me listed with the Hebrew clans that came up from Egypt after the Exodus:

> *Descendants of Asher by their clans: of Imnah, the clan of the Imnites; of Shivi, the clan of the Ishvites; of Beriah, the clan of the Beriites. Of the descendants of Beirah: Of Heber, the clan of the Heberites; of Malchiel, the clan of the Malchielites. The name of Asher's daughter was Serach.*

It's true that I lived through all of our years in Egypt, was there when we left and there at Sinai, a very long time after I was born and a very long time after I should have been dead. For most of my life I've lived an underground existence, not telling anyone who I really am. But from time to time I've confided in others, including (recently) my new friend Estelle, just as I'm now confiding in you. I was friends with one or two rabbis of the Talmud, and they told a few stories about me, based on my very long life. And once, a few years ago, when I was living in New York City, I met two very funny men at a cocktail party. We hit it off immediately and, having a bit too much to drink, which I rarely ever do, I began to tell them about myself. I doubt they believed me, and suspect they thought I was trying to break into their field—they were and are noted comedians—who later developed a character they called the Two Thousand Year Old Man. He spoke with a Yiddish accent. I do not. He was very funny. I am not. He went on to become quite famous. I hope that that will not be my fate. All I want is to set the record straight, and then go on with my private life, however unusual it may be. I have no idea when or if I'll ever die, but I have been slowing down recently, and I don't know exactly when I was born. Our experience of time was very different when I was young. We only knew new moons and seasons: rainy, not rainy. Weeks were a new idea and not many of us used them yet. Imagine that! I'm one of the oldest human beings who has ever lived, but all I can say about my birth is, "I arrived one spring."

At some point a very long time ago I made up a birthday for myself, at the Vernal Equinox, and I suspect that the year of my birth was 1324 BCE, based on things I've read in history books about events that happened at the time. If you add up all these years you will see that I am over three thousand and three hundred years old. Over the centuries I've met a few ancient masters from Africa, India, Tibet, and China who have lived as long as I have. We form a very small private club, and when we meet we always have a lot to say to each other. I've also heard many stories about vampires and zombies and other dark immortal creatures, but I've lived all over the world and haven't met a single one. As for me, I don't think of myself as an immortal. I think of myself as a mortal woman who hasn't died yet. Or, conjuring the image of the Tree of Life, perhaps I am more tree than human; I read recently of a spruce tree in Sweden that is over 9500 years old, which makes me more like a feisty young adult just getting started in life.

Right about now I imagine there are three things you're asking yourself: First, "Why should we believe anything this old woman is telling us?" Second, "Why is she writing her memoir now?" And third, "Why has she lived this long?"

To the first question I will say this: I'm really no different than any other person of advanced years who you may have encountered. I've already forgotten what I did yesterday, and most of the time I'd rather not remember who the president of the United States is, but my memory of what happened to me when I was young is quite perfect. I remember the hairy mole on Grandma Zilpah's left cheek. The way that Grandpa Jacob used to lie on his pallet of sheepskins all day long eating grapes and pulling on his long white nose hairs. The taste of good oven-baked Egyptian bread. The way the sun rose over a little hill that you all remember as Mount Sinai. Yes, all of that is as clear to me today as it was when it happened.

Given that we're a people of words, and given all I've seen and done, don't you think, kind reader, that it would be a waste if I died without telling my story? For I am slowing down, my hair has at last turned gray, there's a pain in my left knee and one in my right shoulder that won't go away. And my digestion isn't what it used to be. So it seems like time to put down my long story; who knows how much time I have left. In addition, I owe it to everyone I've ever known and loved who's been left out of history, or been distorted by it, to put them back into the story, right where they were in the first place. I know that my stories will offend both Orthodox Jews—who believe that the Bible is the literal word of God, and scientific Jews—who see the Bible as a layered and much-edited human document that doesn't reflect the truth at all, or, not very much of it. My book, which is that of an actual eyewitness, will reveal to you both the marvels of our history, and the core truths that inspired the stories we all know (and many of us love.)

As for your second question—and it's a good one—about why I'm writing this memoir, let me say this. In my early years few women could say what they wanted and write what they wanted, and it's been that way for most of the time that I've been alive, with several noteworthy exceptions. But the world is changing. Women are once again taking our place in society, not everywhere, but in many locations, so, having carried my story, *our* story, for so long, I am grateful to have lived this long, for this is a very good time to be a woman writing. But, and this is harder to discuss, I did once before sit down and write another book, on rolls of parchment with a quill pen and black ink that I ground and mixed myself. It wasn't a work of history, but a work of satire. Alas (and this is the difficult part) my book was taken up and used in ways that still upset and embarrass me, so much so that I haven't done any writing since the time of King Solomon, except for a note or a letter every now and then. But more on that later.

A psychiatrist I saw in the last century in Vienna suggested I was suffering from something now called Post-Traumatic Stress Disorder. How could I *not* be, given our difficult history? Just beginning this chapter has given me a migraine. Now, you may be wondering what a woman my age thinks of human progress. We have advanced very little in terms of what's actually important. But looking back over my long life I would say that the three most important human inventions have been (not the electric light, which has deprived us of the wonders of the night; or the automobile, which has ruined the air and made restless people even more restless; or the mobile phone, which connects people all over the globe while disconnecting them from the people right around them, but)—One: hot running water. There's nothing in the morning like a good hot shower. Two: the printing press. When I was a girl it took years to copy by hand a single book! A very rich man might boast a library of three or four short scrolls. Even a king would possess only eight or ten. And three: my favorite invention of all—the camera. What I would give to have had one when I was a little girl. Oh, the things I would show you! The shallow murky (so called) Sea of Reeds when we crossed it. David dancing naked in front of the ark. King Solomon's temple on the day that it was dedicated. Jerusalem burning centuries later with Roman fire. Instead, I'm forced to make pictures with words. (Films

I'm not too crazy about. They go too fast, and get faster and faster. Besides, I like something you can hold in your hand: a book, a picture. You can imagine my thoughts on these new e-books.) So in stories, in painted words (not meant to ever be turned into a film) I will do my best to render what I know in colors appropriate and pleasing, and I hope that you will pardon my at times awkward English, which is (I believe) my twenty-seventh language.

As for your third question—I really don't know why I've lived this long. My best guess is that I'm some kind of genetic anomaly. Given all the generations of human history, why couldn't there have been a slight mutation in the genes of a few scattered individuals, a mutation that allows our cells to keep replicating long long after we should have died? (Not that I or anyone knew about genetics until very recently.) Before I did, my preferred theory about my life was a mystical one, a tale that you may have already heard, as it's one of the very few stories about me that *has* been preserved.

When I was still a young girl there was a famine in Canaan. My grandfather Jacob sent two of my uncles down to Egypt to buy grain and other supplies. While they were there they found out that their brother Joseph was not just dead, as they'd long believed, but in a position of importance. You may remember the story from reading the Bible, although what you read there wasn't exactly what happened.

Uncle Joseph was my Grandfather Jacob's favorite son, although he was always much fonder of his eldest daughter Maacah, Rachel's first and long-forgotten child. Alas, my poor grandfather Jacob had long been in mourning for Joseph, after his sudden and unexpected disappearance, and his wives, my four grandmothers, were all afraid that the news of Uncle Joseph's survival would be too great a shock for Jacob. I was around fourteen at the time, had a clear strong voice, and was minorly accomplished on a stringed instrument not unlike a modern oud. During the day I would do my chores, all the while singing, and every night I used to go into Grandpa's tent to play music and sing songs for him. So my grandmothers sent for me and told me the good news. Although I'd never met my Uncle Joseph, who was only spoken about in whispers, I was as happy as they were to find out that he was alive. What they asked me to do was to weave the good news into the words of a song when I sang to Grandfather that night. So I did. "And Joseph, Joseph, Joseph, lives. He lives. Yes he lives. Yes he lives." Sung to plucked strings made out of sheep gut, inserted into a song about a lonely dove perched in a treetop, the one that Noah had sent out from his ark, which didn't return to him, letting him know it was safe to leave the ark and go back to dry land.

To this very day I can see the tears in Grandfather's once nearly black eyes, turned white with cataracts, his face a web of wrinkles. Sniffling, wiping his hairy nose on the back of his sleeve, he leaned over, kissed the top of my dark hair, right above the line in the middle where it was parted, and said, "If what you are telling me is true, my little one, may death never come to you." Well, never is a very long time. But so is three thousand years. And while my life, but not my name, has been edited out of the Bible, every once in a while someone noticed me, as I already said, a rabbi or more often than not, a storyteller. I've been talked about more in some places than others. The Jews of Persia, a place I lived in for quite some time, were very fond of me and treated me well. But they were wrong when they claim that a fiery chariot carried me off to heaven many centuries ago. It didn't. Instead, I left by camel along the Silk Road, ending up in China.

For more than two thousand years I have moved about the globe as a wanderer, always settling in with our people. And for the last sixty years I have been living in the United States of America, first in Manhattan, then Boston, then Brooklyn—and now I make my home in Venice Beach, in the city of Los Angeles, in a lovely old apartment complex half a block from the ocean. (The older I get, the more I like warmth, and like to be near the water, as far away from wars as I can get.) To support myself I give guitar lessons to young students. (I've always loved stringed instruments.) And now, old, bitter, and blessed, I am ready to begin to tell you my story.

Chapter Two

In which I continue my tale and introduce you to our earliest ancestors

I WAS BORN IN a tent, and that tent seems like a good place to start my memoir, a fine place to peg my story in your minds. It was my Canaanite mother Arsiyah's tent, and her mother Kalanit's before her, a tent made of tan and brown speckled goat skins sewn together, section by section. Rolled up and packed on donkeys, tents like that were easily carried from place to place, from camp to camp. Now, when I look back on it, I'm amazed at the way that we lived, in such simple conditions, as we were actually a large and prosperous clan.

People think of us with tents and with camels. Some archaeologists claim that camels weren't domesticated yet and that when they appear in early stories in the Bible they're anachronisms, proving the text was written later. But they're wrong. Camels were domesticated, only they were very expensive and most people didn't have any when I was small. We had a few. Our family stock was being bred slowly, generation by generation, from camels that were part of Abraham's father's marriage gift to Sarah. I'll have more to say about this in a little while.

Speaking of Sarah and Abraham, now is probably the perfect time, right at the beginning, to fill you in on who they were and on what really happened to them. And surely my ancestors (and yours) are an important part of that picture. Contemporary scholars link the Hebrew people with groups of wandering Semites called Apiru or Habiru, who are mentioned in ancient sources from Egypt to Mesopotamia. This is wrong. The Hebrew word for Hebrew, is *Ivri,* which means, "Those people from the other side of the river," that river being the Euphrates, and *Ivri* begins, or used to, with a deep open-mouthed sound made far down in the throat, a sound you still find in Arabic, Mizrachi Hebrew, and other languages. So you can hear that the word Habiru hardly resembles the word we called ourselves back then. We Hebrews were a clan of Western Semites who roamed back and forth from Canaan to what today is western Turkey. The Habiru were someone else. Very nice people. I knew a few when I was little. But someone else, entirely.

The text that you know, the Torah, and the stories about it that our people have told over time, would have you believe that Abraham was the very first person to speak to God, and that Sarah his wife was only that, a wife and eventually, late in life, a mother. Much of this is a distortion of the real truth, but here I find myself on slippery soil, because I never knew my great-great grandparents, or my great grandparents either. What I'm about to tell you comes to me second hand, from parents and grandparents and other relatives. On the other hand, I'm a lot closer to them than you are, so you may find things here that will interest or provoke you, depending on your outlook or beliefs. This book will not be for the faint of heart or orthodox of stomach, and if you possess either, good reader, I suggest that you put down this book right now, lest it create in you mental indigestion, spiritual heartburn, or possibly both.

That little disclaimer out of the way, let's go on. An old writing companion of mine, back in Jerusalem in the time of King Solomon, liked to remind me that the job of a good author is to establish plot, character, setting, and theme, for whoever will be reading their story. I used to be big on plot and character, but the older I get the more I favor setting and theme. So the setting for the beginning of my story is the city of Ur, the home of Abraham and Sarah. The Torah would have you believe that they came from the city of Ur that was near the mouth of the Tigris and Euphrates Rivers, in what today is called Iraq. Not so. The truth, and there is evidence for it in the Torah itself, is that they came from a town in the north that was also called Ur. It's a lovely spot in what today is Turkey. I've been there many times. If you ever get to the Middle East, I encourage you to visit. Archaeologists say the city wasn't inhabited during the time of our ancestors, but they're wrong. That Ur is my and your original hometown.

Some scholars see a link between the southern city of Ur, known in the Bible as Ur of the Chaldees, and the city of Haran that is near the northern Ur. The Torah says that Abraham's family moved to Haran from Ur. The tie between them is that both were centers of the cult of the moon god Sin. Scholars also connect the word Sinai with Sin and posit that our ancestors worshipped that god. Wrong again. This confusion is very human. Are we talking about Paris, Texas—or Paris, France? Odessa, Texas—or Odessa, Ukraine? (And why are there so many foreign places in Texas, anyway?

They've even got a Palestine.) Back when the Torah was being put together, the real Ur was about as attractive and familiar as Paris, Texas, so the other Ur was written in, Ur of the Chaldees, a large lovely city, far more famous than the real Ur—but the wrong one.

Legends tell us that Terah, Abraham's father, was an idol maker. This is not so. Terah's wife isn't named in the scriptures. She's called Emteli or Amitlai in the Talmud, and Edna in the book of *Jubilees,* but her real name was Kaivah, which was a local variety of crocus, one that's long been extinct. Kaivah was a midwife, while Terah her husband was a traveling salesman, a fairly successful one at that, who covered a territory that stretched from eastern Turkey to northern Canaan—Canaan the name that I still prefer for the land that is now called Israel and Palestine. Today a traveling salesman isn't a job with prestige or power, but in those days a roving merchant in gold or silver or unguents, perfumes, or spices, could become a very very rich man, and Terah was quite successful in what he did.

The Torah tells us that Kaivah and Terah had three sons, Nahor, Haran, and Abraham, whose birth name was Abram. They also had a daughter named Samlah, who did midwifery, following in her mother's footsteps, and a daughter named Istara, who did the bookkeeping for her father. Please remember that writing had already existed at that time for more than two thousand years, and all firms large and small kept records of their dealings, although to call Istara a bookkeeper when her "books" were written on clay and on dried animal skins, is clearly an anachronism, while to call her a tablet-keeper would be more accurate but an anachronism as well if you're thinking of a computer tablet.

Reading the Torah that exists now, you find that our familiar familial story begins with Abraham and that the focus is all on him. Well, that isn't wrong, but it isn't exactly right either. For everything that Abraham did or said, there were just as many things that Sarah said and did. When I was little and being unruly, as all little children are (or should be, if the spark of life isn't beaten out of them too early) my mother and my aunts would shake a finger at me and say, "Serach, remember that you're the descendant of a princess. So start acting like one!" Mothers often say things like this to their daughters, especially if they're tomboys like I was. But in my case, what they said was the truth. Sarah really was a princess, a minor one, but a princess none the less. Still it was hard for me to understand what that meant when I was small. After all, we were living in tents, and even then lots of little girls imagined princesses living in beautiful stone castles, or their ancient equivalents. But when I was older and had seen something of the world, I came to understand just what a princess is—a girl whose life is exalted and whose fate is restricted. You've seen some famous princesses in your time come and go, like Grace and Diana, so you know what I mean. Back then I was very glad that my ancestress was a princess who'd been born in a castle, but that my mother was the wife of a very very rich man who lived in a tent. A fancy tent, class-wise, but still a tent.

Torah tells us that Sarah's birth name was Sarai, later changed to Sarah, but it was actually Innati, the name of a local goddess. Sarai or Sarah both mean princess in two different Semitic dialects, and that was her title—Sarai Innati—but for the sake of our narrative, let us continue to call her Sarah. Now Sarah was raised in a stone villa in Ur, the daughter of a rich Hebrew princess named Ataah, back in the days when women still had some power in the world. Sarah's mother did business with Terah, Abraham's father, who was from a less important Hebrew family. Sarah's father, Haddad, managed his wife's estates. Our ancestors met one afternoon when Abraham came to the villa with his father, with fabric and jewelry to sell. The two took one look at each other, Sarah and Abraham, and that was that. A flame was kindled in their eyes that raced across the gap between their bodies faster than the speed of light, something we intuitively understood, even way back then.

When Sarah and Abraham went off to Canaan they both changed their names, hers to her title in the local dialect and his from Abram to Abraham. Scholars tell us that Abram means something like, "Father is Exalted"—Father being God, and that Abraham means "Father of Many Nations," which is more or less accurate, but they miss the meaning behind those name changes. I remember back in the late 1960's when my young New York City neighbor Barry changed his name to River and his lovely girlfriend Mary Catherine, a self-defined "hippie-chick" changed hers to Owl. When Abram and Innati got to Canaan, they too wanted new names and new identities, and they did exactly what Barry and Mary Catherine did, after running away from their nice Jewish and Catholic families on Long Island to live in a crash pad in the Lower East Side.

All of that has been forgotten, and this has been forgotten too; had Innati been the daughter of a rich family, that spark of love which flashed between her and Abraham, who was still just called Abram, would have been snuffed out by her mother. But fortunately for her, and for all of us, Sarah was the heiress to a long vanished fortune, so Ataah was more than willing to let her daughter marry the handsome son of that very rich trader, Terah. Down through time I've seen this happen again and again that the children of rich, aristocratic, noble, royal, and even at times imperial lines become impoverished and are willing to ally themselves with nouveau riche clans they'd otherwise look down their noses at. You can get a handle on them by thinking of similar right-and-wrongnesses from your own time.

Romans and Sicilians. South Indians and North. Ashkenazi and Sephardi. Sephardi and Mizrachi. Religious and secular. Uptown and downtown. Red and Blue, Left and Right. You know what I'm talking about.

Sarah's mother Ataah set up the newlyweds in a large wing of her crumbling villa, but the two were never very happy there. Ataah had her own ideas for her daughter and son-in-law and they had their own ideas about how to live their lives. Ataah also had her own ideas about how her daughter's husband ought to use his money, and immediately began to renovate the old place. In the Torah we are told that it was God who prompted Abraham to move to Canaan but in fact it was Sarah who came up with the idea. (I don't discount the likelihood that God inspired her, although the workings of God are still unclear to me after all these years.) My mother and grandmother both told me that Sarah was a princess and a priestess and a very devout woman as well, and since the two of them never agreed on almost anything, when they did, I assume that they were telling the truth, even if it was a goddess she prayed to, the Hebrew embodiment of the Great Goddess, and not the idea of what we now call God.

Abraham was quite uncomfortable with his wealth, and was even more uncomfortable when his father died and he came into his inheritance. If they had the word then, we might say that our ancestor Abraham was something of a Socialist, happy to share his good fortune with others, who didn't mind giving money to his mother-in-law. He only wished she'd done better things with it, like help the poor or start a school in town. Instead, she used it to fix up her villa, buy clothing, and go on fancy vacations. (Some things about human beings have changed over time; others have not.) Sarah kept grumbling about it, Abraham kept telling her that it wasn't worth getting upset about, but our history hinges on the long forgotten afternoon when Sarah found out from a servant that her husband had just given her mother money to visit the ancient equivalent of a famous temple health spa in nearby Haran. Furious, she went storming back to their quarters and said to Abraham, the equivalent of, "I can't take it anymore. Let's get the hell out of here."

Back in those days, in that area, a man moved in with his wife's family, but times were changing and the hip, cool, with-it, trendy, avant-garde were doing things differently, so, hoping to calm his wife down, Abraham suggested to Sarah that they could move in with his father. "It's the modern thing to do." In those days the nuclear family didn't exist yet and couples didn't have houses of their own. Everyone lived in extended families of three or more generations. Well, Sarah thought about that and said, "If we go live with your dad, it's going to be the same old story. He's sweet, and kind, and generous, but he'll just keep bugging us. And my mother will keep bugging us too. And you're too nice to tell her to shut up and go away. So, darling, let's just quit this place all together. " Abraham realized she was right and that's when Sarah went off to light some incense at the family shrine and pray. In the midst of her prayers the idea came to her, and she went back to tell her husband, "I think we ought to go to Canaan. The land is beautiful, the countryside is fairly open, and instead of agents going back and forth we can set up a permanent branch of your family's business there." Abraham thought it was a good idea, consulted with his older brother Nahor, who was in charge of the business since their father died, and Nahor agreed, so they moved, along with Abraham's nephew Lot, the son of his late brother Haran, a kind of a hippie in his own right who was always looking for adventure.

If you're wondering how I know about things that happened two or three generations before I was born, remember how life was in those days. No television, no movies, no books, just a lot of time to sit around and talk. Everyone loved stories, and we all told them. My grandmother Zilpah, my mother Arsiyah, and my aunt Channah were all excellent storytellers. When I was little, Grandmother, who was always sick in bed, was the living repository of our family's history. Family members would come to her all day with local gossip and go to her for information. I took over her position when she died, and I'm still at it. I sat around listening to these stories from the time that I was old enough to sit up by myself. I heard them again and again for years and years. And once upon a time, as some storytellers say, the stories that I'm telling you were all written down. Perhaps one day some scraps of them will turn up in a cave somewhere, just like the Dead Sea Scrolls, and then you'll see that everything I'm telling you is the truth.

Here's another piece of history that's been discarded. In the Torah you will read that Abraham and Sarah had one child only, a son born to them very late in life, who they named Isaac. Well it's true that they only had one son. And it's true that Abraham did have another son with Hagar, which isn't a name at all. It means 'The Stranger.' Her real name was Isis, which was changed later on by fussy old men who didn't want their text to include the name that she shared with Egypt's main goddess. Funny isn't it, sad, ironic, and maddening, that these two great matriarchs and later rivals both lost their real names.

As I said, Abraham and Sarah came from different backgrounds, and they were living in a time when the matri-focal element was shifting, rapidly. Patriarchy was the hot new thing and Abraham was influenced by it. He wanted sons, when in fact he and Sarah had three daughters in Ur before Isaac was born, Atirat, Yonah, and Kalilah. They have been left out of the story, not just because they all moved back to Ur to marry men who lived there, but because they were women and women didn't count for much with the later editors of what became our most sacred texts. It's true that Sarah was rather old when Isaac was born, but not as old as the story makes her out to be. A year after they settled in Canaan she gave birth to her fourth daughter, Davah, and three years after that she had her last child. We know a few things about Isaac, but nothing any longer about Davah. Although she was a powerful healer, she never married or had children, so the later editors and redactors of the Torah didn't think that she was worth mentioning. But I do, and I'll have more to say about her in a little while. Remind me if I forget.

According to everything I was told, Abraham was a very very handsome man and Sarah was quite a looker herself. So, while theirs was a love-match, it was different than how we think of marriage now. Well, some of you would understand it. You talk about polyamory and open marriages, and that's what theirs was. Abraham had other lovers besides his wife, and Sarah had other lovers besides her husband. There are garbled stories in *Genesis,* two similar ones about her involvement with Pharaoh and Abimelech the king of Gerar, and a version of that one is also told of Isaac and Rebecca. But here's the truth, Sarah had an Egyptian lover, name Ahmose. He wasn't a pharaoh but a provincial ambassador stationed in Jebus, which later became Jerusalem. And later she did have a relationship with Abimelech, the king of Gerar. The storytellers got that right. But they didn't know what to make of the story in their increasingly patriarchal society, so they bent the story, instead of discarding it, which several of them wanted to do, and then they attributed the very same story to Isaac and Rebecca, for very different reasons that relate to Isaac, which I'll get into in a little while.

The redactors of the Torah did not know what to make of the family tale that Abraham and Sarah had the same father but different mothers. This is not true, but they did have a kind of marriage that made them the equivalent of siblings in the eyes of the law, and the later redactors took that literally. When beatniks and then hippies were popular, and experimenting with all different kinds of relationships, with free love and group sex, I couldn't help but think of our ancestors as a kind of proto-hippie couple, devoted to each other, equally strong in their own different ways, but not constrained by their relationship in the ways that so many people are today when they get married.

Abraham was a great charmer. That's how the family was able to settle in so easily in Canaan. He used his charm with all his family's business connections. Sarah was also a shrewd businesswoman. My mother told me that she chose her lovers because they were good contacts for the family business, which she was also involved in. Her third lover, at least of the ones I've heard about, was Efron the Hittite, another non-local, a real estate investor who was a good friend of Abraham's as well, and who sold them the cave and the land around it that became the family tomb. This tomb is not, I repeat NOT, the tomb in Hebron that two branches of Abraham's descendants are still fighting about. The location of the real tomb has long been forgotten, and I will not tell you where to go looking for it. We've gotten in too much trouble already fighting about the wrong places.

By the way, Abraham's nephew Lot, the one who came with them from Ur, did settle in the area near the Dead Sea, but he had nothing to do with Sodom, or sodomites, angelic or human. He did not sleep with his daughters, nor did his wife turn into a pillar of salt. We will see stories like this again and again, where real people like Nurit, Lot's wife, are slandered by later writers in order to make a point. We'll see this in the story about Shechem and Dinah and in the account of the Golden Calf, where fact is bent for political purposes. Lot's descendants had all remained in Canaan and were hostile to the Israelites when they returned with Joshua from Egypt, and that story of sodomy and incest was those old homophobic writers' revenge.

Now let's talk about Abraham's lovers. I'll start with Hagar, who I already mentioned, and I'll call her that rather than Isis as that's the name you know her by. She was, I've been told, a very lovely woman. To begin with, she was Sarah's best friend, not her maid as the text tells you, but she did come from Egypt. A young widow whose husband had been stationed in Canaan, she remained there after his death and she and Sarah bonded over being foreigners. As I said, the ancient world had different forms of legal couplings, as do we. There's marriage, common-law marriage, domestic partnership, and civil unions, all of them different. We had different forms too, including marriage, sister-marriage, and concubinage. The later writers couldn't understand that, and in your (supposedly) monogamous world (I say supposedly because you all know the truth of human nature) it may be hard to understand these different kinds of relationships.

In a world where increasingly men could have many wives but women could no longer have many husbands, and where the man's lineage became sacred and the women's ignored, Hagar was in a dubious position. She and Abraham were never married. They did have a son, Ishmael, who was for a time his father's male heir. But the writers minimized her role and they diminished him too, for in their day and age Ishmael's descendants and Isaac's descendants had long been hostile to each other.

The story about Abraham, Sarah, and Hagar contains a good deal of truth. Abraham wanted a son, and after four daughters in a row it was Sarah who proposed that her husband and her best friend hook up. Hagar had always wanted children, but her husband had died soon after their marriage, and as women say today, "After that I just never met the right guy."

Well, from all I've heard, Abraham was the right guy for a lot of women, and he had a number of other children besides those mentioned in the surviving text. And while this kind of an arrangement may seem odd to you, I remember several decades ago watching a film called something like *The Long Freeze,* in which a group of old college friends come together for the funeral of one of their old circle. One of them is a single woman who wants to have a child, and another woman decides to lend her her own husband for the night.

Thing weren't so different with Sarah and Hagar. But the story didn't have a happy ending, in the text and in real life too, because thoughts and feelings aren't always the same and a good idea in the head may be really bad news in the heart, the gut, or in the genitals. So it was with those two women who from the best of friends turned into bitter rivals. Hagar left their encampment several times, came back, but finally went off to a village where some of her family had settled, which was called Lahai-roi, from which she did not ever return. (Remember the name of this place, Lahai-roi. It will become important later in the story.)

By the way, Isaac's real name wasn't Isaac. That was his nickname. His real name was that of his grandfather, Terah, and in naming their son after his well-traveled father, who'd made numerous trips to Canaan, Abraham was legitimizing the family's new location and asserting its authority. But since there already was a Terah in the story, and since no one ever called Isaac that anyway, the writers of the Torah left his true birth name out of their tale.

Here's the missing part of the story. When little baby Terah the Second came into the world and the midwife held him up to wipe him off, he had such a funny look on his face that both Sarah and the midwife started laughing, and so right from the start his nickname became Yitzhak, which is Isaac in English, and means "He who laughs" in Hebrew. His name had nothing to do with angels or with his mother laughing at God, as the story now stands, which is a lovely story indeed.

Now Ishmael, Abraham's son with Hagar, was no more the ancestor of all the Arabs than Isaac was the ancestor of all the Hebrews, Israelites, or Jews, those three words both synonymous—and not—but that's a whole other story, so let me get back to this one. In addition to Hagar, who was never a full wife but a concubine, Abraham had other several lovers. Baalat the sister of his very good friend and distant cousin Melchizedek the king of Salem, Mutemwiya the Egyptian, and Tekla the Hivite come to mind. Then there was his second wife, Keturah, who he married after Hagar left and who some later rabbis mistakenly identified with her. Keturah came from a Bedouin clan that Abraham frequently traded with, and was named for their bestselling brand of incense. I'm told she was a lovely woman who put up with a lot from our ancestor, with great patience and kindness, yet sadly, our present Torah has left her as nothing but a dangling footnote. The Torah says that they had six sons, but in fact they had one son, Midian whose descendants will show up in this story later on, and two daughters, Allul who married a Canaanite man and had three daughters, and Kalyah who became a priestess of Asherah in Jericho and had no children. I knew about Allul because she was a fantastic weaver and in our tent we had one of her blankets. (What I would give for one of those beautiful goatskin blankets right now, on one of those cold damp Southern California mornings that don't fit into the mythology of what it's supposed to be like here.) Kalyah was a leading sculptor of her time and some of her pieces can actually be found in museums in Paris, Berlin, New York, and Jerusalem, small delicate carvings, some of them in ivory, most in clay or cast in bronze. Kalyah was still quite famous when I was a girl and all of us were proud to be related to her.

This should give you more of an idea about who Abraham and Sarah were, from the stories I heard when I was growing up in my tent of goatskins, the one that belonged to my mother and her mother before her. One more thing before I go on. After they moved to Canaan, Sarah and Abraham made several return trips to Ur to visit their families and to do business. Isaac met Rebecca on one of those trips and not the way you heard about it in the Bible. It's a lovely story, one that I've always enjoyed, about the camels and the well, but it isn't the truth. However, Rebecca's father Bethuel was Abraham's nephew, the son of his brother Nahor, just as the text says.

This custom of family intermarriage continued in the next generation as well. In fact, it's still common in that part of the world. Recently, in an old file folder in my desk I came upon an article I cut out of the *New York Times* on May 1, 2003, which stated that up to 25 percent of all the marriages in Saudi Arabia are between close relatives, often first cousins, which was true in the past as well. This intermarriage causes many genetic problems today, and it did the same in the past. I'm thinking of my always-angry uncles Reuben and Simeon, and my cousin Initi, Uncle Gad's daughter, who murdered her husband Baalil with a cudgel in a fit of rage. And the results might have been worse, but after Jacob and Esau's generation, our family's links with the north were severed, so that pattern was largely broken.

Chapter Three

*In which you will learn the long-forgotten
story of what really happened to Isaac*

THE STORY OF ISAAC in your Torah is very brief compared to the tales of his father Abraham and his son Jacob. Almost all we know about Isaac relates to his father almost sacrificing him to God, the way that his marriage was arranged, and the manner in which his wife Rebecca and their younger son Jacob tricked him into blessing Jacob rather than his older twin brother Esau, who was Isaac's favorite. The rabbis of the past speculated on why we are told so little about him and concluded that his near-sacrifice was so traumatic that he never quite recovered and accomplished very little in his life. As in many things, the truth is other than that, as I shall tell you in short order. But before I do there are a few other matters that need to be attended to.

Your Torah, (and please pardon me if I keep calling it that. Kindly remember how many torahs I've seen in my time) is very much the story of a people's relationship with God. Up till now I've left God out of the story, so let me backtrack and fill in a few vital points here, which will illuminate your understanding of the text and perhaps infuse your spiritual life with some radiance, if we both are lucky.

People of your time tend to view people of my time as if we were little children, imagining us to be primitive, unsophisticated hicks wandering about in the desert looking at the sky, waiting for a miracle. You fail to credit us with any level of intelligence or sensitivity and don't realize that our world was interconnected in amazing ways. Did you know, for example, that the tin used in the Middle East to make bronze came from the British Isles, or that the ancient Mesopotamians traveled by sea to India to trade for spices, and by land to China as well? Some of the words for different spices in Hebrew come from ancient Sanskrit and our people have loved Chinese food for many centuries. It's encoded in our DNA. And we had trade routes that extended all the way to the tip of Africa, but I'm sure you didn't know that. And you also think, I am certain, that our religions were primitive and highly superstitious. So before I go on I want to fill you in on the basics of religious faith three thousand years ago.

The Bible is filled with talk about idols and idolatry, and you perhaps believe that the little statues we kept in our homes, and the large images installed in shrines and temples, which represented this and that goddess or god, really were those deities in our hearts and minds. Well, the truth is, some of us did believe that, but most of us didn't. Archaeologists have found female statues and figurines in every level of excavation, all over the Middle East. In fact, there are more of these statuettes than anything else. They assume that they were goddesses and that they were worshipped. Not entirely.

People then were not so very different than people are now. You go off on vacation. We went off on vacation. You visit Paris and come back with a tee shirt of the Eiffel Tower and with post cards of the Arc de Triomphe and Notre-Dame. Or you visit New York City, take the ferry to the Statue of Liberty, and come back with a little copper statue of it, which you keep on the windowsill in your bathroom. And two thousand years from now, when archaeologists dig up the remains of your home, they'll find that little statue and say of you, "The 21st century inhabitants of this domicile worshipped a mother goddess, a fusion of two earlier goddesses, whose attributes she carried. One was the guardian of enlightenment, hence the torch she was holding aloft, while the other was the patron deity of scribes, indicated by the book she holds in the crook of her arm."

A lot of the statuettes dug up in modern Canaan were souvenirs as well, mass produced in clay molds, sold by vendors near all of our shrines and temples, and set up in our homes to remind us of our travels. Some of us believed that they were real, and others of us didn't. If you look into the back and front yards of America you will find countless statues of the Virgin Mary mounted on cement, or standing in glass boxes under a tree or next to a rose bush. (Mary, Miriam actually, was a lovely woman, but more about her later.) Now some of the people who have those statues pray to them, and some don't. Some think of her as the Mother of God, others see her image as nothing more than a comforting presence, while for others that statue is a tribal symbol. "My grandmother had one in her yard. My mother has one. I have one." And some, a minority I believe, put her statue out there because they see her as kitsch, a word and concept that I am very fond of.

We, your ancestors of three thousand years ago, were exactly the same. For many of us those goddess statuettes were simply souvenirs—artistic, decorative objects that we kept on a special shelf in our homes that some might call an altar. Others of us used our goddess images as what today you call "visual meditation devices," and some of us had those statues in our homes because everyone else did. Some had bigger statutes than everyone else, because they could afford to, and others had no statues at all and still believed in goddesses, or didn't, just as you might.

I now live a half a block from the Pacific Ocean, in a four-room apartment in a very diverse complex. Across the courtyard from me live the Rodriguezes, a large Mexican family of four generations. They speak almost no English but my knowledge of Ladino is useful here. They're fervent churchgoers and believe in a very literal interpretation of the Bible. Their crowded apartment is filled with images of Mary and numerous saints, with candles burning in front of them. They pray to them constantly, talk to them, invoke them. Upstairs from me is an old hippie couple. Bob teaches yoga, Shelley is a massage therapist. Their home is filled with paintings and statues from Tibet, of Buddhas and other deities. Although he is Jewish by birth and she a former Lutheran of German and Scandinavian background, they approach their Buddhas with the same devotion (if not the same mind- or heart-set) that the Rodriguezes have for their saints.

Then there's old Mr. Rallway next door. He's a fiery atheist socialist, in his late 80's. His lesbian daughter Martine and her lover Patricia live around the corner. Their home is filled with images of goddesses from all over the world, including a museum reproduction of one by Kalyah. Martine's father is always teasing "the girls" about them. The Tomlinsons across the way are Baha'i, Tina Phillips next door, and her mother Betty, are Fundamentalist Christians. The DeBecques are from Haiti and follow an Afro-Caribbean faith. The Rams family are Hindu, and I am—well, what am I? Einstein said, "I believe in Spinoza's God." Spinoza was a splendid man, the first truly modern secular Jew, and his God comes close for me too. But I tell you all of this so that you get a sense of the diversity of the present, with the hope that you will use it as a lens into the past.

Although we lived in a complex world, we didn't have television or movies or radio. For us stories, especially the ones that were told at night around a fire, were our primary form of entertainment. Because we loved to hear and tell stories we always had multiple versions of them, and that didn't bother us. In some ways it was like what happens to you when you compare a book with the movie made from it, the remake of that movie, and the opera that was created around them: multiple versions of the same story, some of which you like better than others.

I remember an experience I had when I had first moved to North America. Being fluent in several languages including English, I got a job teaching music in a private school in New York City. One day not too long after I arrived I was invited to the birthday party of one of my students, a sweet little girl named Lissy. Her father Bruce led all the children in a game that I had never heard of before—Telephone. There were more than a dozen boys and girls at the party, all seated in a circle on the living room floor. My student's father whispered to his daughter a sentence that she then whispered to her neighbor, who passed it on and on around the circle. The sentence Bruce whispered to Lissy was, "My father's new car is shiny and red." Imagine my surprise when the final student said out loud what he'd heard: "My mother's new dog was run over and killed dead." Lissy burst into tears when she heard it, as a sweet little puppy has been her father's birthday present to her. Well, scripture is sometimes like that, stories passed around a circle for hundreds and even thousands of years, changing and changing.

Am I making sense here? Are you following me? I hope so. Now let me get right down to our own history. You may have read those stories about how Abraham first discovered God, but even the redactors of the Torah didn't think so. They had Adam and Eve talking to God, along with Enoch and Noah and all of Abraham's ancestors. In their eyes monotheism came first and idolatry came later. In some ways the religion of your ancestors was more like Hinduism than what you think of as Judaism. In Hindu scriptures you will find the most exalted writings about the absolute unity of God, sometimes known as Brahman, alongside a great riotous conflagration of deities with the kinds of biographies that are found in all of the world's my-thologies. The religion of Sarah and Abraham was rather like that.

For eons all of humanity considered God, the Absolute, to be Female. But just as many of you, born as Jews or Christians, have become Buddhists like my neighbors, or are studying with Native American or Sufi or Wiccan teachers, my ancestors were also dabbling in new and trendy religions. God hadn't become absolutely male yet, although that was the general direc-tion in which things were going. Sarah and Abraham belonged to a fairly new syncretistic religion that worshipped an androgynous deity known as Shaddai or El Shaddai, which literally means, "God, My Breast," and can be interpreted as God the Nurturer, or God the Sustainer. While they built altars to Shaddai, they didn't make images of him, but they talked about him and thought of him as a man with woman's breasts, rather like the Egyptian god of the Nile, Hapi, who will show up in our story later on. Given that Hebrew was and is dual-gendered it was difficult to talk about and write about a Being who is both female and male, or neither. Shaddai was their best attempt to do that, an androgynous being who was never shown in pictures or statues. The closest we came to thinking of him in form was as light. Not firelight or sunlight but the primal spiritual light of the universe, from which all other things emerged.

In our mythology Shaddai, the Absolute and Unknowable Unity of all that is, had two children, which he/she birthed without another parent. One child was female. Her name was Asherah and she was the chosen deity of our ancestors. The other child was male and we called him Yah, Yah-El, or Yahweh. They were the Yin/Yang of the ancient Hebrews, or like Shiva and Shakti in Hinduism. No one made images of them but they worshipped Asherah in sacred groves, and felt the presence of Yahweh manifest through certain big rocks. Both of these elements will reappear in my story so don't forget them. Asherah and Yahweh were the creators of the physical world and the parents of all the other gods, of which we had many. We called them the Elohim, which means "the gods," and we saw all of them as manifestations of Shaddai, the one ultimate Creator.

Now let's get back to the heart of the Torah story of the near-sacrifice of Isaac. It's a very moving story in some ways, and it's maddeningly horrific in others. That it never happened should comfort you, and yet fiction is a marvelous mirror of the soul. Sometimes we can only tell the truth about human life though artifice, which you may have discovered yourself. So I ask you now, how many children, some in body and many more in spirit, have been done in by their parents? You perhaps are one of them.

Writing was still uncommon in my childhood, and it was even more rare in the days of Sarah and Abraham, except by scribes in temples. Stories about their lives were told by all of their descendants, but they were first written down about three hundred years after they died. So think about what you know of your ancestors from three hundred years ago. Most of you probably know nothing about them, not even their names, unless they came over on the Mayflower or were titled nobility, or if you're Mormon or have done a lot of internet research on genealogical sites. Given that we didn't yet have books, or radio, movies, or TV, we did a lot more storytelling than you do, but three hundred years is still three hundred years. And stories evolve just like playing Telephone, a whole story emerging from a single misheard word or phrase. So let me tell you the story that morphed into the sacrifice of Isaac. (Isn't morphed a marvelous word? From Ovid, to Kafka, to visual morphing in films.)

Isaac was spoiled by his father, his four big sisters, his mother, and by Hagar and Ishmael too, when they were all still living together in the same encampment. The Torah isn't clear on this, but Ishmael was three years older than Isaac, and the two brothers adored each other, the younger following the older about like a puppy, the older teaching him everything he knew. But the tension between their mothers increased. Hagar left for a time, returning to her favorite little village, but she missed the others and, hoping to be able to work things through with Sarah, she and Ishmael went back, as I said before.

Sarah had some reason to be concerned about Ishmael's influence on her son. He introduced Isaac to drugs at an early age, to the resins and hashish other herbal blends that were popular at that time. Sarah found out from their servants and went to Abraham in a rage, insisting that Hagar and Ishmael leave for good, which they did. Hurt and enraged when he found out, Isaac confronted his father and shouted at him, "Everyone knows you're not my real father. Abimelech is!" This deeply wounded Abraham, in spite of the fact that Isaac was the very image of him (or so my Aunt Dinah told me) so there was no doubt about his paternity. Abraham couldn't persuade Sarah to change her mind. A few months later Isaac disappeared. No one knew where he was, messengers were sent off to Hagar's village of Lahai-roi, but Isaac wasn't there. Finally Isaac's sister Davah broke down and confessed, when she saw how distraught her parents were. Her brother had confided in her where he was going and what he wanted to do. Below are a few passages from a long lost written account of what happened.

> And Abraham heard that his son Isaac, the only son of his wife
> Innati the princess, had entered the temple of Asherah in the city
> of Luz, to be a novice priest there.

There were many Asherahs in our time, the same way that there are Mary of Lourdes, Mary of Guadalupe, Mary of Fatima, who are the same Mary but also different. So too with Asherah, who was, again, the primary deity of our family. The Asherah of Luz was a goddess whose male cross-dressing priests castrated themselves after they were initiated, and this is the "cult" that Isaac had run off to join. The priestess there, Hattanit, was a kind of local guru, and lots of young men and women were drawn to her and to her temple. She taught what you might call, "the old way," the path of the Great Mother, and the young people who were drawn to that path were Luddite hippies from over three thousand years ago.

For Abraham, who believed in a modern new religion with its androgynous and main, male god, that was the last straw! Drugs he could deal with, but he'd waited too long to have a son with his sister-wife to see Isaac enter a community like that. A typical Jewish father in a world that was becoming increasingly male-focused and patriarchal, Abraham expected Isaac to take over the family business, and then pass it on to his own sons. Isaac's castrating himself would rob Abraham of his grandchildren, so you can sympathize with his fury. Now you might think that from circumcision to castration isn't such a long journey, but in those days the whole foreskin of a baby wasn't removed, only a ring at the end, something I'll talk about later, when I get to the story of Moses. But given what happened with Abraham's expectations, since that time our people have been uncomfortable with anyone who isn't married with children, and have been particularly uncomfortable with eunuchs, although they were popular in China, Ottoman Turkey, and were singers in the Catholic Church until not so very long ago. One of my best friends in the Middle Ages in Europe was a man named Fratello Solli, a short shy eunuch with a glorious voice! But let me go back to the old story.

> And his wrath was kindled against his son Isaac, the son of his loins, the son of his wife Innati the princess. And Abraham took his chief steward and five of his servants, and they set out for Luz to the temple. When they arrived they saw Isaac and the head priestess offering a sacrifice to the goddess. And they hid behind the oracle tree till the sacrifice was complete. And while Isaac and the priestess were eating their portion of the offering, Abraham and his servants sprang out and grabbed and bound the boy.

Not only had Abraham gotten angry at Isaac, but he'd also had a huge fight with Sarah. She understood why he was upset, but felt two things. First, she understood why Isaac was doing what he was doing. She was the devout one and had long felt a calling in her only son. And getting castrated was a part of their world. Men did it all the time. (Although I didn't understand it then and I don't understand it now.) And second, as the product of a matriarchal lineage and the mother of four daughters, Sarah had her own heirs and she didn't feel the distress her beloved husband did. In fact, she tried to talk Abraham out of going, but he was adamant. His argument was rather like one you may have heard. "The boy's too young. He has no idea what he's doing. I'm not going to sit back and do nothing, and let him ruin his entire life by entering this ridiculous cult."

> The priestess of Asherah of Luz raised up the knife of sacrifice, still bloody, and tried to cut Isaac's bindings, but she was subdued. "You cannot have this son of mine," Abraham bellowed. "His is not yet of age. He is still a son of my tent." For Isaac had lied to the priestess about his age. "I will kill him myself before I see him become a priest in your house," he shouted. The priestess was dismayed, however she had acted honorably, having believed the boy when he said he was of age. But she knew that she could not take in and initiate the youth against his father's wishes, and she told Isaac that he must go home with him and obey him. She told him that he could come back in a year, when he had finally come of

age, if he still felt a calling to the goddess Asherah, to be Her sacred priest in Luz.

Without the support of the priestess there was nothing that Isaac could do. He had to go home with Abraham. But what made it even worse for Isaac was that many of the Canaanite boys in the area had come to see him assist with the sacrifice for the first time. They were his new friends and he'd bragged to all of them about it, so he felt deeply shamed to be dragged off in front of them, jeering and laughing at him. And here you can see very clearly how a single remembered line, "I will kill him myself," gradually over time turned into the marvelous story that you all know from the Torah.

As I said, over three hundred years passed before the stories about the matriarchs and patriarchs were first written down. And the story that you know wasn't authored and edited for another two hundred years after that. The world had changed a great deal in that time. The faith of Sarah and Abraham was largely forgotten. All goddesses and especially Asherah were considered false, if not evil, and Shaddai had fused with Yahweh and several other male gods to become God the Father. The first writer of the story about Isaac's sacrifice was living at the time of King Saul, our first king, the first to unify all the tribes. Saul wanted his chief scribe to craft a saga that would inspire a new nation and fill it with stories that would set it apart from its neighbors.

In some ways people then were no different than people are now. We praise our allies by exaggerating their good deeds, and we condemn our enemies by accusing them of actions that they did not commit. The false statements of several world leaders who went to war to destroy banks of weapons of mass destruction that they knew did not exist is a case in point. In the first spoken tales of the life of Isaac, his whole life was told as he lived it, but as time when on, and stories became garbled, and then written down, Isaac's real life vanished just as his real name did. And later editors of the story used his life as a polemic against Israel's idolatrous enemies. The implication of the story was that Abraham was exempted by God from committing the kind of sacrifice of his children that Israel's neighbors were said to commit, offering up their daughters and sons to the fire on altars of Moloch and other gods. And it's true that human sacrifice was done in various cultures, the Aztecs and Carthaginians, but the Canaanites did not practice it. The story is subtle—and defames them, which I say as the Hebrew daughter of a woman of Canaan.

It's true that animal sacrifice was a part of our lives. But having been a vegetarian for most of my three thousand years, I was never a fan of it. The smell of burning flesh on our altars always made me sick to my stomach. But that's another matter, so let me get back to my story, the many versions of which—if you are wondering—I memorized three millennia ago and have not yet forgotten. (I've spent many the night sitting around a campfire telling others—or just myself—these stories.)

Isaac and his father were not speaking to each other when they returned. Sarah and her daughters did their best to reconcile the two, without success. Father and son could scarcely tolerate each other. Mealtime was a nightmare and as soon as he came of age Isaac took off from his father's camp and lived for some time in Hagar's village. You can see this yourself if you read the Torah. Hagar called her village Lahai-roi, and that's where Isaac was living before he was married. Eventually the family reconciled, thanks to Hagar, who let Isaac know how much his father and mother loved him and missed him. And as with many of us, especially when we're younger, rage in Isaac turned into guilt at the way he'd treated his parents, and from that guilt and the obedience he imposed upon himself, the next chapter of his life unfolded, after he moved back to live with them.

It was Sarah who suggested to Abraham that they all go up to Haran for a visit. Their eldest daughter Atirat had already returned and gotten married there and she and Isaac had always been close. Sarah knew that her husband and son always got along best when they were traveling. It took a while for her to get the two of them to agree, but in the end they went. The trip was tense, and you have to remember that on camel, donkey, and by foot, it was a very long trip, a trip of many months. (A nomadic band can travel anywhere between ten and twenty-five miles a day.) When they finally got back to Haran they stayed with Sarah's family, which made life even more difficult. Isaac sulked and spent as much time as he could alone, which only gave Sarah's sisters more ammunition for their criticism of her.

About two weeks after they arrived Sarah finally persuaded Isaac to join the rest of the family when they went to visit Abraham's nephew Bethuel and his family. Bethuel and his wife Kahinah had a son Laban, and a daughter Rebecca, plus an older daughter named Ezob, who has fallen out of the story. Rebecca and Isaac were close in age and they had a lot in common. She too was that day's version of a hippie, a rebellious child who was also interested in the old ways, although from all I've heard the spiritual content of the goddess revival groups back then was as new as that disseminated by most of the ones that are popular today.

Isaac and Rebecca hit it off. (Does it bother you that I'm using colloquial expressions? I enjoy them. English is my twenty-seventh language, and there is much to be said for it, some of which I may go into later on.) Anyway, the relationship between those two young people was not romantic. It began as friendship, the two of them linked by shared values. Seeing what was happening, and hoping for more, Sarah took Rebecca aside and gently encouraged her. Rebecca was the one who proposed. She genuinely liked her cousin and saw him as a good catch. Abraham and Sarah's business in Canaan was doing very well. She knew that she'd be comfortable there, while under her father's control the old family business was faltering. And Isaac, knowing that his parents approved, and needing their approval as much as he needed to rebel against them, because he was still too ashamed to go back to Luz—although he wanted to in his heart of hearts—decided instead to marry his cousin and new friend Rebecca.

It took a while for Sarah to persuade Rebecca's mother Kahinah to let her daughter travel back to Canaan with them. But like Sarah, Rebecca was a younger daughter, not her mother's heir, and so she was willing to allow Rebecca to marry her troubled but rich and charming cousin. I can't say that things were ever smooth after that between Abraham and Isaac. To the day that Isaac died, my father told me, he never quite forgave his father for dragging him away from the temple at Luz and embarrassing him in front of his new friends. But Isaac loved his wife, never took another wife, nor had any concubines like most of the rest of the men in our family at that time. Instead he fully entered into the family business and maintained an awkward truce with Abraham.

From time to time, when tempers threatened to flare up again, Sarah would find a sly way to remind Isaac, "If your father hadn't brought you home that day you would never have met Rebecca. And you know she's the best thing that ever happened to our family. Where would we all be without her?" After their twin sons Esau and Jacob were born, Isaac mellowed a bit, and Abraham, now having male heirs, was able to finally forgive him. At night, in bed, on those nights when they shared a tent, Sarah would sometimes whisper to Abraham, "Isn't it nice how things worked out? Even better than we could have hoped for, all those long years ago when we set out from Ur with nothing to call our own. And look at us now, with children and grandchildren and flocks and herds and friends to share our joy with."

Chapter Four

In which the author reveals one of
the major lost secrets of her people

MY GRANDMOTHER ZILPAH NAMED her first son after the god Gad, who was one of the Elohim or gods, that we believed in, one of Asherah and Yahweh's sons. My father Asher was her second son. Expecting a daughter that time she named him after the goddess herself, but I'm getting ahead of my tale. So let's go back to Isaac.

The family business was flourishing, largely because of Rebecca, who was a natural businesswoman. Merchants were always stopping by her tent to see what she was selling. She and Davah her sister-in-law ran the whole concern after Abraham died. Rebecca was often on the road herself, visiting local princes and the petty kings and few remaining queens who ruled the city-states that dotted Canaan, bartering and trading. After Sarah and Abraham both died and were buried in the cave that they bought from Sarah's lover Efron, Rebecca began to visit Hagar and Ishmael at Lahai-roi, the village they lived in, for she'd met an older woman named Suvah at Abraham's funeral, liked her and liked spending time with her.

Usually Isaac stayed home in Beersheba when his wife traveled, watching over their sons and playing music. He was a very fine composer and had a lovely voice, which I inherited, as I was often told. He and Davah were both fond of a game that's the ancestor of backgammon, and the two of them would play for hours, while servants looked after Esau and Jacob. One spring, however, Isaac decided to join Rebecca when she traveled out to visit Lahai-roi. Which leads me to another subject.

In my youth we had none, but in this day and age I find that there are three main taboo subjects—death, God, and sex. Death I know nothing about, personally, although I've witnessed it far more times than even an emergency room medic in the worst war zone or inner city hospital, so I'm quite an authority on it. I've seen people die in more ways than anyone else I've ever met. And I've seen people kill and get killed in more ways than a person ever should. On that one subject alone I could write an entire book. But I won't. God is a subject that I have spoken about already. This seems like a good time to talk about sex, that other potent three-letter word.

A few years ago I read an article in a women's magazine about how to heal yourself from the toxic values of a sex-negative culture. The author proposed that we remember the days when there were sacred prostitutes, and reinstitute them as sexual healers. I had to laugh, having grown up with what you call sacred prostitutes and counting several among my friends and family, *our* family. But, and I speak with authority here—you can't have sacred prostitutes in a sex-negative culture. They can only exist in a place and time when sex is considered holy, when people are conceived in joy, raised in joy, and come to their own sexuality in that way—joyfully. You can't reinstitute sacred prostitutes any more than the founders of the first kibbutzim could raise non-authoritarian non-bourgeois non-ghettoized children by mandating and enforcing new childrearing practices. In other words, you can't turn a dog back into a puppy, or a sex-constrained adult into someone who's free in their body and hasn't ever felt any shame.

When I was a girl we had sacred prostitutes, although that's not what we called them. We called them Holy Ones, "holy" from the same root as the word you used today to refer to God—Kadosh—Holy, Set Apart. But in my youth the culture was already changing. Shame was first appearing, an unforeseen by-product of the expansion of the patriarchy, which seemed a good thing at the time, just as automobiles seemed good at first. No more horseshit in the streets. Who knew that what you can't see or smell or step in would turn out to be far more toxic? Same with sex-negativity. It seemed like a way to channel energy into more productive avenues. Alas, looking back on two and a half thousand years of sex-negativity I would have to say that all it's done is channel energy into rage, resentment, and destruction. But in the time of Isaac there was almost no shame around sex or the human body. The story of Adam and Eve and the serpent hadn't been told yet, but it would be later on—a story told to defame the goddess and her serpent, not for us phallic but a symbol of her umbilical cord, that serpent a living creature come to share the Goddess's wisdom with the first two human beings. Back in my youth when people fell in love they believed that they were encountering one of the Elohim through their beloved. (You can read about the lasting influence of this idea in some interpretations of *Song of Songs* in the Bible, and by reading some of the wonderful poems of Rumi. Another wonderful man. I met him once in a tavern reciting some of his poetry.)

Among the Elohim were many who took lovers of both genders, and sometimes contained more than one gender within themselves. This is challenging for me to talk about, not because it's about sex but because in those days we had no such labels as straight, gay, bisexual, transgender. Or, we had all of them, tucked away inside ourselves, a reflection of all the Elohim, all their aspects to be embodied as we each saw fit. So, as you will see again and again in this story, people made love-choices in varied ways, which became problematic as the patriarchy became entrenched in our culture.

Having discussed sex, let's go back to the story of Isaac. Remember that he and Rebecca went to see Hagar at Lahai-roi. The last time Abraham's two sons had seen each other was at their father's burial. Before that they hadn't seen each other in years, so that last meeting had been a time of awkwardness and grief. Their next reunion was different. Isaac had mellowed over time, while Ishmael had remained wild and unpredictable. He was taller, darker, more brooding than his half-brother, but both of them shared the same father-wound. Abraham adored his first son, Ishmael, and it had been torture to him to send him away, but he did, and Ishmael never forgave him for that any more than Isaac forgave their father for dragging him away from the temple at Luz, humiliating him in front of his friends.

But over the days and weeks of that visit their families saw very different sides of the two men, which was both unsettling and enlivening. The past was behind them and when they saw each other again the brothers reconnected with joy. They laughed and talked and talked and went for long long walks. Night after night around a fire Isaac would sing and Ishmael would play his bone-flute. Sometimes they played songs they remembered from childhood, sometimes they sang new songs, or made them up as they went along. And little by little their hearts opened up in a way that I hope you've experienced yourself, like flowers in the sunshine. (I have.)

It had been years since Isaac and Rebecca had been physically intimate, but they were the very best of friends—and since friendship was what had connected them from the first, and because they didn't know about sexual shame, you can imagine the mutual joy and laughter they experienced when they sat down to have a conversation one night around a crackling fire, and Rebecca admitted to Isaac that she was falling in love with Suvah—and Isaac shared with her his feelings about his brother. True, Ishmael had a wife, several concubines, and a good number of daughters and sons. But what he felt with Isaac was different. It was the meeting of two embodied gods, grounded in their prior history, and it awakened in each a depth of feelings neither had ever known before. So the long-separated half-brothers became lovers, their union later sealed, ironically and deliberately, by the head priestess of Asherah at Luz. Within a year Isaac had moved into Ishmael's stone house in Lahai-roi, although to your eyes it would be called scarcely more than a stone hut. But it was the grandest building in the village, in fact the only building, in a small village of scattered tents. And that stone house became Isaac's home for the rest of his life, his and Ishmael's.

Now you can see now why there's so little about Isaac in your Torah. Not because he was traumatized by his near sacrifice, which never really happened, but because the later redactors didn't know how to redeem him, a runaway youth who nearly had himself castrated, fathered twin sons, and then became the lover not only of another man, but of another man who was also his half-brother. The writers, editors, and redactors couldn't leave Isaac out of the story but they skipped over him as much as they could, so that only a few clues remain, the mention of Lahai-roi being one of them. The later editors retold the story about Abraham, Sarah, and the king of Gerar as if it had happened to Isaac and Rebecca, to give him what today would be called "solid heterosexual credentials," because they had to leave Isaac in in order to get to his son Jacob, who they really liked. And then they told lots of stories about Grandpa Jacob, that multi-married adventurer, to distract us from everything they'd left out about Isaac, because we still knew those stories, back in the time of the judges and the first kings of Israel. But they did, accidentally, leave one little lingering clue. The word they use for what Isaac and Rebecca did out in the fields, "play" or "sport," depending on how you translate it, is also used to talk about what Ishmael and Isaac did when Isaac was small, which is not what they did then, but which lay the foundation for what later happened—delicious and mature and sexy love.

In spite of what the Torah tells you, Isaac wasn't buried in Hebron, in the same cave as his parents. He and Ishmael were buried in the same grave, at Lahai-roi, and all through the time of the judges and into the early years of the monarchy, young men who loved each other in Judah and Israel would go there to seal their vows. In fact David and Jonathan went there, but as the patriarchy grew in strength and same-sex love was outlawed, visits to the tomb were forbidden and the custom forgotten. But imagine how the world would be now, if the children of Ishmael and the children of Isaac, at war in such painful ways, had always remembered that their founders were not just sons of the same honored father, but also lovers. There would be no war now, no hatred, no fear. Only love and joy would exist between our two peoples. (Although I tremble in telling this story, afraid that I will find myself having to go into hiding, like poor Mr. Salman Rushdie, for telling stories that will outrage the orthodox of both the Muslim world and the Jewish. Although, on the other hand, to make them rage together could be a unifying thing and perhaps what I'll be most remembered for. We shall see.)

All of this background material is gradually getting us up to the time of my own birth, in that tent you're probably tired of hearing about. So please stay with me for a little while longer and I promise you that you'll get there, because you now know the story about Abraham and Sarah, and the story about Isaac and Rebecca, and Isaac and Ishmael. But before I go on to tell the story of the next generation, of Esau and Jacob and his wives and concubines and all twenty-five of their children, who were my father and my aunts and uncles, let me tell you about Davah, purged from history by the Stalinist editors of the past. And then, when this chapter is over, we'll be ready for that tent made of goatskins, washed and scraped with stones, cleaned and stretched out on frames in the sun to dry, then painstakingly sewn together with goat gut for thread.

As you now know, Davah was the youngest daughter of our ancestors Sarah and Abraham. All three of her older sisters, who were born in the north, went back there to marry and never returned to Canaan. But Davah, who was born in Canaan, remained there her entire life. Now, for several generations, as I may have said earlier, the family business was divided into two divisions, trade and pasturing. Archaeologists say that the Torah is wrong when it mentions camels in the time of the patriarchs and matriarchs because they hadn't been domesticated yet, but they are wrong, as I told you in an earlier chapter. (See. People think the elderly repeat themselves but don't know it. Not in my case. I repeat myself and I do know it. I like my own stories. They've kept me company for all these years, haven't they?)

So yes, we had camels, although they were rare and expensive. It was Davah who decided to make camel breeding a third part of the family business. She ran it herself for years, and when she got older Leah helped her and then my Aunt Dinah ran it, before we all went down to Egypt. It's because of my great aunt Davah that domestic camels are now common in the Middle East. She built up the business until we were making more from selling camels than we were from our flocks and our trading combined. And there used to be prayers offered to the God of Davah, El the Generous, for camel's milk was a part of our diets way back then.

So, you know the basics of the story I want to tell you from the Bible, if you've read it, and I hope you have. For all my criticism of the book as it exists now, it is more than two thousand five hundred years old, which can be said of very few other books. It's an artifact, like those wonderful statuettes done by Keturah and Abraham's daughter Kalyah, which are found in museums all over the world. You may not like them, but would you go in and change them? A famous artist once drew a mustache on a copy of DaVinci's painting of the Mona Lisa, and we write *midrashim*, stories about Torah stories, that are not unlike mustaches. But would we change the original

because we don't like it? No. And so it should be with your Torah. For all
of its failings, it is an ancient text, one worth honoring, as you would if you
dug it up somewhere, rather than found it in a library, or in the ark of a
synagogue.

So all of you camel lovers, say a prayer of thanks to Davah and let's
move on with our story. Rebecca and Isaac had two sons, who were twins.
The eldest, Esau, was just as the stories about him say, a kind of a jock,
rough, rugged, ruddy, an outdoorsman. You can see why Isaac liked and
encouraged him as he was growing up. Esau was all the things that Isaac had
wanted to be when he was a boy—strong, determined, and independent.
Butch. Isaac was like some of the tame suburban husbands I see walking on
Venice Beach, kids in tow, but with a crazy wild look in their eyes, gazing
out on the surfers. Each time that Esau went wild, beating up his brother,
teasing the shepherd boys, stealing animals from the flocks and trading
them for knives or bows and arrows, Isaac would take him aside and give
him a good talking to, a talking to that never said in words but always said
in tone, "Son, I'm proud of you! I collapsed after my one big rebellion. So do
what you want to do and don't hold back."

Although Isaac left his marriage after his father died and spent the rest
of his life in Lahai-roi with his beloved Ishmael, his sons were young adults
at the time, finding their own way in the world. And Isaac was devoted to
Rebecca for the rest of his life. She took over the family business and so they
saw each other fairly often, and it's Suvah her beloved and not Isaac who was
buried next to Rebecca in that tomb in Hebron, the real one that everyone's
forgotten about.

Growing up, Jacob had been something of a mama's boy, just as your
Torah depicts him. (See, it isn't all wrong.) You can understand why he was
Rebecca's favorite. Esau had no interest in the financial aspect of the family
business. He liked nothing more than to be out all day with the flocks, alone,
rather like his Uncle Ishmael. Jacob on the other hand was a people-person,
and he was fascinated by the traders who passed through our region, going
up to Mesopotamia, down to Egypt, and to the ports of the Mediterranean
and the Arabian Sea. He would stand behind his mother as she inspected
their wares and worked out deals with them, staring at everything they
brought as if it were food. As soon as he was old enough, Rebecca began
to include Jacob in her work, increasingly allowing him to make deals for
them all.

In alignment with their very different temperaments, the Torah redactors seem to paint Esau and Jacob as fraternal twins, but I remember the
first time I saw my beloved grandfather's twin brother. I must have been
five or six and one day our camp that was really a village was all astir with

the news that Esau had just arrived. Having never seen him before, and not having photographs yet, or even portrait painters, I was stunned to see hobbling toward Grandpa's tent an ancient man with the same bent back, the same long scraggly beard, hairy nostrils, and the same eyebrows, thick and wiry, crawling over his dark wrinkled forehead like twin caterpillars, just like Grandpa Jacob's. Sitting around a fire that evening, I kept staring at him, so very like my grandfather in looks and yet nothing like him in personality. The Torah focuses on personality and draws them as fraternal twins, but—they were identical!

From the Torah you would also think that Esau and Jacob were never close, but that wasn't the case. Although they were very different temperamentally, they were like many sets of twins I've known down through the ages. My father told me that even when they were very old they would finish each other's sentences. They got sick at the same time, and laughed at the same dumb jokes. And they were both pranksters. Here's one that the family talked about for years. As young boys the two of them dyed a newborn lamb a deep blue and brought it back to Isaac's tent, pretending that it was an omen, a magical lamb that had been born that way. Isaac, a joker himself, pretended to believe them, and told them he was going to make a special offering of it, and invite the entire family, even their cousins from Haran. Embarrassed, and in love with that little lamb, the two confessed, to the laughter of the whole clan.

Perhaps you have something like this in your family, a phrase or a slogan that means nothing to anyone else but a great deal to all of you. In my family, even when we were down in Egypt, if you wanted to tell someone how absurd something was you would say, "Look at that blue lamb," and for centuries afterwards blue dye and blue threads held a special place among our people; think of the blue fringes on our garments. There's another story like that in our family. It's not a funny one, but in a funny way it led to a dietary tradition among our people, one that I'll talk about a little later on.

According to the story in the Torah, Jacob, under his mother's direction, swindled his older brother out of his birthright. The good news here, as it will so often be the case, is that however lovely a story it is, it isn't a true one. But truth be told, Esau was happy to tend our family's flocks and leave the trading arm of the business to his brother and the camels to his mother. The story, however, is a marvelous one, don't you think? But the trickery and the discomfort weren't Isaac and Rebecca's, nor Esau and Jacob's. The real discomfort belonged to the later writer of that tale, who didn't know what to do with Isaac and wanted to both distance his listeners from him and yet somehow redeem him. And Jacob didn't go north because he was fleeing from his brother's wrath; he went north because of work. Over several generations the center of the family business had remained in Haran, run by Abraham's brothers and their sons, so contact needed to be kept up with them. That's why Jacob traveled north, and he ended up spending a little more than a decade in Haran, learning more about the family business from its heads, and getting richer himself. It was there that he met and married Rachel and Leah.

The story you know about Jacob working for seven years for Rachel and then being tricked on his wedding night when Leah ended up in his bed is another one of those stories that aren't true. A later redactor of the Torah was very uncomfortable with the notion that his ancestor had married two sisters, which was forbidden in his own day, although not in Jacob's. How to explain it? By inventing a trick, which was one of his favorite plot devices. But there was no trick. Jacob my grandfather was in love with Rachel but they were never able to talk well. However he and Leah had a great relationship. Those two could sit up all night talking, whereas with Rachel, there were always long stretches of silence, and not always the restful comfortable kind.

The two sisters were very close, and being the kind of man that he was, marrying two sisters who suggested the union to him themselves seemed perfect to Jacob, as several of the Elohim had married siblings, sometimes even their own. "My brother Esau is a real man out in the world, but I am a real man in bed," is the kind of thing my grandfather Jacob might have said to himself. And each of them, Leah and Rachel, were given a servant as a wedding gift by their father, something horrendous that fortunately doesn't happen anymore in most parts of the world. (I say this in case you think I miss the past and find it preferable to the present.) The servants, Bilhah and Zilpah, were also sisters, and both of them had children with my grandfather. Liberal Jewish congregations now add to their prayers the names of "the four mothers," Sarah, Rebecca, Leah and Rachel, but they usually leave out my own grandmother Zilpah and her sister. Fortunately for us, Grandpa Jacob saw us all of his wives and concubines and their children as equals. He was a wonderful father and grandfather. My father Asher adored him, and I did too.

My grandfather's life was shaped by four defining events. You know them from the Torah in a garbled fashion. One was his encounter with an angel, the second was the death of his beloved wife Rachel, the third was the rape of his daughter Dinah, and the forth was the tragedy of being told that his favorite child, Joseph, was dead. The first event elevated him and the second three events nearly destroyed him. Fortunately the fourth event had a happy ending and I am grateful to this day that I had a part in it.

Grandpa Jacob was a shrewd businessman, a wise investor, and during the years that he and his wives lived in Haran he became even richer than he was when he arrived, which was how he was able to support all of us. But after eleven years in Haran he decided that he wanted to return to Canaan, to be with his own clan and to get out of the shadow of his father-in-law, Laban, who ran the family concern up north. Laban wasn't too happy about them going; in fact, he had a huge fight with Jacob and refused to let them leave. That strange story about Rachel stealing Laban's *teraphim* is grounded in something that really happened.

Contemporary scholars don't know what *teraphim* were. But I do. Scholars speculate that the *teraphim* were household gods. Not quite. They were winged creatures who represented the goddesses and gods we called the Elohim. They were the power animals of those divine beings, in a way, their living thrones. But to understand what they represented back then I want you to think about the framed certificates you see in restaurants that tell you that they're legally entitled to serve food and alcohol, and in doctors and dentists offices that tell you that they're licensed practitioners. The *teraphim,* usually made of wood or clay or bronze, but sometimes carved from stone, were issued by various temples and let customers know that they were dealing with a legitimate business which was registered with the local authorities, to whom they paid taxes, and whose scales were regularly inspected by them.

Now Rachel didn't steal the *teraphim,* and she didn't take all of them. She and Leah and Jacob had a meeting with Laban to tell him they were leaving. He refused to let them go at first but Rachel negotiated with him, reminding him that the family business had prospered because of her and Jacob's work. He eventually agreed to let her take two of the family's seven *teraphim* out of the wooden chest where they were stored and leave with them. Those two small wooden *teraphim* were enough to set up the family business officially in Canaan, independent from the ties that had bound them to Haran since the time of Abraham's great grandfather Serug, the first merchant in the family and the one who set up the family business. So it was Rachel who actually legitimized the family's concerns in Canaan, and you ought to know that. But the redactors of your Torah were uncomfortable with the story of a woman of power, so they turned her into a tricky thief.

I remember the *teraphim* from when I was a little girl. They were kept in a wooden chest in Rachel's tent. There were similar but not identical, one a bit larger than the other. Both of them had wings that spread out to their sides, and both of them had cuneiform writing on them, which let you know they came from two different temples and licensed their owners to operate two different businesses, one directed toward material trade and the other toward livestock. You'll hear more about those figures and this chest so don't forget about them. We took them down to Egypt with us, and they came out with us all those years later. But I'll tell you about that when I come to it.

Now is the right time to tell you about the first critical event in my grandfather's life. The family left Haran, and since so many people and flocks were traveling, it took a very long time to get back to Canaan, months and months. Then he sent two messengers ahead to let Esau know they were coming, and they returned telling him that Esau had planned a huge feast to welcome them back. Today a man who is stressed out might just go for a massage and then soak in a hot tub. The night before they all met up with Esau and his family, Grandpa went off by himself to visit to the nearby shrine of the god Baal Hadar, one of the Elohim. That's the night when Jacob wrestled with a strange man and became Israel.

Today we might say that Grandpa needed more male energy to return home again after all those years and face his butch twin brother, so he opened himself up to an encounter with a man who served at that temple. His name was Uzzi and he was a holy one, a *kedesh,* which King James's Bible casts into English as "sodomite" but which is usually now translated as "cultic male prostitute." The story in your Torah says that Jacob and the man wrestled all night and that Grandpa's thigh was wrenched out of its socket. But the truth is that "thigh" or "hip" was a euphemism invented by an uncomfortable man several hundred years later, who couldn't acknowledge that a defining moment in Jacob's history happened while he was being the passive partner in anal sex with a sacred priest trained in the Middle Eastern version of what we now call Tantra. Instead of telling the truth, that Grandpa had a marvelous spiritual experience that led him to change his name to commemorate the event, the "holy one" was later desexualized and morphed (I do love that new word) into an angel. But angel means "messenger" in Hebrew, and that's what those *kedeshim* considered themselves to be—body-to-body messengers of one of the many aspects of the Divine.

In the 21st century, when people define themselves with labels, you might be inclined to ask yourself: "Was Jacob gay? Or, closeted?" Not a chance! My grandfather was what thirty years ago we'd call "a notorious heterosexual." Today he would be labeled metrosexual, perhaps, but his father Isaac occupies a different place on the famous (or is it infamous?) Kinsey Scale. Way back then none of that had any bearing on who they were in their own lives. When a man spent time with a holy one and had wives and children, his encounter had very much more to do with his spiritual life than his sexual preference. Remember that. There is much I like about the present, but for all of its freedom, it is restrictive in different ways than the ones I grew up with, and this matter of labeling is one of them.

So let me talk about Grandpa Jacob's wives and concubines, who are all so important to my story. Let's begin with Rachel, who was Grandpa's favorite. Everyone said that she was beautiful, round and shapely, with a busty figure like many of our goddesses had. And we are taught by the Torah to feel sorry for poor Rachel, as she had to wait for so long to have a son, while Leah had boy after boy. But the truth is that Rachel had a daughter Maacah a year after she was married, and then she had Joseph, two years later. Then she had Rabat, and then she gave birth to twin daughters, Tovah and Zillah. After they were born she delivered a stillborn boy, and then, just as the story still says, Rachel died after giving birth to her last child, a son she named Ben-oni, "Son of my sorrow." Jacob renamed him Ben-yamin, which most people say means "Son of my right hand," but which really meant, "Son of the south," which is where he was born.

Rachel was buried in the region that much later belonged to the tribe of Benjamin, and it says so in the Bible. But people think that her tomb is on the road to Bethlehem, which was in Judah's territory, and for generations a tomb there has been a place of pilgrimage, but just as the tomb in Hebron is the wrong one, so too is that one on the way to Bethlehem. Herod rebuilt it, but it was the wrong place even then. I tried to correct him, but that's a story for later on, perhaps. Rachel's death was devastating to my grandfather. It was a sadness that he wore like a garment, even years later when he married again for love, and even after his family had grown and prospered.

I never knew Rachel but I remember Leah, and I always liked her. Rachel was the favored wife, but Leah was the first wife, which is how they set it up themselves, and neither of them minded that. Rachel was very involved in the family business, but Leah loved being a mother and devoted most of her time to the family's children, her own and everyone else's. The Torah says that she was soft-eyed, weak-eyed, or doe-eyed, but I remember Leah very well and she had the most extraordinary eyes—pale pale hazel—the color of green grapes, big and shining. She had very dark skin. We all did. And there was something haunting about her face, with those pale eyes staring out from it. Even as an old woman she had a regal bearing. The Torah says that she had six sons and only one daughter, Dinah, but Leah also had another daughter, Rizpah. The two full sisters were very close. The Torah has some things to say about Dinah, and I have a few more, but that too is a story for later, about love and lust and other tents.

As I mentioned above, Rachel and Leah each had maids who they gave to their husband as concubines. These two women were sisters, just as their mistresses were, daughters of a woman named Helbenah. Bilhah the younger sister worked for Rachel. She was a tiny woman, wiry and quick. She spoke quickly, moved quickly, and she did everything as if there wasn't enough time, which was a very odd thing as we didn't have clocks or watches yet. It was just her temperament: speedy. All the women in the family had jobs, and Bilhah was in charge of food preparation. When I talk about my family I'm speaking of more than eighty-five people, plus servants and guests. Bilhah didn't do all the cooking herself, but she did coordinate it, which was a lot of work, like running a summer camp, which I only mention because it's something I once did, back in Germany, between the two World Wars, work at a Jewish summer camp. Maybe I liked her because I associated her with food. All of us kids did. Or maybe I liked her because of who she was, sweet and warm herself, femme in a way that I liked even as a little girl. She and grandfather had two sons and a daughter named Ahuvah. Sadly, Bilhah got into some trouble later on, but I'll tell you about it when I get there.

In spite of a certain, I would say, natural nostalgia for the past, I can't help but comment on the insanity of slavery, concubinage, and the insane way in which people were bought and sold and given away as gifts. These things all still go on, under different names, but they were horrible then and are horrible now, only it never occurred to me to question them for about a thousand years. So you have to remember that my grandmother Zilpah was Bilhah's older sister, and Leah's maid—her property actually. Eventually Leah gave Zilpah to my grandfather, as people did back then, and they had two sons together, Uncle Gad and my father Asher, and three daughters, my aunts, Bikurah, Hadar, and Yael. Grandma Zilpah was a taller version of her sister Bilhah, but she was very different in temperament. Bilhah was fast and my grandmother was slow. Her words were slow, her actions were slow. She walked with a slow rolling gait and she was always the last one done eating, to the annoyance of her sister, who liked to have all the eating utensils washed up and put away as soon as she herself was done eating. Not that our table was very fancy. To begin with, we didn't have a table. We all ate sitting on the ground, from clay bowls, with our fingers, sitting on woven mats and animal skins.

My grandma's job was shearing, weaving, garment and rug making. We needed a lot of it, cloth for garments, rugs and coverings for the floors of our tents, and for the backs of our donkeys and camels, although we also traded for a lot of the skins and fabric we used, and got a lot of our rugs from the Bedouins. Grandma was always bent over a floor loom, or doing hand-weaving from a loom that was strung between her body and a tree trunk, or sewing or mending, or embroidering. She tried to teach me and my sister Tamimah. I was terrible at it and Tamimah was good. Besides, by the time that I arrived, Grandma was always sick, with one thing or another, and spent more and more of her time in her tent. Looking back on it now I'd say she had rheumatoid arthritis in her legs, but we didn't know about that then. We called what she had "the achy bone disease," to distinguish it from the "stabbing bone disease, the "burning bone disease," and several other similar disorders.

Even when she was sick, Grandma kept weaving. She had a wonderful sense of color and style. I would give anything to have one of her garments, but alas, none of them survived, except in stories. It was she who Grandpa Jacob went to when he wanted to give Uncle Joseph a special gift, and she wove and embroidered the cloak that you can still read about, the coat of many colors is what it's usually called, although that's not the case at all. It was deep blue and had long hanging sleeves, and I may have more to say about it later. Her hands were always stained with dyes, and she was the one who hennaed the hands and feet of all the women in our family. Once, in the late Middle Ages, I tried my hand again at embroidery, and made a cover for an ark using one of her designs. I worked on it for years and it hung for years in a synagogue in Mainz, but it wasn't anything like Grandma would have made, and was sort of an embarrassment to me. I was glad when they threw it out after about thirty years.

Now you know the basic cast of characters for my tale, with one exception. After Rachel his beloved wife died, my grandfather Jacob married a third full wife, a lovely younger woman named Adah bat Idrah. She was a Perizzite, the daughter of a local chieftain, a woman of power and influence in our area. Idrah her mother did a lot of trading with our family. This is how she and Jacob met. Idrah's family were well known for making what were later called idols, but we mostly thought of them as souvenirs or decorative art. I liked Adah a lot, and I liked her three daughters, Gali, Anat, and Batshuah. Now I can hear you muttering, "What the hell is she talking about this time? They aren't mentioned anywhere in the Bible!" And that's exactly my point. In the one that exists today women are only mentioned when something they did or was done to them had something to do with the men around them—and a wife who only bore her husband daughters was left out of the text along with those three daughters, who were my cousins and earliest playmates.

On this note (and notice please how short a paragraph this is) I will stop. The tent awaits. (And if you think I've forgotten about Dinah, or about Joseph's disappearance, I haven't.)

Chapter Five

Here the author finally tells you,

her dear and patient readers,

the story of her birth and

of her early years in a tent

THE SKY WAS BLUE, cloudless, and achingly clear. I know this because whenever we were having one of those days, Arsiyah my mother would stop and say, "Serach, this was exactly the kind of day that you were born on. Unlike your brother Imnah," her firstborn, "who showed up right in the middle of a blizzard." Most people don't think of blizzards when they think about Canaan, but they do happen from time to time. We had a really big one during Roman times. Beautiful, and deadly. To this day I can close my eyes and see the desert all covered with snow, and the clouds so dense and the snow swirling about us, thick and dry. And the silence. That perfect, silencing silence.

My mother was a short round woman with a kindly smile, who was always a bit nervous, but she tried to not let that get in the way of anyone else. Her childhood was a difficult one. Her village had been burned down, its men killed, the woman and children sold into slavery. She and her mother Kalanit were freed by their owner, after many years of loyal service, and it was to my father Asher's credit that he married her. Freed men and women didn't have the highest status, but my grandmother Kalanit had been a priestess and her status remained with her and was part of what inspired her owner to free her. I never knew my grandmother, but my mother talked about her a lot, especially as she got older. My strongest memories of my mother are toward the end of her life, when, with her dark hair streaked with gray, pulled back from her face, she sat in the dirt, bent over a fire, cooking for us, and always singing or humming a song, in her raw, off-key, enthusiastic voice.

My mother liked to tell that story about my birth, and over the years it came to mean more and more to me, a blue thread woven through time, for a woman who never had biological children of her own. It never occurred to me to ask my mother what day of the week I was born on, as days of the week were still a new idea and we didn't number years yet, which I already mentioned, and we honored the new moon but didn't otherwise pay very much attention to months, although they all had names. But I liked it that I was born on a clear day. "It was the beginning of spring," Mother added. And to this very day, when the sky is blue and cloudless and achingly clear, like glass, I think of it as my day, my own special day, a day made just for me to be born on.

Being born is really not such a special thing. Billions of people have been born on this planet. And billions of people have died here too. What's unusual is to have been born here but not to have died. Yet. I didn't realize at first that I wouldn't die. In fact, for the longest time, it simply never occurred to me. I just kept getting older. So when, you're probably wondering, did I realize that I wasn't going to die? Well I would have to answer that question as I did before, by saying that I still expect to die, still think of myself as a mortal creature, not an angel or a vampire. Just a mortal creature who's lived a very, very long time.

Once, in the first few years after I'd moved to California, a lively young woman named Clarice who lived next door to me in Hollywood took me to visit her good friend, a feisty and engaging older woman named Bick. Bick came from an old notable California family, the kind you read about in history books, and she lived most of the year on a large ranch in the Sierra Nevadas, breeding horses. On her land there was a sequoia tree that she said was over three thousand years old. It towered above us, straight and powerful, its branches so high up above us. "Who'd ever have thought," I remember thinking, "that a person and a tree could be the same age?" And it was on one of those Serach Days that Clarice and I had gone to visit Bick, so the day sticks out even more in my mind.

When I was little I didn't know that I was different. In those days we didn't have the concept of being different yet, in quite the way that you do now. For example, I grew up knowing that I loved women, but that wasn't considered Queer back then. It was just how some of us were. And we Hebrews didn't even consider ourselves different then, in any way that would make us feel better or worse. We were different because we weren't the same. That's all. Because every tribe and group was different, and yet all of us were connected. I didn't know I was different when first I fell in love, or when first I made love. I didn't know I was different as I got older and one by one all of my relatives and friends died. People would often tell me that I looked young for my age, and I answered them with the ancient equivalent of "I guess I have good genes," which was, "The goddess must think kindly of me," by which we meant Asherah.

I didn't think I was different when my grandparents died, or my parents and all the people of their generation died, or even when my sister and brothers started dying. But I did begin to wonder about myself when my nieces and nephews started dying. By then we'd all moved down to Egypt, and there were many distractions, so it took a while for me to sit down and soberly ask myself, "Serach, why are you still here?" and for others to begin to start asking the same question. The first thing that came to mind was of course what happened when we found out that Uncle Joseph was still alive, and what my grandfather said to me when I sang him the good news.

The disappearance of Uncle Joseph was one of the defining events of my grandfather's life. And since I've told you about the first two, his encounter with an angel, and the death of his beloved wife Rachel, this seems like the perfect time to tell you about the fourth one. I'll come to the third when it feels right. A storyteller is entitled to tell her tales out of order sometimes.

According to the Torah, Joseph was sold into slavery by his ten older brothers, who were jealous of how much their father loved him. The text you have is a composite one, so it's unclear exactly who he was sold to. Was it Reuben who persuaded the others to spare his life, or was it Judah? And was he sold to Midianites or Ishmaelites? At least two different versions of the story can be found, spliced together in your book, but none of them are correct. The real honest truth is—Joseph ran away from home as many young men do, and sometimes young women. Although in my experience, speaking at least about the past, young men most often ran away from home because they were looking for adventure, while young women ran away from home because they'd already had one—but it was about to show and they didn't want people to start talking.

Joseph was one of those young men who was looking for adventure, looking for excitement, looking for experience in a larger world than the one he'd grown up in, a world of tents and flocks and camels and traders coming and going with stories that he wanted to live himself. You can see the way that a genetic trait is passed on. Joseph was very like his Uncle Esau, and very like his grandfather Isaac. In a later day he would have run off and joined the circus, or the navy, or taken a Greyhound bus to the nearest big city. But in his own day he did what other young men did in Canaan. He went to Egypt. And while today you would think of him, correctly, as a bright and beautiful youth, we didn't think that way back then. We didn't have those categories. Joseph was Joseph, different and hungry to find other people like him.

Over the years I often wondered, and people have sometimes asked me—"Do you believe in reincarnation?" My usual answer, to those few who knew the truth about me, has been—"No. I'm just waiting to learn about de-incarnation." But a more serious answer would be, "While I have no concrete evidence of it, and no past life memories of my own, once or twice in my long life I've met someone who was so exactly like someone else I knew that it's hard to dismiss the theory." One such case was in the mid-Sixties when I was newly living in California and met, walking on the beach, a rather striking young man who was so terrifyingly like my Uncle Joseph that I could hardly breathe. A smaller-nosed and much lighter-skinned version, he walked like him, moved like him, even smelled like him. He was both arrogant and self-effacingly modest in the very same way, and I was deeply thrown. As with my own self, I might conjecture that given the millions of years in which human beings have existed on this planet, it would make sense that every once in a while a person might be born whose genes keep replicating endlessly. And doesn't it also make sense, given all of this time, that two people might appear who are startlingly the same? So that day on the beach when I ran into that handsome and talented young man, later to become quite famous, and die too soon, he introduced himself as "Jim Morrison," but all that I heard and saw and felt and even smelled—was my dear and long-dead uncle Joseph. Proof of reincarnation? Perhaps.

I've known identical twins over the years who were less alike than Jim and Joseph, and while Jim was far more talented than my uncle, Joseph was a pretty good dancer, musician, singer, and seducer, so meeting Jim made me feel like I was encountering the aged wine of a soul that had learned and grown over time, as I fear that I myself have not. If you don't know about Jim Morrison look him up, and the next time you read your Torah you will have new insight into the character of the ancestor in our most sacred book who is given more page time than anyone else except for Moses, and for several good reasons that you can reason out yourself—a character who, in a long lost version of our Torah was actually the major figure, for that book ended with Joseph's death, ended there as if all of human history from Eve and Adam was a journey toward him and no one else.

It's true that Joseph did have a fancy coat, which as I mentioned earlier, was made for him by my Grandma Zilpah, on instructions from Jacob. It was a very elaborate deep blue and turquoise coat that suited him and his handsome arrogance, but in order to have enough money for his trip, Joseph sold it to a band of traveling Bedouin. They sold it to a Hittite merchant, who remembered having seen someone wearing it in Jacob's camp not too long before, when he was there trading incense. Curious, he brought the garment back to Jacob several weeks later, when he returned to the area, which was for years the first and only clue that Jacob and our family had about Joseph's whereabouts. The rest of the story, about his brothers wanting to kill him, but instead throwing him in a pit, and about his being sold into slavery, were not true. Joseph ran away from home, as young men and women do in every generation, long before Jim Morrison. I took in a fair number of them during the 1960's, young people just like my uncle, running off to find something they probably never would find. But he did.

At first, I was told, no one wanted to believe that something bad might have happened to Joseph. It might be different now, in an age of cell phones and texting, or it might have been different in the Sixties with just plain old fashioned telephones attached to the wall as all phones ought to be. He might have even called from a pay phone to say, "I'm fine. Don't worry about me," and then not called again for years. But as the months and years went by and not only did Joseph not return, but no news arrived about him either, everyone assumed that something terrible had happened. Everyone assumed that except for my grandfather, who never doubted that his beloved son was alive.

Speaking of Grandpa and our family, I imagine you're wondering what it's been like for me to be related to some of the most famous people in history. Because they were my family, and because we weren't famous yet, they were ordinary to me, and they've remained that way. And in a curious sense, because who they really were was often different from how they appear in your Torah, I don't feel as if I belonged to the family who are written about there. I feel like I come from a family where everyone, coincidentally, has the same names as the people in the Torah, except for the ones who've been left out of it. But let's go back to the story.

Years passed, Joseph never returned, and then just as every single Torah ever said—there was a famine. Grandpa Jacob kept his heir and business partner, my oldest uncle Reuben, at home, and sent Simeon and Levi, my next two oldest uncles down to Egypt to trade sheep and goats for grain. And there, in a small garrison city in the eastern delta region near to Canaan they encountered an official in charge of the grain stores. He was groomed and dressed in the Egyptian style, shaved from head to toe so they didn't recognize him—but Joseph recognized his older bearded half-brothers and let them know who he was. It was a joyous reunion!

Elated that Joseph was alive and well and in a position to help them, Uncle Simeon and Uncle Levi came home with grain and with good news. But everyone was afraid to tell Grandpa directly, so they had me splice the words into that silly little song that he liked me to sing to him at night. At first it was as if he hadn't heard me. And then, as I repeated the refrain, he did. And his wrinkled face broke into a huge smile. You may remember what he said to me then. "If what you are telling me is true, my little one, may death never come to you." Perhaps, I used to think, when I was lying awake in my tent at night, perhaps that's what's happened, and more often than not, as the years went by, I thought of it as a curse and not a blessing.

There was a time, down in Egypt, when I was around a hundred and fifty, after I'd lived through the death of my second life partner, when I tried to see if I could kill myself. I jumped off cliffs, did reckless things on camels, attempted to drown myself, and once I took poison, but not a lethal dose. All of them harmed me, so I realized that I probably *could* do myself in, but I also discovered that if no bodily harm came to me, I would just keep on living. So I have no miraculous super powers, just good luck, I suppose. I get injured and I get sick, just like everyone else. My body is a canvas of scars from top to bottom, and once in China, several centuries ago, I got such bad food poisoning that I had diarrhea and was puking at the same time for three days, and I kept praying to die, but no one was listening. A sword could kill me, a guillotine, a room full of gas. So it's not because suicide isn't an acceptable Hebrew thing to do that I don't jump off a cliff or throw myself in front of a train—although I think of it each time a train approaches. It's just because the life-force is strong in me, and whenever I contemplate suicide something deeper than my need to get out of this world of suffering stills my hand, asserts its vitality, and I go on. And now, at last, after three thousand and more years, I have a genetic theory about my existence that makes sense to me, which I told you about the in the very first chapter. I know a doctor at Cedars-Sinai Hospital in Los Angeles, a very nice young Jewish man, who is doing research on longevity, and my new friend Estelle has been trying to talk me into telling him who I am. But before I do I want to finish this book, the writing of which is, I think, the real reason that I've been kept alive for so long, by That which some people call God. So let me get on with it.

I haven't forgotten the tent, which will show up later in an interesting way. The tent was made of goatskins, the tent that I was born in, a skinny little girl with dark fuzzy reddish hair. About two dozen goats had to be killed in order to make that tent, but made it was, and home it was, for many many years, our tent one of many in a large circle of the tents of the families of Jacob, really a village, with Grandfather's tent in the middle and the tents of his wives and concubines spread out in a circle around it. As their children grew older, the ones who didn't marry and move away were given or made tents of their own, which clustered around the tents of their mothers. There was an order to our camp, wherever we moved to. Jacob's tent was always in the center, and its entrance always faced south. Leah's tent was to the northwest of his, and my mother's tent was to the southwest. Rachel's tent had been in the northeast and Bilhah's tent was to the southeast. After Rachel died her tent remained the home of her four daughters and two sons, and when Grandfather married Adah her tent was set up in the east, just beyond Rachel and Bilhah's tents.

When he was younger Grandfather rotated the nights that he spent with each wife, with a night in his own tent in between, from Leah to my grandmother, then to Rachel's tent, then Bilhah's. After Rachel died Adah was given her night in the rotation, but by the time I showed up Grandfather was old and had stopped visiting his wives at night. Sometimes Adah came to spend the night with him, but she was so much younger than his other wives and I think like many women married to older men, she was relieved when the sexual part of her life with him stopped.

So picture our camp, with Grandpa's tent like a sun in the middle, and the tents of his wives circling around it like planets, planets which sprouted moons of their own as time went on. The entire camp was encircled by other tents, the tents of our family servants, retainers, and the tents of visitors and guests. One rich old man, four wives, twenty-five children, their spouses and their children, and servants and visitors. Yes, it was quite a camp, an entire village of its own, with sometimes more than a hundred and fifty people in it. For our family had prospered in the land of Canaan. Not that Abraham and Sarah had ever been poor, or Rebecca and Isaac either. But as time went on the family businesses grew and that was how a man like my grandfather could afford to have all those wives and all of those children, named and unnamed in your Torah.

It was quite a process to pick up camp and move. Packing took days and traveling took days. As he got older Grandpa liked to stay in one place more and more. Who could blame him? Business was good. He was a rich and respected man in the region. He and his older sons traded with the local chieftains, princes, and kings. There was less and less contact with Haran and the rest of the family up there, whose business wasn't flourishing like ours was, and more and more trade with the Egyptians and Arabians, our new regional neighbors.

That was the world I was born into. It was the universe to me when I was small. Of Jacob's twenty-five children, all but six of them were living in our camp when I was born. Joseph was long gone and the other five children who'd left were all daughters who had gotten married and moved into their husband's camps or villages, as was the custom with our Canaanite neighbors. But Grandpa made sure that all of his sons remained at home and the rest of his daughters brought their husbands or wives to live with us, so the camp was a place of almost constant activity.

My father Asher was neither the oldest nor the youngest of Jacob's sons, neither was he the tallest or the smartest. But he was a very handsome man, with black black eyes and black black hair, and brown brown skin, with the whitest teeth and a nose like a hawk's beak, large and proud, like an eagle's beak, strong and beautiful. Father was the next to the youngest of his mother's five children, although only he and his older brother Gad are mentioned in the Torah. Gad, as I said before, was named after one of the Elohim, and my father was named for Asherah, which the scribes and the rabbis of old tried to obscure or forget. My father had three sisters, all of whom I've also mentioned before, Bikurah, Hadar, and Yael, who was my favorite. We all lived in our clustered tents, set up in a semi-circle around Grandma's tent.

If you're thinking—"Well, she took long enough to get to herself!" please note that the very first time I set out to write about our family I left myself out almost entirely, and only time has persuaded me that there might be some value in adding myself back in—a sense and feeling of authenticity. Had life unfolded as I wanted it to, like Jim Morrison I would have had a brief career in music and been long forgotten. But fate, the gods, goddesses, or God Him and Her and Itself seems to have had other ideas for me, and here you find me writing lyrics for a painful, endless opera without music.

From an early age I was a tomboy who loved the hustle and bustle of the men and boys going about their work, tending to flocks and camels and their wares. I loved the coming and going of merchants and traders and the visits from family. I didn't at first know that I had been born into a rich family. It was the only family that I had or knew about and as a young girl I had no idea that the web of my family extended for hundreds of miles in every direction. Only as I got older did I realize that the visitors who came to see us came from places I didn't know about were linked to ours by caravan routes, by stories, and by marriages. Yes, that was the world I was born in, but for me the center of it wasn't Grandpa's tent at the physical heart of our camp, but Grandma's tent, and our own tent.

There were six of us. You can read about us in the Torah. I made it in there, but only in a list. The references to me were edited out. But a tiny sentence of the bigger story survives in a very old Aramaic version of the Torah, called the *Targum Pseudo-Jonathan*.

> *And Serach their sister, who spoke and was therefore worthy of entering Paradise, because she brought good tidings to Jacob, saying: "Joseph lives."*

So my name remains in a list, along with the names of my brothers Imnah, Ishvah, Ishvi, and Beriah. But you won't ever meet my sister Tamimah, which is a great shame. My name remained because of one little song I sang, even if the story about it was eventually cut out. So let me tell you about my sister. Tamimah was a lovely girl, with dark curly hair and large dark eyes that embraced you when she was looking at you. Tamimah was shy and sweet, very much the opposite of me. In spite of that, the two of us were very close. I protected her and she made it easier for me to fit in with the others, for even as a little girl I was painfully shy and she was not. And so there we were, two different and adoring sisters, growing up together in a hot dusty place filled with sheep, goats, camels, tents, and lots and lots of family.

Chapter Six

Having entered the story herself,
the author goes on to tell you
more about her family and
about their going down to Egypt

THERE ARE SO MANY stories I could tell you about my childhood, but my point in writing this book is to tell you about our family and about what we all lived through. Now you know more about the tent, and where it was, and something of the life that surrounded it. I mention the tent for a variety of reasons, all of which you will discover in due course.

One story I *will* tell you, because it's an important one, is about my Aunt Dinah. In the Torah what you get is most of a horrible story that's true, true except for what's left out, and a little bit that's been added. Aunt Dinah was a short dark woman with thick black wavy hair, dark sparkling eyes, and a raspy voice that suited her strong character. The Torah says she was the only granddaughter of Jacob, but she had a full sister named Rizpah, who was older, and eleven half-sisters who were left out of your Torah because nothing awful or wonderful happened to them, which isn't of interest to most men, although it provides the background and texture for their own lives of great (or most often, no) accomplishments.

Dinah was raped by Shechem the son of the local chieftain Hamor. It says so in the Torah. But what the story doesn't say is that before that happened, Dinah was in love with Shechem's sister Katirat. The two young women had been romantically involved for several months, but Shechem was jealous of his sister and in love with Dinah himself. He kept following her, begging her to pay attention to him, but she just brushed him off, and as his attentions grew more and more annoying, she would tease him and tell

49

him to go away. One evening when she was on the way home from a joyful day with Katirat, Shechem followed Dinah, grabbed her and forced himself on her, in a ravine between their town and our camp. All that's left of the truth about her real life and not just the terrible thing that happened to her, is the tiny phrase, that Dinah "went out to see the daughters of the land." It wasn't all of them; just Katirat.

This happened when I was a girl not many years younger than my Aunt Dinah, and it was always talked about in whispers. In the Torah it says that Shechem's father Hamor went to Jacob to ask for Dinah's hand in marriage for his son. The arrangement they worked out was that if Hamor and his people became circumcised the two clans could intermarry. While the men of Hamor's town were recovering from their surgeries, your Torah tells us that Levi and Simeon, Dinah's full brothers, murdered all of them.

The real story wasn't quite so bad. First, Jacob and Leah knew about Dinah and Katirat, and they approved of the relationship. So did Hamor and his wife Uzzat. They both knew and liked Dinah. It was Shechem himself, so crazy in love with Dinah, who had himself circumcised, and came to our camp all aching and swollen to beg for her hand, thinking that that would make amends and do the trick. When Jacob and Leah said no, Shechem threatened them, but he was thrown out of the camp, vowing to return and extract his revenge. Levi and Simeon followed him back home and killed Shechem, of their own volition, in the same ravine in which he'd raped their little sister.

Everything that happened was devastating to Dinah, to Katirat, and to all of our families. Hamor understood that there was blood on his son's head but he did nothing to turn the mess into a blood feud, which he could have done. Blood feuds were popular then and even now, in the Middle East. They happen when a family decides that a death they perceive as being wrongful must be avenged. A southern storyteller made the story worse in some ways than it was, to discredit the northern kingdom of Israel, which had its capital hundreds of years after all of this happened—in a city that was also called Shechem. And his story helped to explain the historical eclipse of the tribe of Simeon, and the non-landed role of the tribe of Levi too. But the real story was otherwise.

Dinah and Katirat never saw each other again. At first neither of their families would let them. You can understand why. And then, later, when the worst of the shock and horror died down and either one of them could have gone out to see the other one, they didn't. It's not easy or probably even possible to get over, "Your brother raped me," and "Your brothers killed my brother." Even with someone you love, there is only so much a human heart can endure. There was something very Greek or Shakespearean about a story that was all once told in a Torah that no longer exists. But as our culture changed, as same-sex love was forbidden, that was another tale that the redactor could not keep in his book, so it's fallen out of history until now.

Before I go on there's something important that I want to say to you, my good readers. You may be finding much of what I'm telling you to be troubling, or even worse, heretical. And I can understand that. A major way that we locate ourselves in space and time is with stories, especially the ones we've been told about our family, our country. And I want you to know that at the very deepest level my intention is not to dismantle your belief system or destabilize your faith. In fact, my hope is quite the opposite, that in telling you what happened to our people, you will come into deeper alignment with who we really are, a rare people who have survived for even longer than I have!

My own long life has been a life of faith. It might not seem that way to you, but I was born a Hebrew and I will die a Hebrew. My ancestry informs every moment of my life. After all, if you consider yourself a Hebrew, by birth or by choice, you know that it's a part of your makeup. So imagine what it's like for me. You've been you for twenty perhaps, or forty, or eighty years, but I've been a Hebrew for more than three thousand. And in this chapter, as I tell you stories that may make you question the very core of what you think our religion is about, remember why I'm telling them, and travel with me.

To the day that I die, whenever that day comes, I will remember what Dinah looked like, dragging herself back into our camp, her robe torn and bloody, with long scratches across her face. In spite of her appearance, her face was icy calm, emotionless. I was the first one to see her, as I was always prowling around the edges of our village. She was coming up from the ravine when I saw her. You have to remember that although she was my aunt she was the youngest of Leah's two daughters, while I was the eldest of my mother's children, so there were only four or five or six years between us. Before she got involved with Katirat we used to play together, and I remember the pangs I felt when the two went off together. Today we'd say I had a crush on my aunt. Back then we didn't have words for that, but crush is exactly what I had. And when I saw her staggering up the ravine my first thought was that Katirat had done something to her, and I was furious.

Dinah let me support her as we made our way to her mother's tent. We were almost there when my grandfather's wife Adah came out of her tent, let out a cry, and ran toward us, asking what happened. Our modern Torah doesn't record a single word of Dinah's, but that afternoon, all that she could get out was, "Shechem did this to me." Adah, understanding far more than I did, slipped her arm around Dinah, to support her, and said to me, "Quick.

Get your mother." Not understanding, I ran off to do just that. My mother came running, and soon half the women in our clan were darting like bees to Leah's tent, where Adah had taken Dinah. But they wouldn't let me in when I got there with my mother. Having been the first to see Dinah, I felt like I had a right to be there, and I remember being even more furious.

For days and days they wouldn't let me see her. Not even her father or brothers were allowed into that tent. And I remember the uproar the morning that Shechem came staggering into our camp, demanding that Grandfather see him. And I remember how Simeon and Levi confronted him after Grandfather ordered him to leave our camp, how they threatened him, and chased him out of our village. Later in the day I heard about his murder, and by eavesdropping on my mother and a few of my aunts I finally realized what happened to Dinah. I wanted to go to her, comfort her, but day and night there were women sitting guard around her mother's tent, and they told me I was too young to go in.

A few weeks went by before Dinah came out. When she did she was pale and thin and did not seem to even see me when she walked past. It was months before she seemed halfway back to normal, and even longer till I heard her laugh again. By then I was older and found ways to spend time with her. And so it was, little by little, that we found ourselves bumping into each other, as we came up from the spring with jugs of water. And we would turn to each other at night around the campfire, and start laughing for no reason at all. "What's with the two of you?" my brothers kept asking me. I scarcely knew. But Dinah knew. And there was a night when the stars were shining, and the two of us went for a walk in the hills, in the opposite direction from Hamor's city. While we were walking the moon rose up, bright and full, the color of a juicy ripe melon. And Dinah took my hand and gently pulled me to her, and tenderly kissed for the longest time—my very first kiss.

Much later, Dinah told me how much she fought it. "I didn't want to open up and get hurt again," she said. "Love seemed to bring me only hate. And I don't know what hurt more. Loosing Katirat, or what Shechem did to me." But I took her in my arms and promised her that this time it would be different. And it was. With tenderness and passion we came together, to the joy and relief of all of our vast family, who feared that Dinah would be scarred for life. To celebrate our union all the women in our clan gave a feast in our honor, at the shrine of the local Asherah, the Lady of the Spring. And to this very day I can remember the song that they all sang to us, the women and the men of our growing family, a song about Asherah's daughter Kiddah and her girlfriend Gozalat.

And she came to the spring, the spring of the Great Lady.
Gozalat came to the spring, and there she met the Lady's daughter.
She met her daughter there, Kiddah of the long dark hair.
And her hair was like streams, flowing out from that spring
And Gozalat loved her, loved her, loved her by the waters.

And the air was heavy from clouds of incense, and all the women were singing and clapping, singing the song over and over like what we call today a *niggun*. And Leah, who was very old by then, and my mother, stood beside the spring holding hands. When we approached them, together they dipped a clay bowl into the water and poured it on our heads. But the only hint that there might be anything at all between Dinah and me in today's Torah can be found in *Genesis 46,* where Dinah and I are the only daughter and grand-daughter of Jacob listed among the men who all went down to Egypt. No stories about us, and thirteen men's names between us. But down through the ages, ever since the Torah as you know it has existed, whenever I've missed my first love and wanted to be with her again, and wanted the world to know that we were once together, I go back to read that chapter, just to see our two names—separated—but in the very same verse and most often on the very same page.

People talk about the incest taboo, and how powerful it is, how in kib-butzim children raised together never fall in love. But Ishmael and Isaac, Dinah and I, all lived together in our encampments, in tents, under the sky, and we all fell in love, to the great discomfort of later editors. Lest you think I only have bad things to say about them, even after all of this time, and to spare you any further discomfort right now, I will go back to my long dif-ficult story, difficult to tell and probably to hear.

Before I was born our family used to move a lot, from place to place to place, in order to trade and let the flocks graze. But by the time I arrived Jacob was older and weary of life, so we stayed in one place all the time, in a broad valley in the hills to the east of Bethel. Although my older cousins knew all about moving and loved to talk about all the different places they'd been to, until we went down to Egypt I'd only lived in that one camp. I was approximately fifteen when the famine began, not too long into sharing a tent with Dinah. This may seem young to you, but that's how old Romeo and Juliet were, if memory serves me, and the average life expectancy was around thirty-five, so I wasn't that young, back then.

To this day I can I remember a summer that was hot and dry, which was not unusual. But the rains never came in the fall, nor for a second year. I had never been hungry before, but you can imagine what it was like to feed somewhere between fifty and a hundred and fifty people, twice a day.

(Lunch hadn't been invented yet. Our meals were breakfast and a large mid-day supper.) But once the rain stopped, all of our crops failed, the wells and streams dried up, and our flocks were dying. Parents would push what little food remained at their children, but we all went to sleep hungry. I can hear the sound of Dinah's and my belly gurgling at night from hunger, and when we made love—bones knocked against bones where there used to be flesh.

It was a scary time, and after we heard about Joseph and I sang Grand-father my song, after he sent my uncles Simeon and Levi down to Egypt, we didn't know if we would ever see them again. They were gone for months and then returned with food and with good news about Uncle Joseph and his position, so we made ready to go, feeling hopeful as we left that dry but once beautiful valley.

Dinah's and my tent was rolled up neatly, and was packed on our camel Gilanit. The journey was slow but exciting to me. We stopped at withering oases and dried-up streams. It never occurred to me that I would one day make that journey in reverse, and that no one would return with me that I knew when I was a girl, not even those relatives who had been babies at the time. We traveled through miles and miles of bleak terrain, stopping whenever we found a tiny stream, a dying oasis. And then, as if by magic, all at once, everything changed. Suddenly there was Egypt, all lush and green from a branch of the Nile. I want you to see this as we did. Not a gradual wash as in a watercolor painting, which goes from dry tan to wet green, but all of a sudden the shock of two different colors side by side. Startling. Beautiful. Wet in a way that Canaan is never wet, wet from the waters of the southern lands that fed the River Nile.

The Torah says that seventy of us went down to Egypt. Usually it ex-aggerates but this time it under-represents. Some of our family chose to remain in Canaan and one hundred and thirteen of us went down to Egypt. Egypt. One of my favorite places to live! We called it either Kemet, the Black Land, for the dark soil brought down by the Nile, or Misr, which means "The Two Lands" in ancient Egyptian, and is the origin of the Hebrew word *Mitzrayim*, which you know from the Torah. It was not the evil Egypt of your Torah but Egypt in all its beautiful aliveness. My uncles Simeon and Levi, who had been there already, led us to Uncle Joseph's city. It was a work-ers' city, one of scores just like it all over Egypt, mud-brick settlements cre-ated so that laborers could live near the sites of the temples, fortresses, and warehouses that the king and the priests and the army liked to build. My uncles led us right to where Joseph was living. I had never seen so grand a house, all six rooms of it, white-washed and shining in the sun, with two small green flags in front, one on either side of the door, flapping on tall poles in the wind.

I will always remember that joyous reunion. Not Jacob nor anyone else who'd known Joseph could recognize at first the beardless man in Egyptian clothes who came running across the large room when we were let in, a rough and dusty, dirty crowd of Hebrews. His arms were open to them and all of them were sobbing, and kissing each other, and groups of us were pressing toward him, those who knew him going first. And then one by one the rest of us were brought forward. I remember Grandpa Jacob introducing his new, last wife Adah to his long lost son, and I remember how shy I felt going up to him, that handsome beardless man who smelled so good. Grandpa took me by the hand to introduce me, letting my uncle know that I was the one who had given him the good news. So imagine a large high-ceilinged whitewashed room filled with sobbing and laughing people falling into each other's arms and you will have a sense of what it was like for all of us that afternoon, with Joseph. There was joy and the thought never spoken—of Rachel his mother, so long dead.

Standing in supermarket lines I always pick up the tabloid papers put there with candy and cookies and other things I understand are called "impulse items." If there's an interesting article, I'll buy one. "They're nothing but trash," my friend Trudy always says when she finds one on my kitchen table. But I like them. Gossip stories, real and false, told by famous people's butlers, nannies, children, and former lovers, are the kinds of stories that fuel history. I understand that some of the informants are paid a great deal of money for their inside stories, and there were times when I was very poor and remembered that I've known some of the most famous people who ever lived and I've thought about selling my stories, but who would buy them? Joseph doesn't have name recognition when you're standing in a long line with your grocery cart. And who would believe me, anyway?

But let me tell you about my uncle. In the Torah he comes across as an arrogant youth, but later we see that his arrogance was all part of God's divine plan to save His people. That story always troubled me. If God set up Joseph to save his people during a famine, why didn't He just end the famine? But that's not the kind of story a tabloid would want. They'd want to know that Joseph was gorgeous—which he was—even to a woman's woman like me. He was a very honest and fair man, and he treated all of us well in Egypt. But he was a neatness fanatic. If there was lint or dust on the floor he'd always bend down and pick it up. And if something of his wasn't in the right place, he'd snap, "Who moved that? Why is that there?" which we always joked about when he wasn't around. So I can't say that I ever felt close to him, but I always appreciated and admired him for what accomplished and for what he did for us in Egypt.

But let me backtrack a little bit. It's true that his brothers resented his being the favorite son and resented the fact that he was so compellingly handsome and charming. Grandfather Jacob had my grandmother make Uncle Joseph that fancy coat to celebrate his special status—which further enraged his half-brothers. "Who does he think he is?" they kept asking each other, which always pissed him off. So he did what boys like my dear friend Jim have done since the beginning of time—he ran away from home, heading for the big city. He slipped away one night, and paid for his way down to Egypt by selling his expensive coat. He traveled with a band of wandering Bedouins, and ended up in the eastern delta city I've just described. Joseph was hungry and afraid when he got there, for his money had run out and he didn't know what to do. He was wandering around in the market, drooling over food he couldn't afford, when he was noticed by the man who ran the city, an officer named Potiphar who was inspecting the market with a group of his guards. It says in the Torah that Joseph had an attractive figure and was very good looking and even years later, when I first met him, he was strikingly handsome, as I said before.

Joseph always followed his own path. He knew he was beautiful, and he wasn't averse to using his beauty. Hungry and desperate, enterprising and quick witted, as many of our family were and still are, noticing the way that Potiphar was staring at him, Joseph took off his head scarf, ran his fingers through his dark curly hair, shook it out, and gave Potiphar a smile that could have sold toothpaste, only it hadn't been invented yet. It says in the Torah that Potiphar was the head of the king's bodyguards, but he was only the mayor of that mid-sized workers city, and in his entire life he'd only seen the king one single time, at a distance, when he was invested with the insignia of his position, along with twenty or so other provincial leaders.

Naturally Potiphar offered Joseph a job, and he took it, working in the kitchen. Joseph continued to flirt with his boss, who eventually made him the head of the kitchen, then of his household, and ultimately turned him into his major domo and personal valet, in the hope that the gorgeous and skilled young man would repay his kindness with love. But in addition to being heterosexual, Joseph was one of those vain people who like being adored more than they like intimacy, and the women he had sex with were always what we now call "one night stands," although they almost always happened in the afternoon, when we all took a break at the hottest point of the day. Additionally, my handsome uncle was also power-hungry. Giving into Potiphar would have weakened his position, and he knew it. He wanted to exploit the powerful older man, and he did. Little by little he learned about running the household, and when the famine began in Canaan and the king sent word to Potiphar and the heads of the other workers cities, to start storing grain, Potiphar put Joseph in charge of the operation, which he executed with precision. Was this the working of God? Perhaps. I'll let you decide for yourself.

Now here are a few other things that never happened. First, Joseph was never a slave. He was for years a hired and salaried worker in Potiphar's household, even though a good portion of his pay was in onions and dried fish. Later, as a reward for his good work during the famine in Canaan, Potiphar gave my uncle a house of his own, the one he lived in when I first met him. Second, Joseph did not have the capacity to understand dreams. That was added later by a particular storyteller; I'll come back to this point eventually. Third, over time, Potiphar figured out that Joseph was never going to be his lover, and he stopped mooning over him, and Potiphar's wife Meryt never tried to seduce Joseph, although he flirted with her too, but the redactors were more comfortable with that than with the idea that it was Potiphar himself who was after my uncle. Further, Uncle Joseph was never in jail. He worked for Potiphar for the rest of his life, and after several years of loyal service he married Meryt and Potiphar's lovely daughter Asenat, when he was older and finally ready to settle down. The text makes Asenat out to be the daughter of a priest named Potiphera, but the slight change in name shouldn't fool you, now that you're a seasoned reader and archaeologist of our history, and there are some old stories that make her out to be Dinah's child with Shechem. Not true. Just editors uncomfortable with my uncle marrying an Egyptian and not one of us, even an us who was the product of a rape.

So you can see the major themes of the storyteller and the redactors emerging—exaggeration, distortion, fabrication, and diminishment, in varying degrees and mixed with art, artifice, invention, and propaganda. In spite of that, there are many elements of truth in the Torah, and more importantly, the stories there are often much better than what really happened. There *was* a famine, and it *was* Joseph who organized the grain stores for Potiphar that ended up feeding the people in our city and region as the famine spread to Egypt. But it wasn't the pharaoh who rewarded Joseph, and there was no later pharaoh who didn't know him, just our grateful Potiphar, then his silly son Amenemhet, and his vicious son Ptahhotep after him, who's important in this story. I knew them all.

Because of Joseph's job and power we were given reasonable quarters, on the northeast side of the city, looking out toward the sea. We lived in a kind of an apartment complex, made of mud-brick, one story tall, with palm trees in the courtyard, not unlike the building I live in now. There were lots of them in that city, built to house teams of workers who would come up to do service for a month or two at a time, for the king and the temples and the army. It was wonderful to have food again, new food, fish and duck and different kinds of grains too, that were available to everyone in that city.

The famine in Canaan lasted for almost a decade, longer than it says in the Torah. We lived in Egypt for seven years before it was over, settling in and making friends, finding work, and learning to live in a different way, in a city way. One by one my family started dying. I was heartbroken when Grandpa Jacob died, and my grandmother Zilpah, then one by one all of the elders of our clan. Some of them were taken back to Canaan for burial, the older ones, but most of us were buried in Egypt.

Our family was used to living out in the wilderness, sleeping under the stars or in our tents, able to be close when we wanted or to spread out when we wanted to. But suddenly we were all living in one large compound, working together, eating together in the courtyard. This brought us close in ways that we hadn't been before. Joseph didn't want the Egyptians to resent us or fear us any more than they already did. They called us stupid, ugly, hairy, useless nomads, and in order to counteract that Joseph gave us all jobs to do, very soon after we arrived, helping him out during the famine. He divided my uncles into two groups, one that worked with him in the warehouses that he'd filled with food. That group included his full brother Benjamin, and his half-brothers Dan, Naphtali, Issachar, Zebulon, Gad, and my father Asher. The other group was made up of Judah, Levi, Simeon, Reuben, the four eldest sons of Leah. Joseph had them work outside, dealing with the merchants and hungry people who came to get food. The two groups bonded separately, and their children and grandchildren continued to work together in those two groups, even after Joseph died.

Now you may be wondering what the women in our family did. Some of us took care of the small children. Others cooked, or worked in the city infirmary. Egyptian medicine was very advanced. They were already doing basic brain surgery when I lived there. You can look this up in other sources if you don't believe me. Many of us worked as weavers and others of us worked in the market. We'd taken some of our flocks with us, and they were kept outside the city, often a distance away, but we brought them in from time to time for slaughter, and of course we were involved in that and in selling the meat. Yes, women of our people have worked in markets for thousands of years.

The job that I was given when we got to Egypt was to work in the stables. Potiphar was a soldier and the city of workers was an armed camp. Dinah got a job working in the compound kitchen. My job was perfect for a tomboy, currying horses and getting them ready for the soldiers to ride, brushing them down when they came back, feeding them, cleaning out their stalls. There were three Egyptian girls and one Nubian girl working there, but I was the only Hebrew. And since I didn't know how to speak Egyptian yet, and our overseers thought our language wasn't really a language at all, just the grunting of animals, I spent a lot of time alone, working when the others were talking.

The work was hard, but every night I got to go home to Dinah and our tiny room with its single window. Perhaps it's the same with everyone that their first love remains with them forever as a special part of their life. I've loved a lot of women in my three millennia (and a handful of men too) but years later, when I think about our time in Egypt, it wasn't our arrival or what happened to us later, but being with Dinah that I remember. Sometimes I can even smell her, taste her, all these years later. We shared that small room for many years, and while I experienced many losses before her death, when it came I felt that I would die myself. We had her embalmed and buried in the workers' cemetery outside the city walls. For several years I would go out there to sit by her grave and talk to her. But, let me get back to our story as I'm rather sure that you don't really want to hear about me. Nor do I. After all this time, the simple act of looking in a mirror, (Dinah gave me a beautiful one) and seeing the same old face looking back at me, day after day, year after year, century after century, millennia after millennia, is thoroughly exhausting, even heartbreaking! For what that poor woman in the mirror has seen—would kill anyone else who has bio-normative genes. (I believe I just made up that expression, but I think you will be able to follow it.)

Chapter Seven

Here the author informs you of what happened
to our people in Egypt, and how we finally left there

IT OCCURS TO ME now that I've done something very foolish. If I were a more seasoned and less traumatized author I would go back and fix it, chapter by chapter. But I am not that kind of a woman, focused, neat, and orderly. I don't take after my Uncle Joseph. Nor am I a trained historian. I am simply a very very old woman who has seen a great deal of history and wants to write about it.

So, let me talk about dating. Scholars and archaeologists debate all the time about what happened when, based on details they find in the Torah, as if it were a factual work of history. For example, authors take the lists of stopping points after the Exodus and construct from it very different theories about why their Mount Sinai has to be the real one, using places and descriptions to justify their conclusions. I've recently read two new accounts, one that locates Sinai in northern Arabia, the other in the Negev, that use the exact same information in the Torah. One of them makes much of the details of what happened at Mount Sinai, claiming that the smoke and fire indicate that it was really a volcano. No. The author had seen a volcano and put in those details into the story to make it more dramatic. Fiction writers are thought to be living in fantasy, but a good fiction writer (like one of my all time favorites, Tolstoy, in *War and Peace*) will weave together real and imagined in so tight a way that the imaginary could be real. This is true too with the Torah. Giving a detailed list of stopping points after the Exodus doesn't make them real. It only tells you that the writers did their homework.

I watched the Torah grow, a layer at a time, like a pearl. It is an exquisite text (multifaceted and actually more like a cut gemstone than a pearl) but please remember that it is the marriage of fiction, fable, gossip, and propaganda, woven together with truth, memory, distortion, and divinely inspired passages as well as entirely made up ones. The discovery of ancient cuneiform tablets from Mesopotamia, from Ebla, Ugarit, and other sites have changed biblical scholarship, anchoring it in the world of the past, which was my childhood. But anyone who thinks our ancestors didn't really exist, just because there are names like theirs in other texts—are just plain wrong. A lot of people have similar names in American history as well, but no one would confuse George Washington with George Bush, Junior or Senior. (I myself am particularly fond of Orwell and Gershwin.) And just because elements of the "patriarchal" tales resemble cultural aspects of a certain era, scholars have posited a date for our family's origins that is wrong. They assume that the period of the Hyksos invaders of Egypt, who were Semites just like us, was the patriarchal era, the time of Joseph. They are wrong. The Torah says that we lived in Egypt for over four hundred years. That is wrong. We were there for eighty-seven years. Tradition also says that there were four hundred eighty years between the Exodus and the building of the first temple by King Solomon. It was closer to half of that.

Abraham and Sarah lived during the 18th Dynasty in Egypt, during the reign of King Thutmose III. I will tell you about their lives in relation to Egyptian rulers (even though there is some debate about the correct chronology there) to give you a solid point of reference. Our family went down to Egypt during a famine in Canaan that happened while Amenhotep III sat on the throne. We lived in Egypt through the reign of his inspired but loopy son Akhenaton, that time of disruption and creativity, and stayed on during the chaos that followed his death, through the sad days of that silly boy king Tut, and on through nasty Horemheb's flawed attempt to restore order. The Exodus from Egypt happened while a small plague was brewing in the Delta, which occurred during the very short reign of Ramses I, not II as many historians claim. We wandered in the wilderness for a little more than four years, not forty, which was a nice round number that to us signified, "long enough." We entered Canaan again during the reign of Ramses I's very handsome son, Seti I. I saw him once when he made a visit to our city in the Delta, passing by in his golden chariot. His mummy is gorgeous, but it doesn't do him justice.

Biblical scholars take the text at face value. It says that we built the cities of Pithom and Ramesses. We didn't. A later author put those details in. Those cities were actually built during the reign of handsome Seti's son Ramesses II, not Ramesses I, in the years after we'd left Egypt. And lots of Jews have a quite mistaken notion that our ancestors built the pyramids, which were already more than a thousand years old when we were in Egypt.

We did build things though, but it was nothing to write home about, as we say now.

I hope this chronology gives you a clearer sense of what was going on when. As I said above, the actual dates are debated by archaeologists, but not the sequence of kings. Some say Thutmose III ruled from 1504 to 1450 BCE. Others say it was from 1479 to 1425. But we didn't have dates back then. Each king's reign began with Year One, and when he died and a new king ascended the throne, we started counting all over again with Year One, and one of the four of our own Hebrew new years was based upon that kind of reckoning, although it's no longer observed. But this little foray into history should frame things. And with that out of the way, I shall go on.

On his deathbed, Grandpa Jacob made us promise that we would all leave Egypt when the famine was over, but Egypt had become our home and no one wanted to leave except my Uncle Simeon's son Ohad, who returned to Canaan with his wife Esment and their five children. All the rest of us stayed, which we regretted after Joseph died. But none of us knew what was coming. Again, we didn't stay for four hundred and thirty years, as the Torah states, but only for a few generations. Go look at the genealogies, and remember what I said before. Trust them before you trust the stories. Figure out for yourself how long a generation lasts and you'll be on your way, as long as you remember that we married younger, had children sooner and died much earlier than most people do now. If it says that someone lived for one hundred and twenty years, that's poetic language, except for when it comes to me. Then again, it doesn't say how long I lived, or anything about me at all, which isn't poetry—just censorship.

Here's one example of the gulf between dates and lineages. It says quite truthfully in *Genesis* that Moses's mother Jochebed was the daughter of my Uncle Levi, who came down to Egypt with us. Unlike your humble author, she lived a normal span of years, during which time, especially after Joseph died, things got tougher and tougher for us. But we stayed because Egypt was familiar, our complex was familiar, and little by little we ended up becoming trapped there. But we weren't ever slaves. More like indentured servants. And it wasn't slavery but the loans we took out against our salaries and needed to pay back that made our departure impossible. Workers have been caught in binds like this since the beginning of time. I heard a song once that goes, "You load sixteen tons and what do you get? Another day older and deeper in debt. Saint Peter don't you call me cause I can't go. I owe my soul to the company store." It was just like that with us, but there was no pharaoh keeping us there, just our local tyrant, Joseph's lovely wife Asenat's nasty brother Amenemhet, then his son, the compassionless Ptahhotep.

Ptahhotep, who was in charge of our city in the time I'm telling you about, wasn't a very nice man, but he never ordered us to kill our baby boys. That note was a piece of fiction that expresses the emotional truth about our situation. The storytellers *did* remember Puah and Shifra, the midwives who delivered Moses and all of our other children, but they left out that they were a couple. And they did remember the brutal hardship of living in that workers city that soon became a slum, a ghetto, a prison for us. Ptahhotep and his heartless underlings hated and feared all of the migrant workers who'd come to Egypt to escape famine, hardship, drought, who came there just as migrants come today, looking for opportunity but finding a different kind of nightmare than the one that they fled from.

The city was crowded and grew more so over the years as the king demanded more temples and palaces. There was no sewage, no clean water, and all of us suffered from ill health, and our mortality rate was far higher than it had been in Canaan. That city which I shall not name was dreadful, deadly, but what changed everything for us was that just when it seemed that things could not get worse—a plague came. One plague, not ten, but one horrifying plague that was a kind of viral infection, I suspect, sort of like the disease called SARS that was in the news for a while. It was deadly and frightening. In less than a week people grew congested, feverish, then died, in a state of drenched delirium. None of our old herbal cures worked, nor did our prayers to Shaddai, Asherah, Yahweh, the Elohim, or to any and every other goddess and god, Egyptian and otherwise. And the formulas of the Egyptian doctors didn't work either. Many people died, many of our people as well. Between our hard work and the plague, we were all suffering, and it finally was Moses (yes, there certainly *was* a Moses) who took up our cause.

The Torah says that Moses's name is related to the Hebrew root meaning "to draw forth," for Pharaoh's daughter pulled him up from the Nile. But in fact Moses's real name was Egyptian, as biblical scholars have recognized for quite some time. *Mose* means "Son of…" For example, Tut*mose* means "Son of (the god) Thoth. Ra*mose* means "Son of (the god) Ra." This is true for our Moses also. Generations of Biblical scholars have speculated about his real name, and now I am going to reveal it to you, for the first time in more than two thousand and five hundred years.

Moses's parents were my cousins Jochebed and Amram. They had given their five older children, Miriam, Aaron, Itai, Chavah, and Peninnah, Hebrew names. (Nobody knows about Itai, Chavah, or Peninnah. They died during the plague. But I'm getting ahead of myself.) Anyway, Jochebed and Amram were becoming increasingly assimilated, as most of us were, and when their last child was born they gave him an Egyptian name. (This has happened all throughout our history, as you have probably noticed.) They called their new little baby Hapmose, which means "Son of Hapi." Hapi was the god of the Nile, the generous source of life in a land surrounded by desert, and he was always shown the same way, as a man with breasts, which was exactly how we imagined our own god, Shaddai. As you can see, in the forgotten memory of Moses's real name, lies the origin of that truly splendid story about his being drawn out of the Nile. Not drawn out of. Named for. Son of the god of the Nile. But frankly, over time, there's been so much talk about Moses, while the real story of our departure from Egypt is much more complicated. In order for you to understand that, I have to backtrack a little bit.

One day, many years after my beloved Dinah's death, I was shopping in the marketplace for a few tiny things that we could afford to trade for when I noticed a very attractive Egyptian woman walking ahead of me with one of her maids. After Dinah died I hadn't thought that I'd ever love again (nor did I expect to live long enough to love again either) but when that handsome woman smiled at me, a rather devastating smile, and approached me, my heart leaped up for a moment. And then I was suspicious. Why would a rich Egyptian woman approach me, a poor dirty desert foreigner? Was she looking for a maid? I had a job and wasn't interested. But being a polite woman, I nodded at her and, over the years, my knowledge of the Egyptian language had gotten quite good, so we were able to talk to each other. I was standing at a spice vendor's booth and she asked me if I could recommend a particular spice for a Canaanite fava bean dish her maid wanted to prepare. (Canaanite food during the last years of the 18th Dynasty was very popular, rather like Thai food has become here in America.) Well, I knew the spice she wanted, pointed it out to her, told her how much to use and when it add it to the beans. "Too soon and the taste cooks out, too late and the dish is too hot for most people."

My heart was pounding, my palms were damp, and I wanted to run away. You have to remember that although at that time I looked like a woman in her early thirties (and in looks I have only aged about thirty years since then) I was actually at the time much older than that. And Dinah had been my only lover so I wasn't very experienced in the ways of courtship. But fortunately for me, the very lovely Egyptian woman sensed my discomfort, trusted in her own charms, and said that she would prepare the dish herself, if I would agree to taste it. I said I would and she said, "Tomorrow at the same time, meet me here. I will bring a bowl of it." By "the same time" she meant when the sun was in approximately the same place in the sky. This isn't a very exact way to make a first date, but isn't so inexact if you've never seen a watch before, and if minutes and even hours hadn't been invented yet.

I could hardly sleep that night. "Why would a rich Egyptian woman be interested in a Hebrew worker, a woman who smells of horses?" I kept asking myself. (I know, you're laughing right now about lesbians and horses. Go right ahead!) "Besides, she already got the information she wanted from me," I kept telling myself, and I almost didn't go, so certain was I that she wouldn't be there. But of course I went. She was there when I arrived, alone, carrying a small basket in her hands, with a pretty green bowl whose rim was painted with alternating fish and ducks. (Funny the things I remember, isn't it?) That bowl was filled with the meal she'd cooked. Her stew wasn't very good, but I didn't care. She laughed when I told her, and her hand accidentally brushed against mine. And remained, for a moment. And one thing led to another. A walk by the water. A small picnic. Our first kiss soon followed. See, human beings haven't changed very much, have we? (And as for myself, like some other women labeled "butch," while I was tough and fearless in many ways, I was as shy as a little femme girl in others.)

Her name was Bast, after the Egyptian cat goddess of love. She was a very rich widow in our workers city, the orphan daughter of the chief priest of the city's main temple, to their main god Amon-Ra. Our courtship was swift and I moved in with her a few months after we met, into her large and comfortable villa in the much better administrators' end of the city. (Okay, laugh again, about lesbians and horses and moving in together on the second date. But don't joke ever about lesbians and their cats. Not with me.) Our meeting felt fated to me, but at the time I had no idea that our shared life would have consequences that might seem like the hand of God at work, if you are inclined to think that way. But God for me, Shaddai, in ancient Hebrew fashion, has always been a rather abstract concept, and in three thousand years I've seen many very remarkable things, but I've never seen a single miracle, although I've been in a lot of places where they were supposed to have happened. What I have seen, however, are things that felt miraculous—and falling in love again, with that marvelous woman, was one of them.

It was strange to live in an Egyptian house, away from my own community. In today's language I might say that the joy I felt in our relationship was mingled with a sense of discomfort with my upward mobility. "Have I abandoned my people?" I might have asked myself. "Am I sleeping with the enemy?" I might have wondered. "Is it right to live in this grand hotel when the rest of my people are living in hovels?" But I didn't. I felt blessed and happy and in a sense relieved, because my longevity was attracting the kind of attention that I did not want, an elder of a category that would not make sense to you in this youth-obsessed culture. So moving in with Bast brought with it a release from that unwanted role, and my time with her was my first opportunity to explore my primary survival trait—the art of hiding in plain sight. Now back to the story.

Bast had always wanted children. I never did. Then I heard that my cousin Jochebed and her husband were looking for someone to adopt their baby Hapmose. Things were very tight for them, with Miriam, Aaron, Itai, Chavah, and Peninnah to feed. When I mentioned it to Bast she got very excited. Jochebed brought her four-month-old child over in a small woven basket, and when she peeled back the cloth that covered him—while it's almost a natural human impulse to say, upon seeing a baby, "Oh, what a beautiful baby!"—we saw a scrawny little boy who didn't look like he was long for this world. We were shocked by his appearance and I remember Bast grabbing my hand, uncertain of what to do or say. But then Hapmose turned to her and gazed up at her with his large dark eyes, then turned to me, smiling a lopsided smile as if he knew that his fate was on the line. And in those few brief moments of seeing and being seen, for both of us, it was love at second sight! (And see, there *was* a basket in the story, just no river, or at least not in the way that you think. And in her garbled role in our history you know now that my life-partner Bast has been recorded and remembered as Pharaoh's daughter. Inflation again. Exaggeration.)

Bast and I raised Hapmose together, dear Jochebed living with us until it was time for him to be weaned. He remained small and fragile, but once he started eating food he began to put on weight, and although he was short for his age, he turned into a very active child, running in and out of the house, playing with the other children in the neighborhood. For the most part he was a good boy, and since his adoption was what would now be called an open one, our little Hapmose knew his entire extended family, his birth parents and his siblings, for they were my family too. We saw them all the time. Now he did have a bit of a lisp, which he was shy about, and of which there is some memory in the Torah. It troubled Bast but never bothered me. He was prone to temper tantrums, from even before he could talk, and he liked to break things; a difficult habit of his which caused a lot of problems later on.

Had I been a smarter woman, more like my uncle Joseph, when Bast first approached me in the marketplace I would have thought, "Flirt with her, girl. Use her. Exploit her for the good of your suffering people." And when I found out that our evil overseer Ptahhotep was her late husband's first cousin, I would have started singing her all of my most seductive love songs—and I knew quite a few. But I didn't think like that, and I didn't have to. Bast didn't need me to flirt with her to be the generous woman that she always she. She did kind things for me and for my people—because that was her nature. When Hapmose got older she got a place for him in the Egyptian school for scribes in the temple of Amon-Ra. He had very good handwriting and after several years of hard work he landed a job Ptahhotep's accounting office. (When I hear modern lesbian couples talking about starting families, I have to laugh. We were doing it more than three thousand years ago.) Bast paid for Miriam to be trained to work in the city clinic as an herbalist, and sent Aaron for instruction in the lay guild of people who assisted the priests, skills that they would both make good use of later. Itai was apprenticed to a silversmith and Bast supported Penninah and Chanah during their training to be nurses in the healing temple of Isis. She also helped me with my work. I became the first woman in that period to be in charge of the city stables.

And then a plague came. You have an understanding of viruses and bacteria. Modern medicine isn't perfect, but we now have simple cures for diseases that were deadly back then. In spite of the harsh conditions of our world, we Hebrews had faith in Shaddai, Asherah, Yahweh, the Elohim, Bast had faith in the deities of her own people, who weren't so different from ours, and we all hoped that life would be good to us. When it wasn't, when bad things happened, we believed that it was because we'd done something wrong and were being punished for it. This notion will echo all the way through the Bible, and many old and (as they're now called) New Age people, believe it to this day, that pain and suffering, disease and death, are punishments, externally decreed or self-created, rather than the random events they really are when we can look at them dispassionately, which is never very easy to do.

Our fear inspired the story of there being multiple plagues in Egypt, but as I said, there was only one. How can I take this away from you, the Ten Plagues? Ten is such a handy number. Ten fingers. Ten toes. Ten Plagues, Ten Commandments. There's so much more drama in them than there is in One or Three or Eight. And always remember that before there was history there was storytelling, and a good story needs details, needs suspense. And we are Middle Eastern people, prone to hyperbole. One plague that *felt* like ten just doesn't make a good story. If we'd had cameras then we could have documented it. If we'd had films we could have recorded it. But without them we did what worked best for us—we over-told our stories. The truth sometimes requires that.

Growing up, our Hapmose, but let me call him Moses so as not to confuse you, our Moses sometimes reminded me of things I'd heard about Isaac when he was younger, and Esau and Ishmael, wild and difficult. Caught between two cultures, not fully belonging to either of them, he was moody and increasingly prone to outbursts of anger. We sent him to see one of the priests at the temple of Amon-Ra, the ancient equivalent of going to therapy. But it didn't help much. Adopted, short, with a lisp, our child was a troubled

boy. Then at puberty, overnight, our scrawny baby and then short little boy
shot up taller than any of the other boys around, and went from being a
smooth sleek little animal to one of those young men who are sprouting hair
everywhere, all of which revolted him and all of which he shaved off, in the
Egyptian fashion. Yes, everything about him changed—except for his voice.
It never quite deepened, so now, in addition to his lisp, he had a very high
soft somewhat squeaky voice, which made him even more self-conscious. If
we had phones then and someone called to sell us the daily paper, hearing
his voice, they would have said, "Ma'am" to him, or "Miss." Tall and broad-
shouldered as he was, getting him to talk was now almost impossible. And
he never quite got used to his new body, broad and covered with a thick pelt
of hair, front and back, bottom to top. For years afterwards he continued to
throw himself into chairs like the small boy he had once been. Which was
sad and strange and, I must confess, slightly comical. And for some years
after that he and his razor were never far apart.

Bast and I tried to be good parents to him, but he was in a double bind.
He liked the life he had with us. I suppose we spoiled him. But he longed
to be with his birth family—until he paid another visit to their quarters. He
always came home disgusted and washed his hands over and over, sickened
by the dirt, the smells, the flies, the roaches, the poverty—grateful to be back
with the two of us again. And yet I knew that at the same time he was furious that his birth parents had given him away, and resented us for making
them look bad in his eyes, although they were all good people, his parents
and his sisters and brothers.

Perhaps Moses was what we today would call a manic-depressive, with
some anti-social tendencies. Here is the prime example of this. Ptahhotep's
workers were paid once a month, and as workers all over the world do on
payday, Moses and several other scribes ended up in a local tavern. Staggering out, drunk, he bumped into a fellow worker, Sobek, who snarled at him,
punched him in the shoulder, and called him, "Fur face," which was how the
Egyptians referred to men from bearded cultures. (This was ironic as Moses, in Egyptian fashion, as I said, had his head and his entire body shaved
daily by one of our servants, but he was so hairy that what for other men is
now called "a five o'clock shadow" came to our poor tortured son at noon.)
Enraged, Moses grabbed Sobek by the shoulders, spat in his face, called him
"Alabaster head," which is what we called the clean-shaven Egyptians. Then
Moses shoved Sobek away from him with great force. Sobek staggered and
fell backwards, hitting his head on the stone doorframe at the entrance to
the tavern. Still furious, Moses bent down to grab Sobek and shake him,
only to discover that he was dead. Terrified, instantly sober, Moses dragged
his body into an alley, then raced home and woke us up. Because of her

contacts, Bast was able to smuggle Moses out of Egypt by bribing the border guards. The later storytellers were uncomfortable about Moses being struck and invented the story about his killing a man who had struck another Hebrew, but it was he himself who had been hit first.

Moses fled to Midian, where he lived for more than three years. I chose the place, not Bast, sure that he would be welcomed as he was by our cousins, descendants of the children of Abraham and Keturah. As caravans of their traders sometimes came to Egypt, I'd stayed in touch with them. Or course we missed Moses terribly. Then one day about three years later, two of his fellow workers came to the house to speak with us. They had seen Sobek strike and insult Moses, but had been afraid to come forward, for fear of making things worse for our people. But their consciences had finally gotten the better of their fear. Bast encouraged them to speak to Ptahhotep about what had really happened. I never liked the man, but in that one instance I was grateful. Ptahhotep ruled that our son had acted in self-defense, that Sobek's death was an accident, and gave him a very large fine, which Bast paid, and then he was allowed to return to the city. Bast sent out a messenger to Moses, who was living in the village of Jethro, whose daughter Zipporah he had gotten involved with. Again, the Midianites were our relatives, descended from Abraham's son Midian from his marriage to Keturah.

It was a shock to see Moses when he came back. In the fashion of the desert people he had let all of his hair grow in, head hair, facial hair, and body hair. Our shaved tall son, from three years of working in the wilderness as a shepherd had turned into a massive hairy giant of a man. A real Hebrew. If it weren't for his voice, Bast and I wouldn't have known him at all. Ptahhotep had been lenient in his ruling, which pleased us, but he was harsh in its consequences. He wouldn't give Moses back his job. We were upset by this, but Moses wasn't. He didn't want to go back to work in Ptahhotep's accounting office. If he started shaving again, Bast thought she could get him a job in the scribal school, teaching beginners the basics of the intricate system of Egyptian writing that you all know, with its birds and snakes and bees and pointing hands. (I'll have more to say about those hieroglyphics later.) Moses refused to shave and refused to do any other work. When we tried to talk about it with him he would bellow, "If you don't like me being here, I'll go back to Midian." Losing him again was more than we could bear, so we always backed down. Instead, he started spending more and more time with his biological family, which was awkward for everyone. He'd grown up so differently from them, and now, after his time in Midian, he was even more different, even though he now thought he was more like them, which none of them did. After a few generations in Egypt they, we, may have been poor Semitic outsiders to the ruling class, but in terms of culture we had all assimilated, whereas the clan of Midian had held onto all the old stories from Abraham, held on to the old ways, and shared them with our son.

When Moses was home with us he would retreat to his room for days on end, and when he was angry, which was often, Bast and I and the servants would try to keep him away from anything breakable. Smashing bowls and plates seemed to comfort him. But it terrified the rest of us. And we were also deeply troubled by something else. He had told us when he returned of his marriage and of the birth of his two sons. We longed to see them. (Even a photograph would have made us feel better.) And we were troubled that he could so easily walk away from them, as if they were all inconsequential. But Moses never talked about them, and didn't seem to miss them as we had missed him. We had no idea where all of that would have gone, his anger, his brooding, into what disaster, but then the plague began, about six months after he returned to Egypt.

I can still recall an afternoon a few weeks into it, when people were starting to die, but before we had any idea of how horrifyingly widespread it would soon become. I was out in the garden, picking herbs for our dinner, and that was where Moses found me.

"Mother," he asked, "is it true what I once heard you say? That Grandfather Jacob made us promise we would return to Canaan after the famine was over?" I said that it was and he said, "That's why this plague has come to us. Shaddai is punishing us for breaking our promise." I laughed when he said that, which was a big mistake. "If Shaddai is punishing us, Dear," I said, "why are the Egyptians dying too?" If there'd been a jug there Moses would have hurled it across the garden. Instead he kicked his sandaled foot into one of my rosemary plants and said, "We have to go back," and stormed into the house to find Bast and tell her the same thing. She and I talked about it that night in bed, concerned. We'd seen our son go through his moods before, and they always passed, but something was building up in him, and we were both afraid.

Over the next few weeks, like a man with a mission, Moses started spending all his time at the complex where the rest of our people lived, telling everyone what he'd told us. Soon, word came back to us, from relatives and friends. As bad as things were in Egypt, people thought he was crazy. We'd lived there for several generations. Except for me, not a single one of us had ever been in Canaan. Imagine a fiery young man going from house to house telling you that it's time for you to go back to whatever little city or shtetl your ancestors came from. As poor and unhappy as you were in the New County you would probably laugh at him. Oppressed but surrounded by wealth, you would work till you dropped, dreaming that someday some of that wealth would be yours. I know this—because we all did. But then gradually, out of a combination of fear and hope, as the plague continued and as more and more of us were dying, one by one our frightened people started to agree with him. One night at dinner Moses turned to Bast and said, "Mother, will you go to Ptahhotep and ask him to cancel our debts? He knows that we can't pay them back." Bast tried to talk our son out of his request, but he was adamant and finally, worn out, she acquiesced, even though the idea of going back to Canaan seemed absurd to both of us, and the idea of approaching Ptahhotep left a very bad taste in our mouths.

A woman of her word, the very next day Bast paid a visit to Ptahhotep, to ask him to cancel our debts. But he refused. He wouldn't even tell her how much we owed the city. But Moses still had friends in the accounting office and he went there to find out. They let him review the books, which were kept on papyrus scrolls, and he came home with the total amount. I can't remember what it was now, but it was a lot. That night he sat with Bast and me and we discussed the situation. By that point so many people were dying that it seemed silly to try and hold us to the full amount, so Bast went back to see Ptahhotep and made him this offer. "I will give you all my land, my houses and fields, my servants, my vineyards, my boats, my share of the profits from the temple that are due to me as a high priest's daughter, if you will absolve this people of their debts so that they can go back to their homeland." Ptahhotep refused her again. In a way, she and I were relieved. We thought that Moses would get over his ridiculous obsession and stop making everyone feel guilty and even more afraid than we already were.

In the meantime, people all around us were dying like flies in winter, including both of Moses's parents and his sweet sisters Chavah and Peninnah and his charming brother Itai. Their deaths nearly destroyed Moses. It seemed to Bast and me that his very heart had been ripped out. Miriam was serving in the workers' clinic and Aaron became our unofficial priest, performing last rites, for the Egyptian priests would have nothing to do with us. Ptahhotep's soldiers kept guard around the workers' city, but they were dying and we were dying and when Bast went back to see Ptahhotep again her final argument was persuasive. "If we stay much longer the rest of us will die and you won't ever get your loans repaid. And so many of your guards are dead that the ones who remain won't be able to stop those of us who survive from leaving."

Ptahhotep finally consented to accept Bast's offer. What she hadn't said to him but had implied is that he himself might die any day. And, he was drowning in grief, as we all were. Not a single household I knew of had gone without at least one death in it. But there are a few things in the story that you know that are true, or based in truth. The plague took all of Ptahhotep's children. Cold as he was, he adored his little son Harakhty and his daughters

Baketamon and Tahery. Weakened by his losses, Ptahhotep took everything Bast had and canceled the debts we'd amassed over the years, the repayment of which was really what kept us in Egypt. Bast came home exhausted and ebullient. Moses and I were pacing back and forth in the courtyard of our house when she returned. We knew (like the story of Ruth told later on) that this woman had just given up all her worldly possessions to follow us out of Egypt. We three embraced in the courtyard, and then Moses ran out to tell Aaron and Miriam to organize the people.

So you see, there weren't ten plagues. Only one. There were no magic tricks, no rods turning into serpents. There was no pharaoh, just his wicked local representative, Ptahhotep. And it wasn't even Moses who dealt with him, but his adoptive mother, Bast. Now, there are several old legends about me, told in the Talmud and a few collections of midrashim. They state that I was the only one remembered that Joseph had asked us to take his body back with us to Canaan when we finally left Egypt. This is true. Some versions say that I was the only one who knew where he was buried. This is not true. We all had a shared burial ground near the Nile, and all of our dead were there so lots of us knew where Joseph was. My favorite accounts says that he was buried in a metal casket that was sunk into the Nile, and that I knew that magic words to give to Moses so that he could raise it up. So, of the true part, yes, I did remember, and I went to Moses and informed him of what we had to do. We took the six biggest men with us, as he'd been buried in a large double sarcophagus. It wasn't easy to open it, and when we finally did we discovered that his mummified body had crumbled into bones and dust. I was secretly relieved. How would we have carried that huge double coffin with us? Instead, we put his remains into a wooden storage box that Bast had had for years. Much easier for people in exile to carry. What the Torah leaves out is that Joseph's sister Dinah was interred there as well. Her bones too came with us, in their own little carved wooden box.

We left quickly. It says so in all accounts, and that's true. We were afraid to stay there any longer. Moses had convinced many of us that we were being punished for remaining in Egypt, and a frightened people can be easily manipulated. We left the next day. We *did* take flat bread with us, and as much as we could carry. But just as there was no pharaoh, no one followed us with chariots. The garrison soldiers were all too busy dying. We'd gone down to Egypt with flocks and camels and great wealth, but we'd sold almost everything over the years and would have to start all over again. And there weren't six hundred thousand men of us who left Egypt, as your Torah states. The story was revised in two layers. First one editor said that instead of us being six hundred people we were six hundred "contingents" of ten men each. Then a later editor took our old word "contingent" and interpreted it as "thousand." So, six hundred and nine people first became six contingents of ten each, and then became six hundred thousand. But again, 609 of us, the descendants of Jacob and his five wives and many of our Egyptian spouses, all of them workers themselves but Bast, left Egypt on that cool but sunny spring day. I can't tell you the exact year we left Egypt, but as I said earlier, it was during the reign of King Ramses I. The sky was clear, that I remember. It was the Egyptian version of one of those Serach Days my mother told me about. (We have a lot of them in Los Angeles, which is part of why I like it here.) Moses was in the lead, and Bast and I followed, with Miriam, Aaron, and then everyone else coming after us, some with donkeys, a few with our last camels, and most with their possessions on their back.

We were proud of our son, although later on some people said that we had pushed him into the role of leader, to give him purpose, to keep him out of trouble. Maybe we did. Parents do a lot of things for and against their children. But what did it matter! We'd escaped from the nightmare of our servitude and we'd escaped from the plague, which had mostly worn itself out by the time we left—and we'd gotten out of Egypt debt free! That was a miracle, and that's how we remembered it, and we remembered it that way, the way that it had happened—for several centuries.

As for Bast, she and I were together for almost twenty years, which was a very long time in those days! I buried her in the wilderness near Kadesh-Barnea. I've loved a number of women since that time (and few men, too, as I said before) and while my first love Dinah will always have a tender spot in my heart, Bast was the great love of my life. Imagine that! Almost three thousand years later, and it's Bast I think about when I think about love. And that's why it's such a joy to finally be able to put her back in the story of our people. For without her and her love and her great kindness and strength, she who has been remembered as Pharaoh's daughter—we would never have left our hellish life in Egypt. Little by little we'd have married into their families and lost our separate identity—but Fate (or God or.....???) had other things in mind for us, and used that generous and magnificent woman to satisfy Its desires.

Chapter Eight

The first wilderness year, Mount Sinai, revelation,

and everything that happened to us there

FOR A LONG TIME we didn't write things down. We just told stories, as we walked, one of us at the back of the line calling them out in a chant-like fashion. And we told them in our tents, old dried up tents we'd brought with us from Canaan and kept rolled up in our Egyptian houses, the wind whipping the flaps. But mostly we told them as we sat around a fire at night, under that vast dark vault shot with its own tiny fires, and we told them that way for generations. The very first time that someone decided to write down the stories of our people in a systematic way was long after the Exodus, long after our return to Canaan, during the reign of King Saul. After having lived for years as semi-independent tribes, we had come together as a nation like other nations, with a king and a capital. Saul and his ministers and the priests decided that we needed a regal epic to go along with our new status.

The very first official chronicler of our stories was Elishua the son of Avner, from a priestly family that lived in the village of Nob. Elishua was a direct descendant of Moses and Zipporah and when he sat down to write our national epic he told the story in a way that would highlight the achievements of his noble ancestor, and downplay those of Aaron and his descendants, who in his own time were a rival band of priests. Sadly, Bast had to go. No Egyptian widow could save the day. It had to be their own man, Moses, appropriated by them to serve their own purposes. And I had to go, too, because the patriarchy, as we've come to call it, was in full swing. It had become a man's world, but to tell you the truth, a lot of women liked the change. They said, "We invented art and agriculture, music, science, government, and religion. If it hadn't been for us we'd all still be running around like a bunch of wild animals. But we're worn out from all this inventing. So let's sit back and let the boys do some work for a change. It'll be fun to see what they come up with." You know the rest. It's history. Not so fun.

Speaking of history, our leaving Egypt, which was such a big deal for us, was an inconsequential event for the Egyptians. A bunch of wandering Semites leave a minor workers' city in the midst of a deadly plague wasn't newsworthy. Even the cancellation of our debts wasn't recorded in their chronicles. The papyrus that listed our debts was given to Bast, who used it to wrap up some figs that we took with us, and later on I used it to start a fire, out in the wilderness. Had I known its value, I certainly would have kept it. On the other hand, if I'd kept everything of value, I'd not only be one of the oldest human beings alive, but the most loaded-down human being too.

So, we left Egypt, most of us on foot, a few on donkeys. Passing through the wooden gates of our workers city, dust rising up around us, Bast took my hand and we turned to look back one last time, smiling at each other, remembering all that we had shared there. We walked thought those gates with a sense of disbelief. No men stood guard there. Too many had died, but not for a single moment had we ever thought that Ptahhotep would let us go, and because of that we'd never really asked ourselves if we wanted to leave our home. But we left, with the majority of our people, and we followed our son on the dirt road that headed east and north, toward Canaan, the land of my birth.

The Torah says that we wandered in the wilderness for forty years, until an entire generation of us had died, except for Joshua and Caleb. Not true. Not all of us died before we reentered Canaan, although I was the only one who went down and then went back. And again, there weren't six hundred thousand men of us. Have you ever been to the Sinai? There's no way that that many people could have lived there. Not even six thousand of us could have done it. No, it was six hundred and nine of us who left Egypt, right before sunrise, with no angels or miracles to guide us.

But when we got out of Egypt, finally, with all of our debts to the Egyptians canceled, we all felt so good, so wonderful, that it seemed to us that a miracle had happened. We walked east and then north for several days, weary and afraid. Suddenly the reality of our situation hit us. We were going back to a place that no one knew but me. As you can see in the Torah, and as you can see again in human history, the known but awful suddenly seemed far more appealing than the unknown and perhaps wonderful.

Moses took the lead. It had been his idea for us to go, so it was only natural. There were several small branches of the Nile to cross over, and then one large one. None of us knew the best fording place and it took several days of wandering to find one that didn't seem too deep, so we prayed to Shaddai and pushed into the water. It was cold and waist-high in some places, but shoulder high and swift in others. I remember that a boy named Tibni lost the small bundle of things he'd had time to gather before we left. It was carried away in the current. Miriam watched him struggle after it and called out, "Let it go, cousin. Let it go." A young woman from the family of Dan named Iscah stumbled, and her little daughter Elat, clinging to her back, was nearly swept away. But Shifra and Puah, the elderly midwives who had brought her into the world, grabbed the child and saved her. And we all pushed on, panting and cold, following the path that Moses had taken through the reeds and across the open water.

Bast and I stayed at the rear, waiting till everyone else was in the water. From where we were standing I could see Moses and Miriam grasp at reeds on the opposite shore, and pull themselves up on the far bank. Then, gasping, coughing up water, muddy and dripping, alone, in groups, hand in hand, the rest of our people pushed and pulled themselves up on the far side of the sea. Some were sobbing. Others were standing, shivering, numb and afraid. Others were wandering in the crowd, looking for their loved ones. Moses, beaming, reached down to Aaron's little daughter Batshuah and raised her high up over his head. Then he spun her around and the spray of water made rainbows in the morning sky.

Miriam was a marvelous singer. Much better than me. And she could also spontaneously compose songs, which I could never do. To this day I can remember the look of joy on her face when we signaled her that everyone had made it across the water safely. She threw back her head and let out a long loud ululation of victory. Everyone stopped, and then, pushing their way through the crowd, all the women gathered in a big circle around her, dripping wet, babies on their backs, little children in hand. We had no drums. We had no timbrels. Or sistrums or hand bells or any other instruments mentioned in the Torah. Most of us had been too poor to have things like that, and if he had, we'd left Egypt with what we could carry on our backs so we probably wouldn't have taken them. But we had our hands and our voices and when Miriam began to clap, all the women clapped with her. Then she began to sing and after each line all the rest of us repeated it, as we always did when she was singing, in Egypt and for the rest of her life, in our travels in the wilderness.

> As if the waters had parted for us—she sang.
> As if the waters had parted for us—we repeated!
> As if Shaddai had parted them with a strong hand.
> As if Shaddai had parted them with a strong hand.
> We crossed. We crossed toward freedom.
> We crossed. We crossed toward freedom.

The waves rose up around us like horses.
The waves rose up around us like horses.
Yes, like horses with soldiers coming after us.
Yes, like horses with soldiers coming after us.
But we crossed. Every one of us crossed.
But we crossed. Every one of us crossed.
Yes. The waters parted for us, and together
    we crossed into freedom.
Yes. The waters parted for us, and together
    we crossed into freedom.

All the men and boys were gathered around the women as we sang and danced, clapping and cheering us on. And when the power that flowed through her began to ebb, when the song and dance began to slow down, Miriam let out a final loud cry that echoed out over the hills. The Torah says that Moses led the people in song. He did not. (The spectacular song that's attributed to him was written many years later, by a descendant of his named Oriyahu, a scribe who was living in Bethel.) First of all, as I told you before, Moses had a soft voice and a heavy lisp and was always embarrassed to talk in front of people, and second, he could never carry a tune and wouldn't have tried. No, our impetuous Hapmose had led us out of Egypt into freedom, thanks to Bast and her profoundly generous act. And now, after three thousand years, you can once again read the real song that we sang that day.

You can also see how, over time, inspired by elements of Miriam's song, being as we are such great storytellers, one person added this, another one that, a third embellished like a tailor sewing a fancy braid on a lapel. And soon enough there was a Pharaoh and chariots and a great sea parting. But that story is so wonderful, with all its embellishments, so you may not want to hear what really happened, or what happened next. I should have warned you before, but if that's the case—in this and in the next chapter I'll be telling you the story of Mount Sinai, so if you don't want to know what really happened to your ancestors, please skip ahead to Chapter 10.

Before I go on I want to say a few words about how memory persists. The Torah, as you know, prohibits men from having sex with each other, but it says nothing about women having sex with each other. However, *Leviticus* 18:3, states, "You shall not copy the practices of the land of Egypt where you dwell." This, the much later rabbis of the Talmud stated, was a prohibition against lesbianism, written more than five hundred years after the Torah as you know it had been compiled. On the surface there is absolutely no connection between that verse and women who love each other—unless you remember Bast and me, as some of those rabbis did. Although we were left out of the text, no—deliberately taken out of the text—the rabbis of old still remembered us and so did some of our people. Edited out, and banned, that has been our fate. But truth will always triumph over lies, if you wait long enough. And Shaddai has somehow preserved me so that I could tell you what really happened to our people, all those many many many many years ago.

But let me go on. First of all, I want you to remember that from the start we were divided into two camps, based on the divisions that went back to Joseph's time. We traveled that way and camped that way, in spite of what the Torah says about our neatly organized community. One group, of the same families that had worked outside with Joseph, all camped together, as they'd remained connected since his death. They included the descendants of Joseph, Benjamin, Dan, Naphtali, Issachar, Zebulon, Gad, and my own family, the descendants of my father Asher. The other group who all camped together was made up of the descendants of Judah, Levi, Simeon, Reuben, the four eldest sons of Leah and Jacob, who had always been tight, as we say now. And by the time that we arrived back in Canaan, our community was even more divided. Gad, Reuben, and part of the family of my Uncle Manasseh went off on their own and the whole tribe of Levi set themselves apart, wanting as Moses's kinfolk to be the intermediaries between the two groups. Bast and I tried to stop all that fragmenting, but now I know that it's just human nature.

Remember that there were six hundred nine of us who left Egypt, Hebrews and others who had married into our family, including Egyptians and Nubians and one husband from Yemen, a sailor who'd married one of our women. Many of us had children, and a few were babes in their mothers' arms, walking dusty trails back toward a land that only I had ever seen, back to a strange land, very different from Egypt. We crossed out of Egypt and headed east to Midian, where we hooked up with our relatives, who were led by Moses's father-in-law Jethro. We were welcomed as family and that was joyful. They shared stories with us and passed on teachings from our ancestors that we had lost in our years of servitude, which was essential for us, a form of bonding with our own lost selves, lost souls, for bondage, servitude, had diminished and dehumanize us—which is a lesson we learned in that time of renewal, and which is behind the many many times in every single Torah that ever existed that the text has said some version of—"Love the stranger as yourself, because you were strangers in Egypt." This is essential, this is the core of the very best of who we are as a people, and it was our kinfolk in Midian who brought that home to us, through the tender care of Jethro their elder.

Jethro was a good man and his daughter Zipporah was a splendid woman. (Pay no attention to the racist comments about her written by later editors.) She knew her way around the Sinai wilderness very well, and joined Moses, our primary leader, his brother Aaron, their sister Miriam, and Bast and I as our guides as we continued back toward Canaan. One thing the Torah relates very clearly is how contentious our community was, challenging Moses and complaining about our lot. Bad as things were in Egypt, Ptahhotep needed us as workers and in his workers' city we were reasonably well fed and housed and clothed, after the time of the famine that made Joseph so famous. But there was so little to eat out in Sinai, and people grumbled and complained all the time.

Things were getting worse and worse. Finally it was Jethro who sat Moses down and told him that he had to do something, knowing that he had led us out of bondage to our debts, and that he alone could be our leader. Moses called the elders of each family together and created a tribal council to back him up. It was a very good idea, but unfortunately, it didn't work. The very same people who turned to Moses for leadership eventually turned against him. The rebellions you read about in the Torah happened, but again, not nearly in so dramatic a fashion as you will find there. No one died after Korah and his cronies tried to overthrow Moses. Once he reasserted his power, a group of them took their families, left the rest of our traveling community, and headed back to Egypt, never to be heard from again. But all of that violence in the story served another, later purpose. It served the priests and their control over the rest of us.

Night after night we would sit up with Moses in council, Bast, Aaron, Miriam, Jethro, Zipporah, and me, talking about what to do, where to go, how to keep our rag-tag community together. It was Jethro who suggested that we change our plans and not head back to Canaan yet. He said we were too scattered, too disorganized, that we would be easy prey for brigands and marauders on the way there, like the Amalekites, and easy targets for the soldiers of the Canaanite petty kings when we got there. "Stay in the desert till you can meld your community," he counseled his son-in-law, and instead of being hot-headed, for once, Moses listened. So we settled in Midian for a while, and things were all right. People were tired of walking, tired of dust, and most, just as the Torah states, wanted to go back to Egypt. Then Dathan and Abiram began to organize the people against Moses. The Torah fuses their rebellion with Korah's but they were separate. When those two challenged Moses his solution wasn't to seek the backing of the council, or to turn to the people directly and appeal to their loyalty. Instead, he insulted all of the council members to their faces, told them that they were useless to him, and when Jethro tried to calm him down, Moses turned on his father-in-law, screaming at him, and said, "I've had it with you, always telling me what to do. I never wanted to be in charge, and now I won't be. I'm getting out of here." And he stood up, loudly wiped his hands in front of himself, shook them out—then turned and marched back to his tent, leaving us sitting on the ground in shocked silence.

Soon Noiyah, another of Aaron's daughters, came running toward us yelling, "Uncle Moses is leaving! Uncle Moses is leaving." Zipporah got up and ran toward their tent. Bast and Jethro joined her. I sat there stunned, and then got up myself. We ran through the camp, raising dust, and caught up with Moses as he was leaving. "Don't think you can change my mind. I wish I'd never said a word to any of you and just left for Canaan by myself." I took a step toward him. Bast grabbed my arm. I turned to her, furious, but the look on her face said, "Let him go. Let him get this out of his system." Time was very different then, but weeks went by and we didn't see Moses. One night in our tent I had a fight with Bast about it. "You were so sure he'd be back. But where is he now? Halfway to Canaan, or lost, or dead!" I screamed at her. She burst into tears and I instantly wished those words had never come out of my mouth. I grabbed her up in my arms and we held each other, sobbing. Those days were hell, a concept that we didn't have yet. But hell they were.

Nearly three moon cycles went by, in which we remained at that small oasis, tending our flocks, mending our tents, intending every day to move on, but remaining. Miriam took control of our community, and as there was a good source of water there, and as we were all exhausted, it made sense for us to stay. Miriam was a powerful woman, and if you asked me at that point who history would remember, her or Moses, I would have put money on her. Not that we were ever close. We weren't. Today we might talk about the tension between adopted and birth families, but we didn't think that way then. So there was awkwardness, tension, but I always respected Miriam and she always respected me as our community's most elder elder, and we all thought that Moses would come back in a day or two, after he had blown off steam. But when days went by, and then moon quarters and another new moon, we feared that if we moved on he might not ever find us. (We never spoke about the possibility that he might be dead, but we all must have thought it.)

One morning, not long after sunrise, I was sitting in my tent, newly awakened, when I heard people yelling on the far side of the camp. At first I thought there was some kind of trouble, again, but then I could make out one loud voice yelling, "Moses is back. Moses is back." Well, actually what they said was, "Hapmose is back. Hapmose is back." Well, actually, that isn't what they said at all. They said it in our version of Early Hebrew, with some Ancient Egyptian thrown in, sort of a hybrid early version of Judeo-Arabic or Yiddish or Ladino.

I was already up on my feet, in a panic when I thought that something was wrong, but I ran faster than I knew I could when I heard those words. Bast was down by the stream, getting water. For a woman who was raised with servants she adapted far better than many of my poor cousins to the harsh desert conditions. She grabbed her water-skin and too came running. We met up by the rise to the east of the camp and clasping each other's hands we flew toward the gathering crowd.

Even at a distance Bast and I could tell that something had happened to our son. He stood taller. There was a clarity in his eyes and an aura around him that was almost visible. The Torah is right when it says that his face glowed. Miriam put it best in the song that she sang that morning.

> *Oh my brother, stranger, wanderer*
> *Now come back to us from the sea of sand*
> *Your face afire*
> *Like a tree that burns but is not consumed*
> *Oh my brother, stranger, wanderer*
> *Now you have come back home.*

Moses was hungry. Zipporah took him back to her tent and fed him. Bast and I stood back, our hands locked together in joy, relieved at his safe return and amazed by his transformation. We held each other, crying, patiently waiting for him to emerge. And others, hearing the news, soon joined us, everyone eager to hear where he had gone and what had happened to him, and of course we all wanted to push into that tent with our questions— but the change in him was so palpable that it had already changed us too, and we all kept our distance, not wanting to interfere with or interrupt what was going on inside him. Instead, we sat in the sand outside that tent and waited. And waited. Expecting to hear the two of them talking. But all there was was silence.

Finally . . . Moses came out. By the time he emerged all of us were gathered there, all six hundred and ten of us—for Noamah and Rami had had a little daughter, our first child in the wilderness, who they rightly named Sarah. Now, our son was never a man of many words, and he wasn't that day. He never once told us the story of what had happened to him while he was gone, and we knew to never ask. All that he said was, "Shaddai came to me in the wilderness and told me that we must all return to that place at the next new moon."

Chapter Nine

In this the ninth chapter you will learn

all about Sinai, where it was, and

several other things you may not want to know

It took us several days to head west and then north. We approached from the south and as we got closer and closer our hearts sank, wondering if Moses had spent too much time out there and lost his mind, as sometimes happens in the heat of the desert. The area was flat and open, strewn with small rocks. It was dusty, barren, bleak, even frightening, especially compared to the lovely oasis we'd just been camped in.

Thinking about that place reminds me of my early years in this country. I was living back East with my late partner Clara, in the suburbs of New York City. Brave thing for two women to do in the 1950's—we bought a house in Westchester that we turned into a music school. People knew me as Sarah. I'd given up years and years before that trying to get people to hear and understand the difference between Serach and Sarah, especially after I came to America, where most people couldn't make a good KH sound, not even some Jews. So I became a widow, Mrs. Da Silva, using the last name I picked up before the Expulsion, when I'd been living in Spain. And Clara remained who she'd always been, Miss Clara Litwak. That was long before the days of Ms, a title I suspect she would have hated. Clara was proud to be an unmarried woman. "I worked hard for my life," she used to say. I taught violin and viola, always in love with stringed instruments. Clara taught piano. Our living room became a recital studio, a grand piano at the far end, its walls lined with chairs that twice a year were filled with beaming parents and trembling students.

Right across the street from our house was the last undeveloped plot of land in the neighborhood. The children on our side of the street would yell out to their mothers, "I'm going off to play in the cross woods." But the children who lived on the same side of the street as that lovely open area would call out to their mothers, "I'm going off to play in the side woods." It was, "the same exact place," to use an expression those kids were fond of, but they had two different names for it, and so for them, in a way, the same exact same place was two different places.

To this day the Torah has two names for the place that Moses took us to. Sometimes it's called Mount Sinai, the name by which it's best known. But sometimes it's called Mount Horeb. Textual critics see these two names as a reflection of two different traditions. In a way, they're right. Some scholars think the name Sinai is related to that of the Mesopotamian moon god Sin, who was worshipped in the southern city of Ur and in Haran in the north that are a part of the story of Abraham and Sarah. Not true. Sinai has nothing to do with Sin. It comes from an old Semitic word for "dusty."

Then there's Mount Horeb. It comes from another Semitic word, one that means, "desolate." So, we have Mount Dusty and Mount Desolate. In the book of *Deuteronomy* there's a nice passage which says that God chose Israel not because it was the greatest nation, but because it was the smallest. And there's a similar tradition in the Talmud that says that God chose Sinai/Horeb not because it was an Everest of mountains but because it was an anthill. This is closer to the truth than any of the Mount Sinais that have been identified down through the ages, from the one that towers over St. Catherine's Monastery to the volcano that one scholar insists was way out in Arabia.

Our initial response to that place was despair. "Where has he taken us to *now*? Egypt was familiar. The Midianite oasis was safe and comfortable. But this place is terrible." Only it was too late to turn back, so, weary and weak, we dragged ourselves on behind Moses. And then, at last, as we kept walking, we saw with great relief why he had taken us there. In the center of that flat plain there was a hill. Not a tall one, really no more than a five or six foot rise. In our minds the earth and our bodies were not separate. The name of our Creator God, Shaddai, comes from the root for breast, so we used the same word for breast and low hill, just as we used the same word for tooth and jagged hills, and the same word for head and for the summit of a mountain.

Moses, we all soon realized, had led us to a Shaddai hill. What made the place even more perfect was that on the top of that hill there was a single large boulder, and growing right next to it there was single tall acacia tree. For us the boulder represented the god Yahweh and the tree was the symbol of Yahweh's sister-wife the goddess Asherah, both of whom we saw not just as Shaddai's children but as Shaddai's manifestation in the world. The Middle East remains rocky and today there are acacias all over Sinai, but they aren't native and were rare in those days, which made the hilltop even more magical, and it was there that the energy of The Creator, as I would call it now, had flowed through Moses and then through the rest of us too.

I wish I could say that what happened there flowed through us easily and unified us, but it didn't. Even physically we were divided. As we had done in all of our camping places, we set up our tents in two groups. One settled on the north side of the rise, and they called the area they camped in Horeb, Desolate. The other group set up their tents on the south side of that small hill. They called the place Sinai, Dusty. What made it livable was that to the east of the rise, about a quarter of a mile away, in a deep ravine, there was a small spring-fed stream. Miriam and some of the other women elders decided to set up their tents down beside that stream. She was in charge and she made sure that no one would get more than their fair share of water. Even today people talk about Miriam and her well, forgetting that she was also our herbal doctor, psychotherapist, and music director, leading us in song and dance at full moons and other special times. Bast and I were in charge of food and provisions. Jethro and his sons had come with us and they organized teams of hunters and foragers. Moses's Levite relatives served as his back-up crew. And so, with that structure in place, we settled in at Horeb/Sinai to chart our future.

We were in that spot for more than a year. During the first month, all of us, day after day, gathered together each morning to talk and dream and plan out our lives. We had little future vision. All we could think about was the present. We were scared, hungry, tired, felt dislocated, and Moses, who had been dislocated himself, was our perfect guide from servitude to freedom. Whereas in the past he would push his brother Aaron in front of him to speak, this time he took charge, calling out to the circle of our people, more than six hundred of us sitting on skins and woven mats on the ground. Daily, Moses made sure that we all participated in the conversation about what we were going to do and how we were going to organize ourselves now that our debts were cancelled and we were going back to Canaan, as Jacob had told us to do so long ago. And out of our time at that mound came ideas and attitudes that shape the lives of Jews almost three thousand years later.

There's another old legend about me, that I would be able to recognize our eventual savior when he appeared on the scene. I wish I could say that that was true. But at the time, and with all these years to look back on it, much as I loved our son, I would never have said that he'd become the strong and decisive leader that he was. If you told me at the time that it was going to be one of Jochebed and Amram's children, as I said before—I would have bet all that I had on Miriam. Aaron was sweet and charming, but he lacked Miriam's strength and charisma. She was the glue of our people in the wilderness, and we owe her far more than just a cup on the table at Passover. In fact it was Miriam who gave me my job for the next thousand years. Puzzled about my longevity I went to her one day, our herbalist, thinking that my problem was the opposite of ill-health—too much health! I asked her what was wrong with me and she said, "Auntie, you are our memory." (She did suggest a tea made of rosemary, which I enjoy to this very day.)

So there was no thunder, no lightning, no flames or visions of God at Mount Dusty and Desolate. But was God in that place? I'm not one for miracles, none of which I've ever seen. I'm a down-to-earth very practical woman, not any kind of a mystic. But something remarkable did happen to us there, something that I never encountered again until the world watched the radical transformation that Gandhi led in India, where in a much larger way humble, poor, and frightened people gathered together to chart their own destiny, without blood or violence on their parts. Our rabbis say that all the Jews who ever were and ever will be were at Sinai, and in a way this is true, that a people beaten into submission by fear, debt, and then disease, could transcend that and rebirth themselves—opened the door for every one of us who followed.

After almost four generations in Egypt, our roots were weak as a people. We knew that we couldn't return to the past, but we didn't know what the future might hold, back in a land that no one but me had ever seen. Moses, like a powerful and loving mother, held us all in his enlightened embrace, and allowed us to craft a new way of living, which inspires the world and inspires oppressed people to this very day. First, we crafted a list of principles to guide us. They aren't the Ten Commandments that you know, but a much-edited version of them is actually preserved in your Torah.

Nothing was included in the covenant we came up with until we'd discussed it and everyone had agreed upon it, and sometimes our disagreements were loud and long and went on far into the night—for days! To give you an idea of the primary law of our people, I will show you what our original Ten Guidelines looked like, because I remember them very well. After we'd agreed upon all of them, which wasn't easy, all of us memorized them and Moses carved them into two large flat rocks that he found. So pick up a Bible and go to *Exodus 34:10-26*, where you will find the only text in the Torah that is actually labeled "The Ten Commandments" (Although Instructions would be a better choice of words.) Most of you have probably never noticed these verses because for millennia we have honored and labeled two nearly identical but different texts, the ones found in *Exodus* and

Deuteronomy. But if you read the text I just mentioned and compare it to the ten guidelines below that we came up with all those dusty desolate and luminous years ago, you will know what was guiding our people at the time and that continues to guide us—for a covenant once made can be violated but can never be broken, even if later editors change it, over and over again.

> *We the house of Sarah, affirm these to be our sacred laws, for all time.*

1. *When we enter the land where our ancestors dwelled we will remember that we are Hebrews, wanderers, strangers, there to live among the people of the land.*

2. *We honor Shaddai the god of our ancestors, and Shaddai's children Asherah and Yahweh, and their children the Elohim.*

3. *We will observe the Feast of Unleavened Bread, at the set time in the month of Aviv, for it was in that month that we left Egypt.*

4. *We will dedicate all of our children to Shaddai, and become through all our generations a nation of priests, women and men together.*

5. *We will observe new moons as a time of celebration, for we left Egypt under a slim new moon, and we count our days from its appearance.*

6. *Six days we will work and on the seventh day we will cease from all labor, to remember throughout time that in Egypt we served taskmasters and now we are free.*

7. *We will observe the Feast of Weeks, of the first fruits of the wheat harvest, when we return to the land where our ancestors once dwelled.*

8. *We will observe the Feast of Ingathering at the turn of the year as well, singing and dancing in celebration of our deliverance into a land of milk and honey.*

9. *We will observe the Feast of Yahweh and Asherah at the dark time of the year, purifying ourselves in preparation for the return to planting.*

10. *We will not boil a kid in its mother's milk.*

In all ancient Middle Eastern covenants there was a preamble that announced who was doing what with whom. You know the preface from the Ten Commandments you're familiar with, "I am the Lord your God who brought you out of the land of Egypt, out of the house of bondage." The preface to the very first set of commandments was:

> *We the house of Sarah, affirm these to be our sacred laws, for all time.*

The words we began with, "We the house of Sarah," were important to us, for we all agreed that she was our shared ancestor, although some of us were not really her descendants but people who had married into our clan and come out of Egypt with us, that "mixed multitude" you can read about in every Torah. And while we debated about whether to call ourselves "the children of Sarah and Abraham" we ended up agreeing on using just her name and on using the word "house," for it conveyed a solidity that we found ourselves lacking out in our tents in the wilderness.

> *1—When we enter the land where our ancestors dwelled we will remember that we are Hebrews, wanderers, strangers, there to live among the people of the land.*

Of all the commandments, this one was the easiest for us to agree on. From Sarah and Abraham first going to Canaan, we were outsiders, and our problem in Egypt wasn't being outsiders but being oppressed. Today I might say, "It's our karma to be wanderers," which isn't very different from what we said way back when. Centuries later I remember arguing about this commandment with an editor of an early Torah, who hated it. He thought it came from the minds of newly freed slaves. But I see it as something that for most of our history has kept us from being harsh taskmasters ourselves. I see it as something that's encoded in our DNA.

> *2—We honor Shaddai the god of our ancestors, and Shaddai's children Asherah and Yahweh, and their children the Elohim.*

We fought about this commandment a great deal. Some of us were comfortable honoring the deities of Egypt, and others felt that when we returned to Canaan we should serve the many deities of the land, some of them the same or related to ours. But in the end a consensus grew that we would return to the faith of Abraham and Sarah. We saw Shaddai's children and grandchildren, Asherah, Yahweh, and the Elohim, as reflections of Shaddai, and not separate. Was that monotheism? Probably not, according to your contemporary definition of that word. But for us, this commandment wasn't about theology, but about identity. We were reminding ourselves to be faithful to our own tradition, and over the millennia I have watched us visit, revisit, revise, and abandon these ancient words.

> *3—We will observe the Feast of Unleavened Bread, at the set time in the month of Aviv, for it was in that month that we left Egypt.*

Once we'd come up with a framework for solidifying our identity, we decided it was important to enshrine our recent liberation in our code. Aviv was the original name for the month we now call Nisan, that name brought back with us centuries later from the Babylonian Exile. What seemed most telling to us, memorable, especially to our children, even at our poorest, was how lovely and delicious good Egyptian bread was. But what we took with us after Bast negotiated our freedom was un-risen bread, and after many arguments about what to call our festival of liberation, we agreed upon that name and symbol, although the matzah of today, those hard crackers, is nothing like what we took with us, which was a kind of flatbread rather like Ethiopian injera.

> 4—*We will dedicate all of our children to Shaddai, and become through all our generations a nation of priests, women and men together.*

Our next commandment further established our religious practice and our sense of purpose, of vocation, as a people. In those days the eldest child, male *and* female, served as the priest or priestess for that family. In Egypt they had a class of priests, and anyone could become a priest or priestesses. We fiercely debated this for a very long time and finally decided that we wanted to go back to the way it had been with us before. But as I've said, the patriarchy was gaining in influence, and soon only first *sons* would be considered priests. Then gradually, over time, only members of Moses and Aaron's tribe and family, the Levites could be priests. Looking back on it, there was much to be said for the Egyptian way, and I wonder if we should have followed it. More egalitarian. Like what we eventually came up with— rabbis who are not a hereditary class. But the idea that we are a nation of priests—remains embedded in our DNA and in our souls.

> 5—*We will observe new moons as a time of celebration, for we left Egypt under a slim new moon, and we count our days from its appearance.*

The New Moon had been a major festival for our ancestors. Jacob and his wives and children all celebrated it each month, and I stressed the importance of coming back to that observance. The Egyptians preferred the full moon as a time for revelry. The return of the moon was something we could see, in the days before we had calendars. It linked us with the cycles of nature, which is still important to me. I was sad, later, when this commandment was edited out, just as I was sad some years ago when I stopped bleeding each month in alignment with the moon—which we actually considered male back then.

6—Six days we will work and on the seventh day we will cease from all labor, to remember throughout time that in Egypt we served taskmasters and now we are free.

Our lives in Egypt were organized around work, around working for someone else, and it was Moses's genius to enshrine for us a notion of no-work. Abraham and Sarah came from a culture that honored the four phases of the moon, but Moses invented the Sabbath as we know it, to comfort a weary wandering people who did not know how to rest. Even today it's a radical concept, in a world of cell-phones and email, where people are more bonded to their jobs than we were when I first came to this county in the years before the Second World War. All through Jewish history it's the Sabbath that's healed us and saved us. At the time none of us knew that it would be so important, and there was actually less debate about this commandment than any other. True, there was a vocal minority in our tribe that said, "We have a lot to do. There's a lot that we need. A day of no work is a really bad idea! How will we ever accomplish anything?" But with this commandment our Moses used the force of his authority, and I am glad he did.

7—We will observe the Feast of Weeks, of the first fruits of the wheat harvest, when we return to the land where our ancestors once dwelled.

8—We will observe the Feast of Ingathering at the turn of the year as well, singing and dancing in celebration of our deliverance into a land of milk and honey.

The holidays we decided to observe were not the ones we'd grown fond of in Egypt but the ancient Semitic agricultural festivals that Abraham and his wives and children celebrated. Some of us were against celebrating them—after living in Egypt, we saw farmers as low class; not so low as shepherds, but close. Others of us, infused with longing and nostalgia, yearning to eat things we grew and harvested ourselves, were eager to return to the old ways, but as you must know, this tension between celebrating historical events and agricultural ones continues to this day among our people, all over the world. We celebrated them when I was a little girl and because Jethro and I encouraged our returning to celebrate them, we were able to influence the vote, and in a good way I think. Oh, but the milk we talked about was from goats and sheep and what we meant by "honey" isn't what you mean. We meant a kind of date-paste that was made all over the region. The word only came to mean "honey" later.

*9—We will observe the Feast of Yahweh and Asherah at the dark
time of the year, purifying ourselves in preparation for the return
to planting.*

What can I say about Commandment Nine, about a Feast that none of
you have ever heard of? In my youth it was a grand celebration, held near
the longest night of the year, to celebrate the sacred marriage of Asherah
and Yahweh, the children of Shaddai. By our shrines to them of tree and
boulder we kindled new fires to honor their connection, to honor the days
getting longer. It was a time of joy and pleasure that marked a return to
planting season, but as the world grew more and more patriarchal, and as
our religion grew more and more monotheistic and male, that holiday was
forbidden—then forgotten! But curiously, I've read that the Jewish holiday
that's celebrated the most today isn't Passover, which I would have bet on,
or even the New Year or Yom Kippur, but Hanukkah, with all of its candles.
Do you think perhaps a deep tribal memory remains, encoded in our DNA,
a spiritual need to have a holiday around the time of the winter solstice? (I
do.)

10—We will not boil a kid in its mother's milk.

Our last commandment is a puzzle to everyone to this very day, rabbis
and scholars, historians and archaeologists. It appears three times in different places in the Torah, so it was clearly important to your ancestors. It's a
major part of keeping kosher, at the root of the practice of not eating milk
or meat together. While the first nine commandments are easy to explain to
you, dear reader—this last one is not. In order to make sense of it for you, I
will have to tell you a very long story.

Every family has particular memories that help to define it, that set it
apart from other families. I told you an ancient one from my birth family,
the story about Jacob and Esau and the calf they dyed a beautiful deep blue
to play a game with their father. And whenever any of their descendants
wanted to say, "That's crazy," "That's ridiculous," or "I don't believe a single
word you're saying," we'd roll our eyes up in our head, sigh and say, "Look at
that blue lamb." The business of the kid and its mother's milk is another such
story, only it's not a funny one. But it was so critical for us in that time that
we put it into our covenant, and here's the story behind it.

We'd all gone down to Egypt with flocks of sheep and goats, and with
our camels, but over time we'd sold most of them to survive in our worker's
city, and so we left Egypt with very little of the richness we'd arrived with.
Jethro and his clan gave us new breeding stock, but their numbers were
small, and while Moses had learned to be a shepherd during his time with

Jethro, except for me, no one else knew anything about taking care of animals. Many of our new flocks died, and when they did we cooked them and used their skins to make tents and clothing and other things that we needed, but we were always hungry for meat and always complaining about it to Moses. Your Torah got that right. And often, he exploded, even after his transformation. "Go back to Egypt if you don't like it here. Go back to your stupid city jobs and your inhuman overseers and see if I care." For unlike Joseph who had loved urban life, Moses always had an aversion to it, and that split in our people remains to this very day.

I remember once traveling to Japan with Clara and a small group of our advanced students, so that they could compete in an international music competition. The judges were strict, our students weren't doing as well as they'd hoped, and every day they would kvetch and moan. "We want pizza!" Well, try and find pizza in Tokyo in 1953. Well, there was a dish we all loved in Egypt—lamb simmered in milk and spices till it's soft and flaky and falls off the bones. But it can't be from an old lamb. It has to be from a very young lamb, a few weeks old. Well, given that we were trying to build up our flocks again, we had a clear understanding that no one would ever kill a young lamb.

There was a woman in the family of Naphtali named Besem, camped on the north side of the hill, whose few sheep were doing very well. In that first spring when we were working on our code, several of Besem's ewes had given birth, and a man named Ozer from the tribe of Judah, camped on the south side of the hill, who was married to Besem's sister Niath, decided to steal one of her baby sheep and cook it up for his wife and children, who also missed that Egyptian lamb dish. That he did it would have been a crime, but what made it worse was that he sent his young son Shallum to get some milk from his Aunt Besem to cook the lamb in, which she had plenty of and was glad to share with her beloved sister's family.

We were crazy then, afraid, lost and not sure of what was going on. And Ozer was even more crazy if he thought that in the midst of six hundred people he could slaughter a baby lamb, cook it, and not have anyone find out, even though he did it far away from the camp.

Besem didn't immediately realize that one of her baby lambs was missing, and at first she thought it had wandered off and gotten lost. But soon the whole camp was like a hive of angry bees, because, naturally—someone had smelled Ozer's stew. As soon as Besem heard about it, she put two and two together. Enraged, she stormed across the hill, where an angry circle were already gathered, jeering at Ozer and his family as they sat around a small cooking fire. Besem pushed her way to the front and started screaming at her brother-in-law, who stood up and said something to Besem about how selfish she was. Well one thing led to another, and Besem shoved Ozer. A huge crowd had gathered by then and they all saw him fall backwards onto the fire, knocking over the stewpot and badly burning his back. Miriam spent weeks taking care of him, and Moses, remembering his own shoving match, was plunged into what today we call an episode of PTSD!

The whole camp was in an uproar. All of our fears exploded outward. Everyone was angry at everyone else, and the old divisions between us going back to the time of Joseph, which led to us camping in two groups on either side of that dusty desolate hill—those old divisions flared up even more strongly. There were people from the north side who wanted to kill Ozer and others from the south who wanted to kill Besem. Leaders from each group threatened to leave and poor Moses did his best to try and calm things down. For days and days on end we battled about what to do, who to punish, and what the punishment would be.

Finally our rag-tag community calmed down after Moses got the parties involved to agree that for killing her lamb and for all the lost lambs that might have been born from it, Ozer was to give his sister-in-law, within three years' time, five new baby lambs. And for causing her brother-in-law the burns which scarred him for life, Besem was to give Ozer five new baby lambs. Bast and I were so proud of Moses, who was so patient all through that episode—and never once lost his temper.

Today it all seems ludicrous, but it didn't then, and when we finally sat down to talk about our covenant, this issue kept boiling up—that word of course chosen deliberately. Moses made all of us agree that in order to heal and get beyond the incident we wouldn't discuss it until we felt satisfied about everything else we'd agreed on. Each time someone brought it up, he'd remind them that we'd get to it later. And when we did, nearly a year after we began, these were the words that we came up with, never for a moment realizing what a curious impact they would have on our people down through the generations.

Looking back on it, thinking of Besem and Ozer, who never forgave each other, and thinking about the Ten Commandments that you know, with their ethical code, you may wonder how we came up with such a strange first covenant. You may wonder how a set of guidelines that once began with "We" was later turned into a version whose commandments all begin with "You." You may also wonder why the redactors of your Torah didn't focus on the edited version of our instructions that came down to them, but came over time to favor a later list of commandments, the ones found in *Exodus* and *Deuteronomy*. But frankly, as someone who was there when it was written and contributed to the final version we all agreed upon—ours doesn't have the glowing ring to it of the Ten Commandments that you know, which are grounded in ethics not practice and deserve their hallowed place not just in Hebrew culture but in Western Civilization.   Please don't think that we were oblivious to ethics. We knew that murder, adultery, lying, and stealing were wrong. We didn't need to write that down. But our final verse, still found three times in the Torah, which seem to us today just a silly little tag-line for a certain way of eating that most Jews in the world ignore today—was for us a stern reminder to behave, be honorable, and not let ourselves be torn apart by resentment and rage. Oh, if only Besem and Ozer had remained in the Torah!

We will not boil a kid in its mother's milk.

Chapter Ten

Now you will learn everything else
that's important about the time we spent in the wilderness

OPPRESSION YES, AND A single plague, but no pharaoh, no soldiers chasing after us, no parting of the sea. It's true that Moses had a spiritual experience out in the wilderness. Someone was bound to. Someone of our people always does. And we did make an ark for our sacred treasures, but it wasn't very fancy. I'll tell you about it in a little while. But please bear in mind two things. If you read your Torah alongside my book you will see the way that it explains things that didn't make sense before. And second, even if everything I tell you was made up, it wouldn't change the strange mystery of who we are as a people. Somehow we've survived for all these years, while nations far greater than us have vanished, and our influence on the rest of humanity has been far greater than our numbers would suggest. So something is going on here, and I truly believe, with every cell in my three-thousand year old lesbian Hebrew body, that we're here because of what we all did together while seated around that barren hillock, under the guidance of Bast's and my adopted son Hapmose, your Moses.

I call myself a Hebrew, which is what we called ourselves when I was small. You probably call yourselves Jews. I've learned to do that too, just as I've learned to call myself Sarah. But it still doesn't feel right to me. Jews are the descendants of my funny and often tipsy Uncle Judah while I'm a descendant of Asher, but over time the heirs of the tribes that camped to the north of our little hill and then in the north of Canaan either merged with the locals or were carted off into exile, including my own Asherite tribal relations, so it's true that most of us today are the descendants of people who camped to the south of our hill and then in the south of Canaan, most from the tribe of Judah, otherwise Judahites, hence Jews. But I'll have more to say about tribes and exile later on.

Before I end this chapter, at the same place in the story where your Torah ends, there are a few more things that I want to tell you. First, there is much mention in the Torah of the Ark of the Covenant and the tablets of the law that were inside it. No one knows what happened to the ark, but there are many interesting theories, from it being hidden beneath the Temple Mount in Jerusalem to it having been carted off to Ethiopia, where it remains. I spent some time in Ethiopia myself and if it had to go somewhere that would have been an excellent place, but it isn't there, although a few years ago I saw an adventure film set in that region about the lost ark that was lots of fun to watch.

If you read the Torah you will find very detailed instructions for making the ark, the tent of meeting, and the tabernacle. Moses, it is said, commanded the people to bring him all sorts of things that would be needed. His list included gold, silver, copper; blue, purple, and crimson yarns; fine linen and goats' hair; tanned ram skins, dolphin skins; acacia wood; oil for lighting; spices for the anointing oil and for the aromatic incense—as if we had any of those things when we were wandering in the wilderness of Sinai. We were poor, starving, grieving from our losses after an awful disease swept through our dreary workers city—and we staggered out of Egypt with almost nothing but a few pots and pans, our old dried up tents, and the clothing on our backs.

Fortunately, it was spring when we left, the weather was good, and we did feel a sense of miraculous freedom, although like all human emotions, it didn't last long. So we had joy, and hope, but we didn't have gold or silver or copper. We didn't have yarns or oil, or wood, or spices. But we did take the wooden casket with Joseph's remains in it, and another with Dinah's in them. And I took six other things that were in my possession as the eldest elder of our people, all of which proved to be very useful, a few of which I'll tell you about later. But do you remember the wooden box that Rachel took with her from her father's house, with the two wooden *teraphim* in it, which gave her the power to control the family business in Canaan independently of her relatives in Mesopotamia? Well, I'd kept them, and I took those things with me, the box and the two figures, knowing it would give us power and business authority when we got back to Canaan.

At Sinai/Horeb, after we came up with our first covenant as a people, all of us memorized it, and being trained as a scribe, Moses found two flat stones and wrote everything down on them, scratching in the words with a knife. To keep his tablets safe, as there's very little useable wood out in the desert, we put them in Rebecca's box. To make it look more impressive and official Aaron suggested that we take out the two *teraphim* and mount them on top. There were different kinds of *teraphim*, as I mentioned earlier, and ours were winged bull figures, about eight inches high, with human faces. We called those strange composite creatures *keruvim*, which is where your word "cherubs" comes from, although they were nothing like the pudgy little pink boys with wings that are found on Valentine's Day cards.

In your Torah there are also very detailed instructions on how to make a tent to house the ark and all the other sacred possession that the Levites and priests needed to serve God. Well, out in the wilderness we had none of the things that are listed to make the elaborate tent. Most of us slept in lean-tos we built each night from leaves and brambles, if they hadn't held onto the tents their ancestors had brought down with them from Canaan. The lucky ones among us slept in tents loaned to us by Jethro's family. As our sheep and goats grew we slaughtered them and were able to make ourselves new tents for shelter, but we didn't have enough skins to make anything big. Fortunately I still had the tent that had belonged to my mother Arsiyah and her mother Kalanit before her. It was a big tent, big enough to sleep a dozen people, old and frayed and dusty. When I first moved in with her Bast said to me, "Darling, isn't it time you got rid of that filthy old thing?" And I said, "No. We may need it someday." Little did I know that it would become the tent where Moses sat in council, the tent where we kept our ark and new covenant, a tent made by women, a marvelous old tent that eventually ended up in a storeroom in Solomon's temple, which is a story I'll probably come back to later.

There were two men in our camp who did all the work of making those old things useable again. They were Bast's and my closest friends, and they're still named in the Torah: Bezalel and Oholiab. What the Torah doesn't tell you is that they were lovers. I debated about telling you myself. Gay men who decorate are such a stereotype, especially since there was a silly program on television not so long ago about five gay men who do makeovers for straight men. I don't want to give power to the stereotype, but deeper than stereotype—is archetype—and over the course of my very long life I've rarely seen anyone else be able to make beauty the way that some gay men do. Oholiab and Bezalel were masters of beauty. There, out in the middle of almost nowhere, they could turn an old wooden box and two silly figurines into something holy that people still read about.

True, in later texts almost all mention of same-sex love was written out, as was the truth about the ark and the tent that housed it, where small groups of us met inside, although most of the time we all sat around it with the flaps up, women and men still sitting together, to meet, talk, pray. Later, when we were settled in Canaan again, the tribes had a huge fight about power and property and the correct interpretations of our covenant. As before, we split along the old lines that went back to the time of Joseph. The tribes who had camped to the north of Dusty/Desolate feuded with those who'd settled to the south. After much conflict it was decided by Moses's successor Joshua that the ark would go to the south and the tent to the north. I was broken-hearted. To me they belonged together. I tried to mediate, but it did no good.

Times had changed and men were in charge. Along with women in leadership positions, Asherah was officially banished from our faith, and for the most part so was our breasted Shaddai. Only Yahweh remained, merged with all the male Elohim into one god, one God. By then the tent was falling apart and a new one was made, much bigger than the first. That was during the period of the first judges, and one of them, a man named Gideon, had the *teraphim* gold-plated. His nasty son Abimelech, who wanted to be the first king of our people, had a new and bigger box made, also gold plated, that the original box fit into. Later on, when we built our very first temple at Shiloh, in the period of the later judges, the ark and tent were reunited, which made me very happy.

Now let's talk about the contents of that box—the Ten Commandments. Our tradition says that there were two versions in it, both of them carved in stone, a first set broken by Moses, and a second to replace it. Our Moses did have a temper when he was younger, but after he came back from his time alone at Sinai he was a changed man. That story was made up later, to try and reconcile duplications in the text that came from different versions being spliced together. So there weren't two sets, and there was no golden calf that so angered Moses that he broke the first set when he saw it. Knowing about his temper, a later southern editor made that story up to reconcile two different traditions.

By the way, Aaron did not have two sons named Nadab and Abihu, but there's an awful story in the Torah about them being killed by God for doing the wrong thing in the tabernacle. That story was written much later by the same southern writer who invented the golden calf, all to discredit Jeroboam the ruler of the northern tribes after Solomon's united kingdom split in two. Jeroboam had two sons named Nadab and Abiyah, and he did have two golden calves made to serve as Yahweh's throne in each of the two temples he built in the north to rival the one in the south in Jerusalem—in opposition to the southern tradition that Yahweh's throne was—the cherubim! (I remember that scribe, remember his name, and it gives me great pleasure to leave it out of my story.) What you call "calves" were actually young bulls, and here's the truth about the tablets of the Ten Commandments and why they later vanished.

Moses was a well-trained scribe and he wrote down our covenant in the Hebrew language—by transliterating our words into Egyptian hieroglyphics, with all of its fish and birds and eyes and snakes and squiggles. What's now called the Proto-Hebraic alphabet was first being used around that time, but Moses didn't know it. We would only learn how to use those lovely simple letters when we settled back in Canaan, and all of our first Torahs were written in them. What Moses did was the opposite of what happened later on, when we used Hebrew letters to write Ladino and Yiddish and other languages.

If you read the Bible you will discover the very last time the ark is mentioned was during the reign of King Josiah. In the *Second Book of Chronicles* it says that he ordered the ark to be put back in the temple. It had been taken out of the Holy of Holies by his father, and kept in a storeroom in the basement of his palace. When the priests finally found the ark they were very troubled by what was inside it, not two sacred tablets written in Ancient Hebrew but two rough stones inscribed with strange unreadable Egyptian writing. So what was Josiah to do? He had a precedent in his grandfather Hezekiah, who'd destroyed a very lovely bronze serpent that Moses had made and he did the same thing. He destroyed the original commandments and replaced them with a new set of tablets, with the Ten Commandments you know from Exodus carved on them, and not the original version. (I do miss the elegant old letters of our first alphabet, which were replaced centuries later by the ugly boxy letters we adopted during the Babylonian Exile, the descendants of which we sadly use to this very day.)

As a woman I wasn't allowed into the temple in Jerusalem, but it gave me pleasure to know that Rebecca's box was there, along with the *teraphim* and my son's tablets. Then they were gone, destroyed by a king whose piety has been remembered, but not his destruction. To this day I dream about the first tent that housed that box and the *teraphim*, the last remaining objects from my youth but one, which I'll tell you about another time.

Before I complete this chapter, there are a few more stories I want to tell you, to flesh out this memoir, which will cover our history from the time of Joshua to the very present. Knowing that I've come to the last chapter of the part that will probably most interest you—the back-stories of your Torah—I've spent the past few days reading over everything that I've written so far, wanting to put in this or that other story, but reminding myself always, "Serach, this book isn't about you, it's about us." So let me go on with our story.

I hope you've gotten some feel for how things were in the past, and some feel for how real stories get morphed into legends over time and by changing political and philosophical mandates. My intention, in writing this work of history, has been to fill in the missing gaps in your understanding of the past, so that you can more fully own our history for yourself, in an era where once again there is room for women, for women who love women, for men who love men, and for people are neither women nor men, and for people who love everyone. Some of you may be troubled to read that Isaac and Dinah loved members of their own gender. But I'm just telling you the truth about how things were, and if you count all of my grandfather Jacob's twenty-five children you will find that only Dinah was exclusively homosexual, a very low number statistically, although a good number of my relatives were what we today call bisexual.

I've told you about Miriam, who had a lovely voice and wrote songs that we were singing hundreds and hundreds of years later. They were so popular that we never thought to write them down. Now they're almost all forgotten but I've given you parts of two important ones that I remember. And here's a place where I can commend the editors and redactors of your Torah. Nowhere in their text does it say that Miriam was married. Much later rabbis, uncomfortable with her singlehood, gave her this or that husband, but Miriam was one of those people who move through life in a self-contained way. If we Hebrews had orders of monks and nuns, which we only did briefly during Greek and Roman times, she would have made a perfect renunciate. As I said earlier, she and I were never that close, for a variety of reasons. But I always admired her selflessness and generosity. Also one time, when I was suffering from some kind of skin infection, she took splendid care of me.

I've also told you about Dinah, wonderful Dinah, my first love, and I've told you all about Bast, who saved us all. Now let me tell you a bit more about our son Moses. He was, as you may remember, a hairy giant of a man with a soft almost girlish voice, which he was very embarrassed about for a very long time. His spiritual experience at Sinai changed him. While he never told any of us what had happened to him there, he came back from it fully accepting himself. Lucky for us too or we might all have died in the wilderness, or crept back to Egypt like dogs with our tails between our legs, which some of us did, only to vanish there.

Moses, as I said earlier, had been a moody young man, prone to fits of anger. You can read in the Torah about Sobek, the man he accidentally killed in Egypt, but it's connected to a later story that didn't survive in any texts, a story that will help to make sense of several enigmas in your Torah. When Moses fled to Midian from Egypt, weary and afraid, he came to a well, desperate for water, just as your Torah says. But one part was left out, that there was a man there abusing his wife. His name was Shual, and the woman's name was Zipporah. Shual was slapping his wife, screaming at her, while their young son cowered behind her. A few other people were also at the well but they knew Shual and didn't want to get involved. Moses however couldn't tolerate such violence. He verbally challenged Shual, who came charging at him like a bull. Moses fought back, trying to fend off his enraged attacker, dodging his blows and then grabbing him by the throat with his large hairy hands, he told us later, and not letting go.

Zipporah's family all knew about her violent husband and weren't terribly sad about his death, and they were all grateful to the stranger who had rescued her, and delighted when they discovered that he too was a descendant of Abraham and therefore family. No blood feud ensued with Shual's family, who had clearly begun that fight—and so many others. Over the next few months Zipporah and Moses grew closer. She taught him many things about living in the desert, and it seemed logical that they would marry. From the start, he told us later, their marriage wasn't an easy one. Zipporah was headstrong and so was our son.

It says in the current Torah that Zipporah and Moses had two sons, Gershom and Eliezer, while he was first living in Midian, which is true. They also had a daughter, Naamah, left out of history, to whom I taught all the songs that I knew and who went on to be a marvelous singer herself, for many years the head of the women who sang in front of the tent of meeting. As for Naamah's brothers, because Moses had been raised in Egypt where circumcision was not universal, he hadn't circumcised his sons. This had always bothered Zipporah, whose people had kept close to the traditions of Abraham, many of which we'd let go of in Egypt. They fought about it several times and finally one day, in exasperation, Zipporah took a knife and did the deed herself. Moses was horrified and screamed at her, calling her a "bloody wife." Zipporah screamed back at him, "You killed my husband, you bridegroom of blood." All that remains of this story in the Torah is the part about Zipporah doing the deed and calling her husband "A bridegroom of blood," but later editors were uncomfortable with the notion that their great leader had killed not one but two men, and this part of the story was edited out.

One more fragment remains. There's a chapter in the Torah called "Balak," about a Midianite ruler of the Moabites with that name. In the story Balak was an enemy of the wandering clans of the children of Jacob. It's a wonderful fanciful tale, with its talking donkey, and the only portion in your Torah from the time that Moses is born until the very end in which he isn't mentioned. In the story Balak hires a famous seer named Balaam to curse our people, but God puts words of blessing in his mouth instead. Balaam was a regional folk hero, we and our neighbors told lots of stories about him and he was spliced in later, to flesh out the text after the heart of the story was cut out. But the real story is that Balak, called in your Torah "the son of Zippor," was actually Balak the son of Zipporah and her first husband, Shual.

Balak had always hated his stepfather Moses for killing his father, and as soon as he was old enough he left our camp and took up with the Moabites. He was never the king of Moab, but some years later, when he was in his early twenties and we were preparing to enter Canaan, he did attack us with a band of men who wanted to take our few possessions and destroy us. The fragments in your Torah don't tell you any of this, but there's enough left so that you can see where the truth fits in.

As for Zipporah, I always liked her and so did Bast. She treated us as her honored mothers-in-law and as the grandmothers of her children, and we always loved her and treated her as part of our family. I liked her father Jethro a great deal. He was always good to me, honored me as the elder of our people, and knew almost as many good stories as I did. In your Torah he's called by many names, Jethro, Jeter, Hobab, and Reuel. Later writers also called him Raguel. You can see how Jethro and Jeter are versions of the same name, but what about the rest? Well, Hobab was actually Jethro's son, Zipporah's brother. Father and son got mixed up. It sometimes happens. As for Reuel and Raguel, quite frankly, even I can't tell you where they come from.

Let me say a little bit now about Joshua. In every classroom there are always one or two students who stand out from the rest, and Joshua was like that. From an early age he showed all of the leadership skills he displayed later on. Tall and slim, with a scrawny beard and mustache, Joshua was very different in appearance from Moses, and it was to his credit that he passed over his two sons (who Bast and I adored but who could be petulant and whiny) to train Joshua to succeed him. He was loyal to our people, always reminding us of our covenant, and had the rare capacity that Moses lacked, the ability to awaken in others their best qualities. Moses was the hub at the center of our community. Joshua was the outer rim, holding us together in a very different way, the right way for a different time.

My heart broke when Bast died. I still can't talk about it. When Moses died I wanted to climb into his grave and have dirt thrown over both of us. We buried him in the wilderness, Joshua, Zipporah, my grandchildren Naamah, Gershom, Eliezer, and the rest of our people. Your Torah says that no one knows were his grave is. I used to visit it from time to time but I'm glad it never became a place of pilgrimage. He would have hated it.

For more than two thousand years I've been going to Passover Seders, and often leading them, now that women are once again able to. Most people think of a Seder as the quintessential Jewish ritual, although the notion of sitting around a table and telling a story is something that we borrowed from our Greek neighbors in the later days of the second temple, the best surviving example of which you can read about in Plato's *Symposium*. There a group of men sit around talking about love while at a Seder we talk about freedom, telling story after rambling story and asking question after probing question—which I adore. And it always pleases me to note that when our later rabbis wrote down the core text of the Haggadah—they left Moses out of it—which would have greatly pleased him, I can assure you.

Now, please.

Pause with me here for a moment.

Sigh. Take a deep breath.

Go on.

This part of the book hasn't been the most difficult to write—but it has been the most challenging. Although I've known a few parents who wanted to destroy their offspring, consciously or unconsciously, almost all parents want the very best for their children, want them to be happy and succeed in life. That was certainly what Bast and I wanted for Moses. For the last few years I've been reading books on neurology and I'm fascinated by the work-ings of the human brain. It seems that the more we retell a story the more that it gets hardwired into our neurons. So imagine what it's like to raise a child who you love, and see him grow up to be one kind of man—only to have history remember him as someone else. You might think that over time I'd get used to the discontinuities, but in fact the opposite is more accurate. Over time, with each repetition, my primate brain is jarred again and again by the differences in real and recorded, which may be why in the millennia of my very long life I've loved many children—but never parented again.

If you'd asked me when Moses died if I thought that our people would still be here three thousand years later, I would have laughed in your face. We were a little lost band of scared and hungry wanderers who'd forgotten so much of our noble past in our years of servitude. But the people of Israel couldn't forget Moses. They made him more, and less, and other than he really was, and it's through the power of the stories we've told about him down through the ages that we've been able to survive and sometimes even thrive—which is a legacy that Moses would have approved of, the man who was changed by his time at Sinai and brought us there to change us too. To change us in a way that is always available to us, in every single moment, which is why we say that every Jew who ever was and ever will be was with us at Sinai, however we visualize it. Because it's true.

And now, all these years later, still alive for reasons beyond my own de-sire or understanding, I have decided to sit down again and write. But before I continue I need to get up, stretch my weary old bones, and go down to the water. I need to walk barefoot on the sand for a while, listen to and look at the crashing waves, and the pumped-up bodybuilders, and the parents with their strollers, and the young people on skateboards and rollerblades gliding by. Then I want to get something to eat at my favorite little boardwalk cafe. Have a cup of tea. My favorite is rooibos. Read a little something, about neurology or my other favorite subject—trees. Listen to the conversations around me. Get a cookie.

Enough talking.

Chapter Eleven

In which your author continues with her tale,
from the death of Moses into the time of Joshua and beyond

THE TORAH AS IT exists today ends with the death of Moses, with the ringing words of his blessings to the tribes (none of which are authentic—he was in a semi-coma for several weeks before he died and said nothing) and with a short concluding paragraph that reminds us that there was never again in all of Israel a prophet like Moses, who saw God face to face. There was once a proto-Torah that began with Sarah and Abraham and their wanderings and ended with Joseph and all of us living happily in Egypt. As for prophets, I knew almost all of them, many of them women who are long forgotten, and some who were quite spectacular, which Moses would have agreed with if he'd lived long enough to know them too. The son of three mothers, our Moses was a proto-feminist. For example, here's what really happened when the five daughters of Zelophehad approached him. He listened to their story and decided that *all* daughters have an equal right to inherit, not just the daughters of men with no sons. Bast and I were so proud of him—and think what the world would be like if his ruling had remained in the text and a part of our tradition!

The earliest version of a Torah that you would recognize ended with us reentering Canaan and building our first altar in the land that our ancestors knew—which I alone had seen before. We built that small stone altar outside a town called Gilgal, where we camped for several months. There were six hundred and thirty-eight of us at that point, who entered the so-called Promised Land with no wars, no battles, and absolutely no conquests of any kind. Those stories were all told later, as such stories usually are, by men bragging about ancestors they never knew, casting them in the image they want for themselves—larger than life. As someone who in a certain sense is (not *larger* than life, for I am just two inches over five feet tall, but) *longer* than life, I have been asking myself for more than three thousand years— "Why do men need to brag in this way?"

In the 1970s I was in a women's support group in Brooklyn and one of the members, a physician, said that since upwards of 80 percent of the violent crimes in the world are done by men—the Y-chromosome is clearly defective. She advocated for funding a program to do research into treating that defect, which still makes sense to me. Women, in my long experience, lie far less often than do men, and distort history less often as well, not to mention that women commit far fewer crimes. Men, not all of them of course, but too many of them I would say, looking back over my extended life—want noise and bigness and blood flowing, perhaps from a sense of deprivation, as a woman's body lets blood flow monthly for years, which may be why we have less need to shed it. We cannot escape so easily from our bodies into our heads as men can, because we are reminded each month of our embodied physicality and its sacredness, which I may have more to say about later on.

So there we were, our ragged tents set up in a large field, back in the land where Sarah and Abraham had once settled. When you look at a map you can see that that strip of land is a bridge between Egypt and Mesopotamia, with the Mediterranean on one side and the Jordan on the other. Because of its location Canaan was a crossroads for people from the time that our first ancestors wandered out of Africa, and so it was then, that people were coming and going all the time—so we fit right in. We were resident aliens, immigrants, refugees, who had two things going for us that many others all around the world to this very day probably don't have. First, our family had been there before, so we felt like we were coming home. And even more important, we had the *teraphim*, the licensing statues that Rachel and Leah had bargained for with their father—those two little statuettes that allowed us to do business in Canaan under Joshua's guidance.

You may have noticed that throughout history the followers of great leaders are often very different in style and temperament than their predecessors, and Joshua was different in every way from Moses. He was calm and grounded while Moses had a quick temper. He was not a mystic, by which I mean that Moses's experience at Desolate/Dusty wasn't anything that ever happened to Joshua. Nor was he a visionary. If it had been up to him we would have remained in Egypt, perhaps lobbying for workers' rights. But Moses saw Joshua's potential from an early age, recognized his leadership abilities, and trained him well. Miriam too instructed him, as did I, and by the time we were ready to enter Canaan, Joshua had done his best to unite us as a large extended family.

Our biggest challenge after we got there was—where to go next. The only property that we owned in Canaan was the cave and the land around it that Abraham and Sarah bought from her lover Efron the Hittite, and we could have all settled around it. But we were all clear that we didn't want to ever live in anything like the tight little ghetto of our workers city. We wanted to be free from living in close quarters—and we wanted to be free from each other as well!

The word "ghetto" was first used in 1516 in Venice when the city's Jews were forced to live on a small dirty island that was called that, and Jews were confined there until Napoleon abolished it in1796. That much is clear, but there is no agreement as to the origin of the word. Some trace it back to *getto* or *gietto*, an Italian word for a foundry, as there was one located near the site, while others say that it comes from a regional form of *Egitto*, Egypt, or from *borghetto*, "a small section of a town," related to the German *borgo*, which is connected to the English word borough. Or, does ghetto come from the Italian word *Giudeica*, which means Jews? Sadly, while I have much to say about the past and am often able to clear up historical puzzles that no one else can, in the early 1500s I wasn't living in Italy and know nothing of that word's origins.

After many conversations that often turned into shouting matches, Joshua convinced us that the very best thing we could do was to move off in small groups to every part of Canaan—with none of the stirring conquests preserved by history. So, just as we had in the wilderness, those who camped north of Moses's little hill decided to go to the north of Canaan and those who camped to the south of that little hill traveled to the south of Canaan. Joshua gave each group one of the licensing *teraphim* and sent the tent of meeting off with the northern group and the ark-box with the southern group. He and I wandered from group to group, from village to village and city to city, helping our people to settle in, find work, make new friends, and rebuild our old trading network.

Today the idea that a particular woman could live for thousands of years, if not hundreds, seems absurd, insane. But in the ancient Middle East our sense of time was very fluid. In the broader culture, particularly in Mesopotamia where Sarah and Abraham came from, everyone knew that Alulim the first king of Eridu reigned for 28,800 years while his successor Alalngar ruled for 36,000 years. And in almost every version of the Torah from the very first one ever assembled, we told stories about our own fore-bears, beginning with Adam who lived for 930 years, Methuselah who lived for 969 years, and Noah who lived for 950 years. So the fact that I had lived through six generations and was approximately one hundred and fifty years old was almost ordinary. We honored our elders and I was always honored as our eldest elder and nearly a goddess, for remember—your idea of God wasn't yet a part of our thinking.

One of the lovely things about returning to Canaan was that everywhere we went we met people who had grown up hearing about Sarah and Abraham and Davah and Isaac and Ishmael and my grandfather Jacob. They remembered our family business from their own family stories, wondered what happened to us after we went down to Egypt, and were open to trading with us again, which gave us all such a feeling of hope. And to my great delight—from out of Jacob's large clan, no one remembered a young girl named Serach.

If you've ever gone back to a place that you once lived in you may be able to relate to my mixed feelings. I was born in Canaan, spent my girlhood there, and it was Home to me. I had so many memories of it and was glad to be back. But it was also painful to return. Very few places had changed. Some were exactly the same. Some were a bit different—a new stone house, a new shrine or temple. Trees were taller in some places and gone in others. During our years in Egypt I'd cared for, buried and mourned many of my loved ones, so death wasn't foreign to me. But coming back to a land that I remembered so well, coming back to a land where everyone I thought about when I'd thought about this town, that village, this wadi, that water well, was long dead—was very disconcerting. Sometimes as we moved about I would meet someone who looked just like her great grandmother, a bit like his great great uncle, but most of the time in a land that was welcoming and familiar—I was met by strangers. Later, I would come to appreciate and even enjoy that, but not then.

Today we call it a land flowing with milk and honey, but as I said earlier, the milk was from sheep and goats and the honey was really a paste made from dates—but the land was abundant in a very different way than Egypt. It took everyone else quite some time to get used to not living by the great River Nile, and it took everyone even longer to get used to the very different climate and terrain. But they'd all grown up on stories about Canaan and about Sarah and Abraham, so returning to Canaan was a kind of homecoming, and while the language the people spoke there had shifted while we'd been gone—it wasn't Egyptian but almost the same language that we spoke! Which was so comforting, welcoming, an experience that most immigrants don't have, that I almost never had after that.

The books of *Joshua* and *Judges* give you partial, skewed, and often false views of what we did and what happened to us in those years. Joshua continued to guide us, and under his leadership we lay the foundation for who we became two hundred and more years later—a unified people married into the peoples around us and growing more and more successful over time.

The *Tanach* is mostly right that in that period we were ruled over—"guided by" would be a better term—by a succession of judges. There were many more than your current text tells you about and you will not be surprised to hear that several of them were women, not just Deborah. And although we were welcomed in most locations, we were unwelcome in others and did have to fight a few battles over the years, which intensified as we grew in power and influence.

There are so many stories that I could tell you about that time and about the centuries that followed, but I've been writing for hours, straight through the night, and it's time for breakfast and for a walk on the beach with Malkah my ten-year-old Golden Retriever. But before I wrap up this chapter there's one more story that I want to tell you. Oh, before I get to it there's another thing to add. When people meet me and hear me talk they always say, "You have an unusual accent. Where do you come from?" My standard response is, "Where do you think that I come from?" To which I'm most often told, as they stare at my face with eyes that are exploring it like the hands of a blind person, "Turkey, or Iran. Yemen, Egypt, or Morocco." Every once in a while someone says, "India" or "Pakistan." Sometimes it's "Palestine" and sometimes they ask if I'm Israeli. My usual answer is, "My ancestors came from a lot of different places. And I've lived in a lot of different places myself." Then I try to change the subject.

In an earlier version of the Torah there was a story. It went like this:

> And Sarah the princess gave her seal, carved in carnelian, to Da-
> vah her daughter, who gave it to Leah the wife of her nephew in
> the next generation. And Leah gave it to Dinah her daughter, who
> gave it to Serach her niece and beloved as a sign for all generations
> of the lineage of the priestesses of the goddess Asherah who we all
> serve. And Serach took it with her into Egypt, a seal of red car-
> nelian with an image of the goddess's sacred tree carved upon it.

That small red seal that we all wore on a cord around our necks, I am wearing still, all these thousands of years later, the cord replaced many many many times, with leather sometimes, yarn, twine, and recently in an experiment soon abandoned—nylon. You can see similar seals in museums all around the world, carved in stone, mine with its little tree and the words carved in cuneiform: "Sacred to The Mother." Seals like that had great power in the ancient Middle East, even more so than the *teraphim,* for the *teraphim* granted privilege while that seal established <u>power</u>. So the clans that went north took one *teraph* with them from temple to temple to register and reestablish our business, and the clans that went to the south took the other *teraph* to do the same in the south, and I went from place to place that we had settled with my seal, to make certain as a priestess that our people would be honored and protected.

Chapter Twelve

In which the author goes on with her narrative,
from the time of the judges to the cusp of the era of kings

No pharaoh, no chariots, no waters parting—we slogged through marshland. No thunderous revelation, not forty years of wandering, and absolutely no conquest. (Although in working on this narrative I may have had a little revelation of my own—that History was the mother of Moses while Jochebed, Bast and I were the mothers of Hapmose, a somewhat different person.) Yes, there *was* a plague, just one, and there *was* a kind of a miracle—that we happened by chance (or by divine providence, something I'm still not sure that I believe in)—to migrate back to Canaan in one of those rare periods in its history when there were no big wars going on there, and in that short time of peace, around (almost literally, this time) forty years, we were given the chance to reestablish ourselves.

When you step beyond the Torah itself into the next section of the *Tanach*, you come to the book of *Joshua* and then the book of *Judges*. (Which I privately call *Smudges.*) Anyone looking for a sense of chronology there or for any sense of clarity will come away confused. Those books are what they appear to be—edited fragments of older texts. But beyond the fragments there are lost connections, the first of which is essential to my story. Moses would have been less than he was without the mentorship of his father-in-law Jethro the Midianite, and Joshua would have been less than he was without the mentorship of his elder Moses. The next step in this chain has been lost, however, and now for the first time in thousands of years I will restore it.

The story about Moses sending twelve spies into Canaan contains a kernel of truth, but they weren't spies they were emissaries, their mission overt, and the response to it as varied as the text recalls. With one representative from each family being sent out (because we/they weren't really tribes yet) ten of those emissaries came back saying, "There is no way that we can return to our old family business," while two of them said, "Of course we can. We have the *teraphim* and everywhere we went we found people who remembered Sarah and Abraham and Davah and we can definitely make a go of it!" The two who came back to Moses with words of encouragement were just as the text still relates—Joshua and Caleb—who were the best of friends and married two sisters, Hannah and Shoshana. Late in his life their father married another wife, Leah, and they had a daughter Shalomeh. (Notice that I left out their father's name. He was not memorable. He wasn't even very nice. Recall the difference between "to father," an act that can take seconds, and "to mother," which may take decades.)

From an early age everyone could tell that Shalomeh was special, old beyond her years, a wonderful listener and a thoughtful friend. Down through the centuries people have asked me if I believe in reincarnation, as I said before, and I've already told you the story about how much Jim Morrison resembled my uncle Joseph. I would have to tell a different story about Shalomeh. It wasn't that she reminded me of anyone in particular, but the look in her eyes, even as a baby, was penetrating—as if she were seeing right into your soul (an object I'm not sure if I believe in either) not with judgment but with compassion, as if she'd been a person many times before and knew how challenging it can be. Later, as a young girl, she would say things that startled us, as if she had come back with all of her past wisdom tucked inside her lithe little form.

Just as Moses looked around for a successor, passing over his own sons, Joshua did the same and singled out his and Caleb's wife's half-sister Shalomeh to be his heir. Yes, this is our leadership lineage and my informed response to the one created by the rabbis at the beginning of that wonderful little anthology of sayings, *Pirke Avot*—"Jethro taught Moses and passed on the leadership of our people to him, and Moses to Joshua, and Joshua to Shalomeh the first Judge." As our eldest elder and a priestess in my own right, something that I've avoided mentioning until now, I was called upon to work with Shalomeh. We'd sit for hours under the shade of an old olive tree, me telling her stories long before they were first written down, stories that she seemed to know already and was able to memorize immediately, having what we now call a photographic memory—almost three thousand years before the camera was invented.

When I say that I was a priestess, a priestess who wore around her neck the seal that had belonged to our matriarch Sarah, what I am saying is that my ritual duties involved our worship of Asherah the sister-wife of Yahweh. (By the way, that isn't how we pronounced his name, but in order to honor our tradition to never say it, I am not going to tell you how. See, sometimes I come across as heretical, but other times I fully honor our customs.) So when I say that I was a priestess of Asherah—and not Yahweh—I want you to remember that more often than not it was to her and not to him that our people turned in our early history. For as any historian or archaeologist will tell you—while only 10 percent of the names in the *Tanach* belong to women, 90 percent of the images from ancient Israel are *of* women, of priestesses and goddesses.

It was a joy to initiate Shalomeh into the teachings and rituals, the songs, dances, chants, and prayers that we offered to Asherah, and it was a privilege to initiate her into the priestessly lineage—"From Ataah to Sarah to Davah to Leah to Dinah to Serach to Shalomeh." She set up her tent outside the village of Gilgal where we'd built our first shrine after crossing the Jordan into Canaan. Beside the altar to Yahweh was a huge old magnificent oak tree where we prayed to and made offerings to Asherah. The sons and grandsons of Aaron and Moses served Yahweh there as priests, and in addition to Shalomeh I initiated five other young women to be priestesses of Asherah—two named for our ancestors, a Sarah and a Bilhah, along with Azibah, Yaffa, and Avishag, who were all the granddaughters of Moses and Zipporah, my own great grandchildren. None of them are remembered in history, all were lovely, and Azibah was noted as a dream interpreter. Princes and kings from all over Canaan would come to consult with her, her interpretations were recorded and referred to for centuries, and I wish that I had kept a copy of them. Remember Azibah please, as she will have some bearing on one of my stories, later on.

Toward the end of his life Joshua lay hands upon Shalomeh just as Moses had done with him, and anointed her with olive oil as was the custom, and Shalomeh became the living heart of our people as we spread out in Canaan, finding places to settle and work, to grow crops and shepherd our flocks. As both priestess and leader she was the one everyone went to for counsel, and she was the one, because of her dual roles, who was fully able to reestablish our people in Canaan. She purchased camels from Canaanite merchants that came from stock bred by Davah, and spent all of the year when it wasn't raining traveling from north to south, from river to sea, visiting our people and spending time with the elders in every village, town, and city in Canaan. An early version of the book of *Judges* begins with the death of Joshua and the judgeship of Shalomeh. "But what happened to that book?" you may ask, and I will tell you.

War returned to Canaan in the last years of Shalomeh's life, and the judges who followed had to struggle to keep our people safe and alive and connected. Some of them were men, just as the book of *Judges* relates, and others were women—Naarah, Keziah, Sheerah, Avital, and Zeruiah, along with Deborah, the only woman who wasn't removed from the text—and this is why. Rather than align herself with the priestesses of Asherah she chose to work with the priests of Yahweh and went so far as to destroy Shalomeh's shrine to Asherah at Gilgal. Because of that war and its psychological necessities, Yahweh increasingly gained ascendancy among our people, Asherah was shunned, then banned, and then gradually (as I've mentioned before) all of the male Elohim merged together into one great god, one great God, and once that happened we were ready for the next two steps in our evolution as a family—we were ready for full-blown patriarchy and we were ready for kingship. It was then that so many of the women in our older stories were purged from our texts, including Shalomeh and a woman named Serach, while a woman named Deborah was left in—a difficult woman who I never liked and who never liked me. (See, if you thought I had only good things to say about women, there were and are women I have never liked.)

When *Fiddler on the Roof* first came out my partner Clara and I had been living in America for thirty years. Going back to the era of the judges I'd seen petty fools like Adolf Hitler rise to terrifying power hundreds of times before, from Canaan to China and back again. After the Reichstag Fire I knew that it was time for us to get out of Germany, and we left in 1934. It wasn't the first time I'd lived in Europe. I'd settled there for a time during the Middle Ages, which I will tell you about in its own right time. But each time that I lived among Ashkenazi Jews I felt alone and isolated, different, an outsider, even among our own people—and the play seemed an odd celebration of one particular aspect of Ashkenazi experience, so I refrained from seeing it when it first came out. Then it became a huge success, won five Tony Awards and became the first musical in history to run for more than 3000 performances—and I was even less inclined to see it. I didn't have these words then but what I was feeling was resentment toward what a friend of mine in San Francisco later taught me to label "the Ashkenazi Dominant Narrative."

Now Clara, my wonderful Clara, was a good Ashkenazi woman whose Yiddish-speaking grandparents had moved to Germany from Poland and when the film came out she talked me into seeing it with her. In 1971 it wasn't hard to persuade me. We'd been talking about moving to California for a few years, as a way of keeping me safe, for even though we'd moved up and down the east coast eight times since 1934, people who'd known us for a while had watched a lesbian couple with an older and younger partner shift roles. When we met in 1929 I looked like I was in my fifties and she was thirty, but in 1971 I was over 3000 and she was seventy-two. Clara adored the play. She saw it three times, and when the film came out I felt that I owed it to her to see it, as a thank you gift for living through all the disruptions that a shared life with me required. As a lesbian who came out early in life in her hometown of Hamburg she'd experienced life in the closet, and our time in Nazi Germany had given her the experience of terror, of needing to hide. But having to move again and again for more than two thousand years is not easy. No wonder almost all of the other so-called immortals I've met have chosen to live in caves in the mountains, far away from everyone else. I will tell you a few stories about them later on in my narrative.

It helped when Clara told me that one of the stars was an Israeli actor, a Mister Topol whose last name means "poplar" in Russian. Asherah and her trees seem to follow us through history, and Mister Poplar was guaranteed to appeal to me. Now, there are a good many things that I regret in my long life, although a Buddhist friend suggested that regret is a waste of time—but for Goddess's sake, I am a Hebrew and regret is built into our DNA! When the play first came out Clara bought the cast album on a record (a record! my dears, and not what is now called "vinyl") which she listened to so many times, singing the songs in the shower, that I learned them all myself, long before we finally went to see the movie, in a theater on Lexington Avenue— and I absolutely loved it!! (Notice that this is the first time in this book that I have used two exclamation points!)

My favorite scene in the movie was and remains the one in which Tevye pretends to be having a nightmare about his wife's dead grandmother coming to tell him that his daughter Tzeitel is supposed to marry someone other than the older man she's been betrothed to, whose dead wife also appears to warn Tevye that she will curse the couple if they wed. Naturally this made-up dream sways his wife Goldie, who, with her dead grandmother's blessing, approves of the marriage between Tzeitel and Motel, the young man she's in love with, a match that she initially opposed.

I remember sitting in the darkness with Clara, holding hands beneath our coats, for even in the darkness it was 1971 and we were afraid to touch each other in public—and I was laughing and crying, thinking—"This is all of our history." Thinking—"I was so wrong to discount the Ashkenazi experience as being Other, when in fact as the ultimate Hebrew other myself I ought to have embraced it." Thinking—"This story of love and loss, and having to leave home again is the story of my life and the lives of all of the children of Sarah and Abraham." Thinking—"I wish I'd seen the play with Zero Mostel and the rest of the original Broadway cast!" And on the way home, walking as two women would then who did not call each other "partner' or 'wife' as people do today but "lover"—not touching, not holding hands, as we slowly wandered downtown, occasionally brushing against each other, quickly and tenderly, I told her how much I loved the movie, and

Clara, being the good lover that she was, never once said, "I told you so." Instead she walked quietly beside me, softly humming her own medley of "Tradition" and "Matchmaker, Matchmaker," of "Sunrise, Sunset" and "Do you love me?" as I told her what rose up in my mind at the end of the movie, my own short prologue to the film—about the very time in our history that I'm writing about right now.

With Shalomeh forgotten and Deborah the warrior the only woman remembered as a leader, we have two very different ancestors of Tzeitel and her sisters imbedded in a story of transition and transformation, of exile and expectations. And we have two stories told in reverse order. For *Fiddler on the Roof* begins in the familiar instability of a little village and ends when its residents have to go off into exile, while my and our story in this chapter begins with us coming out of exile and returning to the instability of life in our little villages in the midst of conflict and war.

Chapter Thirteen

The beginning of the monarchy in Israel and Judah,

with a few personal revelations

that may delight and/or surprise you

AT THIS POINT IN our history I was already old, quite old, perhaps too old, although if you looked at me you would have thought that I was in my early thirties. But I had seen so much, lived through so much, and I was worn out by grieving, by again and again having to say goodbye to everyone I knew. I thought of suicide but also thought—"There must still be a reason for my living on and on." As our eldest elder and eldest priestess I continued to consult and train and guide, but I went back to living in a tent by myself, glad to be home, on one hand always on edge, anxious and afraid, and on the other hand, deeply grateful, not for the big things but the small. I always had family around me, descendants of Moses and Zipporah, which was a great comfort, but as I lost them, one by one, comfort turned into grief, over and over again. I was particularly fond of a young man named Iddo, a fourth generation descendant of Bast's and my son. He was a thoughtful sensitive boy, a poet and mystic. I remember sitting with him on a hill one evening, late in the rainy season. It was a clear night, the moon was full, then a soft haze drifted in, and for about ten minutes the moon was surrounded by two bright rings of rainbow light. There were sheep and goats wandering around but they didn't notice, so I noticed for them, which is rather like this book. And Iddo noticed, his face shining with the same kind of inner light that Moses's face shone. Iddo went on to write a series of songs, of psalms, many of which are incorporated into the biblical book of *Psalms,* and later on his great grandson of the same name, who very much resembled him and was very good to me, became a prophet of Yahweh, quite a good one, in the time of Solomon's disappointing son Rehoboam.

In addition to wondering about reincarnation, I've long pondered another concept that comes to us from the lands to the east of Canaan— Karma. Is there such a thing? How does it connect with our belief in free will? How do group events shape it? And how does karma relate to genetics? Napoleon—I knew him slightly—has been falsely quoted as saying that the British are a nation of shopkeepers. But we, we Hebrew Israelite Jews—have been a nation of traders since long before we were a nation. First in Canaan, then across the Middle East, over the Silk Route, the Indian Ocean, and later the Atlantic, we have been doing again and again what we were doing then. And I wonder now, at three thousand and more, is this encoded in our genes?

Although the stories in the book of *Judges* distort and over-state our power, rather like Tevye does in his invented dream, sometimes our merchant families raised up groups of soldiers to work with the rulers of Canaan, and at other times our people served in Canaanite armies, as slowly over time the descendants of Jacob and his five wives scattered all over Canaan, marrying our way into almost all of the ruling families. But the next question that I ask myself, and which you may be asking, is—"Why have we always been ambitious and so often been accomplished?" Wherever we've lived, some of us have risen to positions of power among the people and nations we settled among and served, from Canaan to China to Germany to the United States. Is this karma? Is it something in our DNA? A neighbor of mine, a Danish philo-Semite whose three wives have all been Jewish, and who goes to synagogue far more often with his children than do any of their mothers, likes to haul out the statistics about the percentage of Jews who've won Nobel Prizes, which is far greater than our population in the world would predict. (I use the word "Semite" with discomfort, for we are not the only ones. But that's the word that comes to mind, and having been edited for so long by others, I refrain from editing myself right now.)

Before I go on, a brief comment. Every time that the Hebrew word Elohim is translated as **God** or Yahweh is translated as **The Lord** or sometimes now **The Eternal**—those words are mistranslations, anachronisms! When the stories that became the Bible as you know it were first being told we had no conception of a singular, eternal, all-powerful *male* being to which the word God could be ascribed. We still believed in that androgynous Prime Creator, Shaddai, and even after we'd banished Asherah and the female Elohim, when Yahweh had merged with the other male Elohim, we still didn't say there were no other gods besides Yahweh, we had him say—"You shall have no other gods before me." Before, but not after. Now back to the story.

It's not the first time in history that commercial success has turned into governance, and that's what slowly happened to our ancestors. All the small Canaanite city-states and regions were separate, and without ever planning to do this, just as Sarah's poor aristocratic family allowed her to marry Abraham, the son of a wealthy family—poor aristocratic Canaanite families were happy to marry off their children to ours. And soon enough we who had been immigrants, refugees, outsiders—became members of the ruling class all across Canaan.

During most of that period there were battles and attacks, invasions, and hostility, between the various cities but primarily between Egypt and Mesopotamia, all reflected in surviving texts, but after almost two hundred and fifty years under the guidance of our judges, there came another period of relative peace. It was then that Samuel, the last of the judges, appointed a charmingly complex trader from the north named Saul to a new position of power—as the head, the CEO, of our entire family business in Canaan. Saul was never called *melech,* king, by his contemporaries, but rather *nagid,* commander, *nasi,* prince, but usually *adon,* lord, the title given to our ancestor Abraham. Samuel was to Saul what Moses was to Joshua, but whereas Joshua marvelously fulfilled his mentor's expectations, Saul did not. Strands of truth can be found in the stories about him in the *Tanach.* Saul was charming and handsome, a sort of dark bearded brooding Cary Grant type. I was always quite fond of him. Under his early leadership our family business flourished and it was he who established our most lucrative trading route, caravans going back and forth from Yemen, which we called Sheba, with perfumes and unguents and spices. But for all of his accomplishments, Saul was prone to depression and to fits of rage. (A bit like Moses, but Saul's were prolonged.) Today we'd say that he was bi-polar.

Now here's a true story embedded in the text. When Saul was in one of his deep dark despairing moods the only thing that could cheer him up was good music, and Samuel, wanting to keep him as steady and stable as possible while he looked for a replacement, invited the leading male pop singer of the time to come on a weekly basis to entertain Lord Saul. This young man was named Elhanan, and he came from an important trading family in the south. But rather than go to work with their father like his older brothers did, Elhanan wanted to be the ancient equivalent of a Rock Star. He was beautiful and charismatic like my Uncle Joseph, had a magnificent voice, was a genius at evocative composition like Leonard Cohen, and was also an amazing improviser like only two people I've ever heard, Fratello Solli, a eunuch I knew and occasionally performed with in taverns during the Middle Ages, and Ella Fitzgerald, who remains one of my all-time favorite musical artists.

Not so very long ago on television I watched screaming crowds of mostly teenage girls swarming around the Beatles when they arrived in the United States—which made me think of Elhanan. Many popular singers over time have taken on or been given other names—Eleanora Fagan became Billie Holiday, Robert Zimmerman became Bob Dylan, and Prince Rogers Nelson who gave up his spoken name for a time to use a glyph called "The Love Symbol" was most often known as just Prince. So it was that Elhanan's fans did not call him by his given name. They called him Beloved, *Dah'hweed,* David! And, as today we speak of The King of Rock, The Queen of Soul, The Prince of Pop, it was the same in a year not too far away from 1000 BCE that in addition to calling handsome sexy promiscuous young Elhanan the name we remember him by—David—he was also called The King, the king of sound, the king of music, the king of voice and words and artful fingers. Yes, we called him simply, *Melech David,* King David, our Beloved King.

You can imagine how proud this made Lord Saul, the CEO of our entire family's business from one end of Canaan to the other, to have as his house guest one of the most famous musicians in the land. Now, every year in early summer down on the coast there was a large festival to the goddesses and gods that always ended with a singing competition, the songs all on one specific theme—love, divine love. In one particular year the last two contestants were our David, sent there by Saul himself, and a tall striking young man from a Philistine family, a drummer and singer called by everyone all over Canaan "The Giant," just as David was called "The King."

I know you're laughing at me now, laughing at my story about Goliath—but it's the truth. I was there. I remember the song that David sang. It became one of his most popular tunes, with a melody that haunts me to this day, a song called "You, girl," that he wrote and named for his current lust object, Saul's daughter Michal. "You girl. Staring at me across the room. You, girl, dark hair streaming down your shoulders, bare." When the applause eventually died down, Goliath came on stage and sang a song about the man he was in love with, Yair, a sailor who had gone off to sea. David's song was upbeat, Goliath's was soulful. I remember part of it too, with its sad refrain, "I look out over the waves. Dark waves. Are you coming back to me, back to me?" But after the thunderous applause given to David, and the three judges' unanimous decision—runners took the news to every part of Canaan. And just as we say today, "I died laughing," or "That movie killed me," or "The Broncos slaughtered the Raiders," we used death and death imagery in the very same way. So the news those runners took to every part of Canaan was—"David killed Goliath. Slaughtered him. Wiped him out completely." And then slowly, over time, for a variety of reasons, including ethnic rivalry and increasing homophobia from our priestly class (not that David hadn't had his little flings with other men and not just Jonathan) that story morphed into the one you know today, a story that celebrates not music but xenophobia and war.

So laugh. Say—this crazy senile old woman is making things up again. But go to your book shelf and pull down your Bible. Open it up to *First Samuel 17:20* and read the story about how young David killed Goliath the giant with a rock from his sling shot. Then flip ahead to *Second Samuel 21:19* where you will read that a man named Elhanan killed Goliath. True, that Elhanan's father isn't called Jesse, the name by which we remember David's father, but in a text written and repeatedly edited hundreds of years after the events that it describes, a dangling fragment will now make sense to you—the story of how Elhanan became David, the King of Pop—or in this case, given the slingshot later ascribed to him, let us call him instead—The King of Rock.

Saul was happy to send David off and furious when he returned, for crowds were waiting for David, screaming and waving, "The King is back! King David is back!" Now David did not help the situation. He was delighted by all of that attention, which plunged Saul into a murderous rage. David fled the palace—really a seven room stone structure—which was actually big for that time—and returned to his family in Hebron, where he hid out, waiting for Saul's rage to pass. But it didn't. It grew worse and worse and for a number of years David did what many other performers have done over time—he retired from performing, but not from popularizing himself. Given his fame, his brothers were glad to go into the souvenir business, selling in the marketplaces all over Canaan small images of David stamped into clay, lockets of his thick dark wavy hair, and little bone and wood flutes which they claimed that David had played. Eventually David took over the operations himself, creating a big business from his fame, as performers have done throughout time, selling fashions and fragrances under their own names.

Watching all of this unfold from a distance, Samuel came to a conclusion that would have seemed not just illogical but insane a decade before—that David was the perfect man to replace Saul, because he had two things going for him—name recognition—and great marketing skills. Samuel came to me and asked for my advice, and I said to him the ancient Hebrew equivalent of, "Go for it, Dude!" It wasn't easy for Samuel to approach Saul with the suggestion that he step down, even though his mental health had continued to deteriorate and his sons were struggling to do almost all of his work for him. And the thought that he would have to let Saul and his sons know that the successor he had chosen was the very man Saul had come to loathe, the very man who had seduced and abandoned not one but two of his children, first Michal and then Jonathan, was a truly daunting task, and Samuel asked me to intervene on his behalf.

Later rabbis in the years after the destruction of the Second Temple, men who still had access to old texts and knew some of the truth of my life, ascribe to me an exploit in that period that I will get to shortly, but there is one other story told about me that they did not credit me for, a story that will give you some idea of why I love so much the story of Tevye's dream from *Fiddler on the Roof.* I almost never claimed rank at any point in my life, but when Samuel asked me to go to confer with Saul I suggested instead that it might begin to shift the balance of power if Saul came to me instead, our oldest elder. That made sense to Samuel, and we sent word to Saul, but a few days after our conversation—Samuel died. After the period of mourning was over, Saul came to see me.

Born in the spring, probably in Aries, two astrologers I knew, one in Safed hundreds of years ago and one right here in Venice Beach, both told me the same thing—"You like all Arians are a creature of impulse." (That word Arian is rather like its sound-kin, Aryan, so I use it with trepidation.) Saul arrived with his body guards, still deep in mourning and looked worse than I'd ever seen him look, stooped, haggard, in a deep depression that could at any moment turn into rage. As we sat, at first in silence, it occurred to me that I could use Samuel to speak for me. And being a priestess, being our most elder elder, I plied Saul with wine and when he was a bit tipsy I said to him something very like, "Lord, Commander, here we are, both of us, deep in mourning for a beloved friend and teacher." Then I told him how Samuel had come to see me in a dream, the very night that he died, and I went on to say, "Good Saul, our dear friend was concerned for you. Concerned for your health. Concerned for your well-being." Then I added something that I alone could have said to him. I said, making things up as I went along, I said, "Good Lord Saul, just as my wise son Moses knew when it was time for him to step down, Samuel and I believe that you too have come to that holy moment."

Saul nodded and went home with his guards to confer with his family, but before he had a chance to act, Saul himself died, not in battle but while sleeping in his own bed. Almost all of the stories about him that you know, about the wars and conquests, the battles, the killing, were stories told backwards in time to help their later authors and their audiences make sense of their terrifying present. And of this story, only fragments remain, none of it ascribed to me, save that I was at that time living in a tent beneath a great big soon-to-be-destroyed goddess tree, just outside a tiny little village called—Endor.

Endor. The Witch of Endor, now sometimes called The Medium of Endor, the Sorceress of Endor, the Clairvoyant of Endor, or even the Psychic of Endor. All of them—me. (I suppose that I could have my own television show now, or run an online psychic network!) And you can imagine how utterly amused and delighted I was half a century ago when a television show appeared called *Bewitched* that featured a lead character named Samantha (clearly a gender-switched version of my old dear friend Samuel) who was a closeted witch with a human husband and a mother named—Endora— along with a collection of odd witchy relatives, all of them some version of immortal.

Chapter Fourteen

More about David and Solomon,
and a painful personal revelation
(made for the very first time ever)

I WAS APPROXIMATELY THREE hundred years old when Saul died, and I watched from a distance as our beloved David, King David, took over his position as CEO, as *adon*. This may seem odd to you, David's midlife career switch, but all through history entertainers have gone on to have careers in politics. Up until now I've always given you examples of contemporary people who remind me of characters from our past, but in this instance let me invoke the memory of someone who died not too long ago, who began his career as a second rate actor and then rose to become the president of the United States. Our David was nothing like Ronald Reagan, but David made the same transition, and was as good a leader as he was a performer.

I saw Reagan speak once, at the dedication of a bell tower in Santa Barbara. He was the governor of California then and, remembering David, I was curious to see him. I got there early and was standing three feet away from him as he delivered a speech in honor of the friend and neighbor in whose name the tower was being dedicated—but he could not remember that man's name, and I watched his wife elbow him and hiss it in his left ear. Even in old age, King David was nothing like that. He was as magnificent a petty ruler of an expanding family concern as he was a performer, and to the end of his life he never stopped performing. I remember his last concert, the tremor in his voice—and the passion. Like Billie Holiday at the end of her life, voice a wreck, with an emotional depth to it that always kills me when I listen to her last recordings, especially *Lady in Satin*.

At three hundred or so years of age there was no way that I could deny the truth about who or what I was. If not immortal, I was certainly ancient. David knew who I was. His son Solomon did as well. They were the last two public figures among our people to whom I told the truth—for a very long time. I was tired, tired of being a public figure, an elder, and an increasingly marginalized priestess. I was tired of attending and often officiating at the funerals of loved ones, and I was dead tired of all the questions people had for me about myself and my past and our people and our history. I was packed and ready to leave Hebron, David's hometown, to go back to my Endor, but he made me promise that I would continue on in an advisory role, which is how I was able to watch firsthand an event unfolding that is only half-reflected in the *Tanach,* a situation that continues to impact our lives to this very day.

When we returned to Canaan, as I've said before, some of us moved north, some south, and we all agreed that we wouldn't settle in one city, Salem, or Jebus (later, Jerusalem) because it was ruled by our distant relations. Perhaps you recall that one of Abraham's lovers was Baalat, the sister of his good friend Melchizedek the king of Salem, who was also a cousin. When we first retuned to Canaan the city of Salem was ruled by Melchizedek's descendant Adonizedek, who knew who we were and was happy to support us in resettling. Some two hundred years later Salem was ruled by Adonizedek's descendant Avizedek, a musician himself and a great fan of David's music. Now Avizedek had a lovely daughter named Anat, which was also the name of one of the leading goddesses of the region—but he had no sons with his wife Inariat or with any of his three concubines! Eleven daughters, perhaps a record. Now Anat too was a fan of David's, and down through history plenty of lovely young women have married older men so I'm sure that I don't have to list any of them for you. David and Anat's wedding was the last one at which I ever officiated. It was held on a small lovely farm outside the city walls of her father's city that was owned by Araunah, Avizedek's half-brother. Not so different from today, Araunah often rented out his farm for festive occasions. Remember him as he will soon return to our story.

I was quite fond of David, as impressed by his business dealings as I was by his talent. I quite adored his and Anat's only child, their daughter Ketesh, which is one of the many nicknames of Asherah. After the wedding, David moved to Salem from Hebron and when Anat's father died he became its ruler. A marvelous example of life imitating art—in two years time our King David became King King David for real, and he spent the rest of his reign living in that city, which sat right in the middle of Canaan, between the land settled by our people in the north and the land settled by our people in the south.

In that short window of relative peace our caravans wandered the region and beyond, and our little pseudo-kingdom was flourishing. Even in his middle years David was a very handsome man who saw himself as the heir to Joshua and Shalomeh, and he took steps to further unify our people by purchasing the farm owned by Aruanah, as well as marrying him off to his own equally handsome but less musically talented son Jeremoth, a practice that was common in those days, although it would soon be forbidden by the priests of Yahweh. To further unify our people David consulted with the descendants of Moses and Aaron who were living in both regions, who all agreed that it was time to bring the ark and the tent back together, along with the *teraphim,* all of which Joshua had divided, sending the tent to the north and the ark to the south, and one *teraph* in each direction. It was on Araunah's old farm, on a lovely little hill just north of that small walled city, that David had our old tent erected and had the ark brought back and set up inside it and had the *teraphim* set up on top of it again. It was then that I felt, naively, that our people were safe, our future was laid out for us, and I was ready to retire back to Endor. But before I did, it was David himself who persuaded me to do something that I'd never done before—give a concert.

Long before there was a word for it, I've always been an introvert, and I was reluctant to perform in public. But David convinced me that it would be marvelous to share three hundred years of music and stories that our ancestors had entertained themselves with. In the end, I quite enjoyed myself, singing songs that I'd learned from Grandpa Jacob and my grandmothers, from my mother Arsiyah and from my beloved Dinah. I also sang the very song that I sang to Grandpa about Joseph still being alive, for which he blessed me with immortality, and then I sang songs that Bast and I had sung in Egypt to our little boy, as well as songs he taught us later that he'd learned from our Midianite kin. Then I sang several of Miriam's songs and to the delight of everyone, I ended my one and only concert by singing a few of David's songs, scattered lines of which have ended up in the psalms that are attributed to him. We held the concert—where else?—on Araunah's old farm, with the tent and the ark in the background. It was a glorious day and while I've never done anything like that again, it was a perfect final act in my public life.

Very often I've told you tales to correct the texts that have survived, but many of the stories told in *Torah* and *Tanach* are more or less accurate. For example, David did have several wives, and most of the story of Bathsheba is true, as is the sad sad tale of his final years, when the rivalry between his sons and their mothers grew into armed conflict. Now there's a tragic story told in the *Second Samuel* about a revolt against David late in his administration that was led by a man named Sheba. He went into hiding in the north,

David's troops pursued him, and the *Tanach* tells us that a wise woman led them to Sheba's hiding place so that they could kill him. A 7th Century CE midrash collection says that I was that wise woman, but for all the same reasons that our historians deleted the truth about David and Anat and the rest of what I've shared with you in this chapter, the rabbis who compiled that collection knew about me being the witch of Endor, wanted in some way to honor me, and switched my identity with that of Padriah, the real wise woman of Abel Beth Maacah who is mentioned in that true story.

It was stories that got me into trouble, big trouble. And I've put off telling you about that trouble since the beginning of the book. But here we are now in the fourteenth chapter, right where this story belongs, chronologically. Before I tell it let me say one thing. Over my three thousand and more years I've probably sat at twice that number of deathbeds listening to wheezing people beg for one more day, one more hour, one last chance to see someone they love. What I would give to be able to hand them some of my hours, and how I envy them. When *you* do something wrong you may regret it for a week, a month, a year, or till your next therapy appointment, but even if you regret it till the end of your life, you can let go of it on your deathbed. But I did something that started out wonderfully well and ended up so painfully distressing that I've been upset about it for almost three thousand years. I still wake in the night from dreams about it, not like Tevye from imaginary dreams but from real ones, and I still lie in the dark starting at the ceiling replaying in my mind all of the ancient ways in which I could have avoided it. Which calls to mind poor Nancy Reagan, who during her time in the White House and during the badly conceived and badly named "War on Drugs" immortalized these words—"Just say No!" And how I wish, three thousand years ago, when King Solomon summoned me to Jerusalem to ask me a favor—that those words had come rippling back to me in the past, during a meal that I had with him, over grilled duck, warm bread, sautéed spring vegetables, and a fine dry wine from a local vineyard.

It sometimes happens that the children of famous parents are stifled by their parent's fame, while others grow up feeling privileged and end up being even more inflated versions of their parents. The Bible tells us an exaggerated version of the truth about King Solomon and his many wives, almost always chosen to widen our trading network through another alliance, so he did not have 700 wives and 300 concubines; more like five wives over the long years of his reign and perhaps twenty-five concubines. However the numbers in the Bible do reflect something about his character and that of many of his insufferable children, most of whom were a trial to their varied parents.

In spite of his chaotic household and overly-indulgent parenting skills, I was very fond of Solomon. For the record, his birth name was Jedidiah, but just like his father Elhanan, Jedidiah came to be called by another name, Solomon, *Shlomo,* from the root- word for peace and wholeness. It was the perfect name for a man of immense skill and a monumental ego, who did, by the way, build the first temple in Jerusalem, out on that hill where his father had brought together ark and tent again. I always laugh when I see pictures of it, paintings, for they are always grand, monumental, based on the descriptions of it in the Bible, which are as vastly inflated as the size of his kingdom. That first temple, added to by several later kings, was a rather humble structure, but it wasn't a tent. It was a stone structure in the rear of a large courtyard, designed to imitate the grand edifices built by some of our older and more established neighbors.

The evening that Solomon changed my life we were sitting on a terrace of his dwelling, looking out over that first temple, rising up on what used to be Araunah's lovely farm. We were eating dessert when he turned to me and said, "Auntie, the work that you set out to do with your son and with Joshua and Shalomeh has all been accomplished. We are safe in our land and we are thriving. We have power and connections, a political center and a religious one, which we've never had before." Then he pointed toward the temple with his wine cup, put it down on the table, turned to me and said, "Auntie Serach, there's only one more thing that we need. Saul commissioned several scribes to start the project, but none of them completed it. Lots of other people have them—a sacred text. And there's no one else who could possibly write it—but you."

"Thank you for asking me, my dear, but as you know, I've gone into retirement."

"How very kind of you to ask. But it's time for me to step back from history."

"I'd be more than happy to work with the priests and give them an outline."

"Perhaps some other time."

"No."

The Torah is not what you think, the one you have now. With the exception of a few scattered verses there and here—it isn't the work of Bast's and my son Moses. As far back as the 12th century in Spain Abraham ibn Ezra wrote of his doubts about it having been written by Moses. And in the 17th century in the Netherlands, Spinoza—a charming man I worked for briefly as a cook—was questioning its Mosaic authorship as well. (Mosaic is actually the perfect word for it. The Torah is a verbal mosaic.) In the last few centuries scholars have come to understand that the Bible is composed of texts from various documents, and in light of the recently discovered texts from the Dead Sea region they have begun to look at our sacred texts in new ways. More recently, two scholars have suggested that the author of one of the core texts that was later woven into the Torah was a woman.

I looked down at the temple. I looked deep into my drinking cup, copper with swirling spirals etched into it. I looked off to the west, the last amber glow of sun tinting the burly clouds. I took another sip of wine and put my cup down. I ate another fig, deep purple and dripping its sweet nectar. And to this day, three thousand years later, I can watch the movie of that evening, for I have played it over and over again from two perspectives, as participant and as observer—watching the way that I looked at Solomon as he, patiently, looked at me—not as handsome as his father but far more accomplished, the ruddy streaks in his dark beard catching the last rays of the sun.

"Yes."

Chapter Fifteen

The story continued, the death of Solomon,

the breakup of the united kingdom,

and what followed

It NEVER OCCURRED TO me that I might want to be a writer until Solomon awakened the storyteller in me. I'd learned to write soon after we returned to Canaan, and as a singer and occasional composer, far less talented than David, I found myself excited by the chance to do something new. (Novelty can be rare when you live on and on and on, and the quest for it can turn into an obsession that eventually becomes boring.) Rather than record stories about our past that everyone already knew—the very stories that I've been telling you here, many of which had already been recorded by Saul's scribes—I decided that I would write a satire, a farce, something that Euripides might have understood, or Shakespeare, Edward Albee, and one of our most talented writers ever, Sanorah, Moses's great, great etc. etc. granddaughter, an older Hebrew sister to Sappho, which you would not know from her only surviving text—the core of the book of *Job,* the really funny parts long ago removed. (Forgive this little bit of family pride. If you'd been able to read any of her other books you would all agree with me.)

As a priestess who had been telling factual stories for years I wanted to tell wry, droll, ridiculous stories that would make everyone laugh. As you can tell already from this narrative, I have some clear critiques of the patriarchy and have had some pointed things to say about some specific men and about men in general. As someone who was and is grounded in Goddess and not God—I wanted to paint Yahweh in the same way that I saw so many of the men around me—whiny, petulant, and perpetually immature.

As the oldest heir to the original founders of our family firm, Solomon offered me an annual stipend so I didn't have to worry about working. Up until that time I'd always worked as the rest of us had. In Egypt we lived by barter of services; our bosses paid us with onions, melons, cucumbers, and fish. When I served as a priestess I was paid in food, fabric, and other usable objects. But with a stipend of gold and precious stones, I realized that I could finally do what I wanted to do—disappear to Endor. The name of the place is actually two words, Ein Dor, which means the Spring of Dor, Dor meaning "generations"—which seemed the perfect place for someone to live in who had lived through so many of them. (I wish I could say that it was the waters of that spring that granted me my longevity, but I was old when I got there.) It was a lovely quiet location surrounded by trees, perfect for writing, and I returned there with a delightful well-paid servant girl, Naima and with Iddo, who I mentioned earlier, the descendant of Moses and an earlier Iddo. It was very nice to have family with me, what today I would call "Queer family," as Iddo's partner Shimron moved there with us. Although I looked the same age as Iddo, Shimron, and Naima, they knew how ancient I really was and were there to keep me company, watch over me, and take care of me—which I let them do—not because I felt my age but because of my project.

I came with long rolls of parchment, made my own ink, had a small writing desk that was a gift from Solomon, and a little cat I named after my sister Tamimah, because non-human relationships are so important. With financial support and companionship, I went to work in what today I believe was possibly the very first writer's retreat in all of human history. Scholars who say that the author of the J Document in the Torah was a woman are correct. What they do not know is that the material they identify as J is not always mine, nor do they know that my finished product was four times as long as the J material you have now. I began of course with the story of Creation and my tale of a serpent tempter was a comic inversion of the ancient and then totally familiar story about how Asherah sent wisdom to the first two people through that umbilical messenger. I continued the tale from their expulsion from the Garden of Eden on through all of our family history until we came back to the Garden of Canaan once again. In addition to my talking serpent and talking donkey (the only speaking animals which survive) there was a lovely story (if I do say so myself) about Sarah's talking cat, which I named Bast, and much later a series of stories about a silly talking fox named Lo, which means No in Hebrew, that followed Moses in the wilderness, offering him her not-so-wise counsel.

I and all of our people were so haunted by the horrible later years of David and by the armed conflicts between his various sons, and one major

strand that I wove all through my history—was the rivalry between brothers, beginning with the very first pair. What's missing from your text are the
stories of all the women I included in my book. Sarah was a central character in my tale, my grandfather Jacob's five wives were all there, Zipporah had
a much larger role and so did Miriam, but later editors—male, all of them—
could not tolerate my stories of Asherah or of Miriam's visions of her so they
removed them—which breaks my heart to this very day. And sometimes, to
my deep regret, I retold a story for comic effect that made no sense later on,
of which I could give you many examples but will give but one.

Everyone in the time of Solomon knew the truth about Joseph, that he
was a charmingly self-centered and at the same time immensely competent
administrator. One thing that he was *not* was intuitive in any way, nor was
he very sensitive to other people's feelings. So when I wove into his tale
elements from the story of Azibah, one of the priestesses who I initiated
during the years when Shalomeh was leading us and who was a noted dream
interpreter, everyone laughed, laughed as you might today if I told you how
deeply wise a mystic George Bush had been, either one of them.

Male sibling rivalry ran through my book, as you can see in the surviving fragments. My intention—to make men look ridiculous—was not
the most honorable of motives, but it was also balanced out by stories of
men who were wise, noble, just, and good role models—chiefly Joseph and
Moses, whose stories I told as mirror images of each other, for literary effect.
I could have told my tales in different ways, but that didn't occur to me at
the time, which troubles me to this day. So let it suffice to say that I am not
a saint, a bodhisattva, or any kind of an enlightened being. I am now even
more who I was then, a cranky old woman who doesn't look her age, and as
the patriarchy deepened I grew more and more tired of men and what they
were doing to the world. Hence the stories I wrote by day and read to Naima
and Iddo and Shimron each night around the fire, or in my tent on colder
nights. It wasn't my old tent, which as you know became our nation's first
collective meeting place and ended up in Solomon's temple. It was a new
tent that he gave me when I went off to live in the woods, a totally up-to-date
modern tent, lovely and well-insulated against heat and cold.

I wrote and I wrote. It took me three years to finish my saga and when
it was done I brought all of the scrolls to Jerusalem and read them night after
night over dinner for almost a year to everyone in court. People laughed and
cried sometimes, but mostly laughed. When I was done reading the whole
thing I gave it all to Solomon, who whispered to me, "Auntie Serach, this
isn't what I was expecting. But it's marvelous." I asked him if he was disap-
pointed and he said, "Absolutely not! It's brilliant, you're brilliant, and you've
filled my head with so many wonderful ideas of things to do and change

and make happen." Pleased, exhausted, tired of urban life, even in a city that you today would scarcely call a town, I was happy to go back to Endor, but returned less than a year later for Solomon's funeral, and then went back to Endor again.

Sadly, the same old rivalry that began under Joseph, that exploded in Sinai under Moses when some of us camped to the south of the hill of Sinai/ Horeb and others of us camped to the north of it, and that sent us back into Canaan in two divisions—that rift never healed. David and Solomon were able to bridge it for a time, but Solomon's son and successor Rehoboam lacked both the charm of his father and the business acumen that kept our family enterprise flourishing. A faltering economy led to conflicts and war and then a civil war that split our people into two small nations clustered on the hills of central Canaan into which we'd married and become established. Given that Endor was in the north, I did not return to Jerusalem for a very very long time.

People forgot about me, which was exactly what I wanted. I went to work as an embroiderer, sending Naima out to sell my handiwork in the market towns of the north and staying alone in the woods by my little spring. First Tamimah died, then Shimron died after a brief illness, then Iddo, called to become a prophet, wandered out into the world himself. Wanting to not be known, I left my spring behind and began a pattern that's continued until the present, of moving every few years so that no one would ever point and say, "There's something wrong with that old woman. Something weird about her. I wonder if she's some kind of a witch, 'cause she never gets any older."

To say that I'm immortal, as people do who read and write about me, is both inaccurate and wrong. As I've said several times already, I am *not* immortal—I just haven't died yet. And I'm not even sure that I believe in immortality, the truth of which seems a question best addressed by physicists, geneticists, theologians, and mystics. If there is such a thing as the soul, perhaps *it's* immortal. But I do have to say that in the last fifty years my body's aging process has speeded up, so I have high hopes that my time on Earth may be coming to an end, which has been part of the impulse to write my second book, and just in the nick of time, as feminism and an interest in Jewish mysticism and folklore have generated a renewed interest in me—which frankly horrifies me.

Speaking of horror, some years ago I went through an obsessive period of reading everything I could get my delightfully liver-spotted hands on—about vampires and other 'immortal' creatures. (A related genre, books about werewolves, had no attraction for me.) I went back of course to explore our own stories about me—so maddening—and to reread those even older stories that I'd heard as a little girl, about Gilgamesh and Utnapishtim.

Then I reviewed the stories from our own people about Enoch and Elijah and went on to read others including the Christian tales of the Wandering Jew. I read Bram Stoker's work on Dracula, which may or may not have been influenced by our own Jewish stories about the golem. Then I leaped ahead to watch films and television shows like *Doctor Who*, and to read all kinds of books and even comic books with immortals in them—a genre I wish had existed sooner—and then I read several contemporary vampire books, but none of them reflected me back to myself. (By the way, all the talking animals in comic books and cartoons, those talking mice and ducks and pigs and turtles, evoke for me my own lost and surviving stories of talking animals.)

I wish I could say that having lived for three thousand years has made me wiser, but all that it's done is given me more stories to tell and many more things to try to forget—more loss, more anger, and more frustration, plus a few amazing views, meals, friends, lovers, and orgasms. Yes, lovers, orgasms—and profound regret and shame.

After the united kingdom split in two I kept to myself. People forgot about me and it was lovely. I'd given up thinking I would die. After five or six hundred years of being a hypochondriac you have to give up the belief that this pain, that ache, this bruise, that bump is going to kill you. I never wrote again, I sewed, embroidered, sang to myself and kept to myself. How many times can you have your heart broken and keep trying to love? Every woman I'd loved I'd lost to the grave, for I loved a woman in David and Solomon's court named Esmid, a musician who played flute with the priests, when that was still allowed, and who died in my arms too young, and after whom I did not take another lover for centuries. No, I lived alone and wandered the land of Canaan, living through plagues, droughts, famines, floods, a terrifying blizzard once that killed so many of our people, and then a fire that devastated the hills of northern Galilee. And being in that ridiculously unsafe land between two endlessly hostile powers, one from the banks of the Nile and the other from the banks of the Tigris and Euphrates, I continued to see threats, invasions, war and endless killing.

Several hundred years after Solomon's death our old friends the Assyrians decided to invade us. I was living, as we would say today, "way off the grid," in a tiny little village on the east side of the Jordan River. I knew about the invasion and the destruction of the northern kingdom that was sometimes called Israel and sometimes called Samaria. Long used to hiding, when many of our people were carted off into exile I remained behind. There's a story that says that I'd lived with my ancestral tribe of Asher in the north, was taken into exile by the Assyrians, and died in Assyria. There's even a tomb said to contain my remains, in a town called Pir Bakran in modern Iran, but obviously I'm not buried there, although I did live in the area several centuries later. No, I hid, survived, and when the situation calmed down a few years later I was curious to see what was happening in Jerusalem, so I gave my tent to the son of a kind neighbor who wanted some independence and I returned to the territory of Judah. Prophecy was all the rage then. Jeremiah, Isaiah, and other women besides Huldah, the only one whose story is even told in fragments, were wandering up and down the land, through Judah in the south and also among the ruins of Israel in the north. I encountered several of them on my way to Jerusalem and remember how inspiring a woman named Ozeret was, long forgotten.

When I got to Jerusalem after a several day's journey on foot, I was amazed at how much the city had changed. There were more walls, more quarters, the temple had been enlarged, although it was never as large as in people's later imagination. Compared to how it was under Solomon, Jerusalem was almost cosmopolitan, flooded with refuges from the north, which had always been richer and far more sophisticated, and they brought some of those qualities with them. My visit occurred during the reign of King Josiah, who I saw for the first time from a distance—a tall slim man with a long dark curly beard, leaning on a walking stick as he headed toward the temple complex. With its larger courtyard and expanded holy place built around the original temple, with a much larger altar and far more priests of Yahweh, I was saddened to not see a single pillar or tree dedicated to Asherah anywhere in sight, let alone a single priestess. As a woman I had to watch everything through the large gateway between the outer and the inner courts, which made me furious, as you can imagine, for it was not that way in the time of Solomon. Women and men prayed together then. I tried to peer up through the steps and into the temple itself, hoping to be able to see the gold-plated ark of the covenant with our old gold-plated *teraphim* on top, and my old box inside it—but it was much too far away.

It was Shabbat and after the sacrifices were over—and they went on for a long time—the priests stood on the steps to the outer court and everyone fell to their knees and recited the early version of our primary . . . what shall I call it? . . . mantra? . . . a single line that would eventually become what you would recognize as the Shema. And then the priests recited a version of the Ten Commandments which sounded nothing at all like what we had originally agreed upon. And then another priest stood up and began to chant from a scroll what you today would call the *parasaha*, the Torah portion of the week. Parts of it sounded familiar, but it took me a while to realize what it was that I was listening to—because every few lines or so a man in the crowd would interrupt the priest who was reading—to shout out (always with a northern accent) something from a scroll that he was holding, from down at the bottom of the steps. I turned to a woman standing beside me in the outer court and whispered in her ear, "What's going on?" And she whispered back to me, "This happens every Shabbat now. It's driving me crazy. One of our priests tries to read the weekly portion, but one of *their* priests"—and she pointed to the other man—"from the north, yells out the equivalent sections from their ridiculous idea of a Torah."

Soon it became a total shouting match, two older men trying to outdo the other, one from the top of the stairs to the inner courtyard and the other standing at the bottom. I asked my neighbor how long this had been going on for. "Since right after Samaria was defeated and some of their priests fled to here." I tried to listen. I tried to not shout out words myself. Because what I was hearing as a sacred text from Jerusalem—was an edited and at times extremely mangled version of—yes, you guessed it—what I myself had once written, almost exactly three hundred years before! Yes, during all the time that I was away from Jerusalem someone—no, some men, I later I found out exactly who—took my old text, gutted it, added to it, and turned it from what I had intended it to be—a spiritual and political satire—into their idea of a sacred text.

I was both furious and in despair. And the story gets worse. I stayed in Jerusalem for about a year, and every Shabbat the same thing would happen—a shouting match between two rival priests, one from Judah and the other from Samaria. Some weeks there were fist fights, and other weeks rival gangs would attack each other, usually outside the temple compound but sometimes in the outer courtyard of the temple itself. One day a fight began about truth, The Truth, about Revelation, about which was the real Torah, and a young man who grew up in the city pulled a knife on a young man who came from a family of refugees from Samaria—and stabbed him to death.

Now, as you may have noticed from this narrative, I am not a very religious woman, not someone who turns to prayer in times of need. But it seemed to me that things were getting out of control, and it seemed to me that something had to be done about it before the entire city erupted into violence. As the prayers I would have offered to Asherah would have had no place in that temple from which she'd been banished, the sister-wife of Yahweh the now-solo god, almost God, of our people, I left the temple, left the city, and wandered outside the walls and up to the east, till I came to an old old tree on the Mount of Olives, a tree that once might had been a little goddess shrine. (Remember these little local shrines; they will return to our story somewhat later.) I sat beneath its outspread branches, grew quiet and asked for guidance. The wind shimmied the leaves of the old tree above me, and all at once the thought came to me—"Serach, go to the king, reveal yourself, and tell him that it's possible to weave these two texts together."

I tried to get in to see the king every day for more than a week. None of the guards would believe me, even when I showed them the seal around my neck that belonged to Sarah, which they knew about because that story still remained in the Jerusalem version of the two proto-Torahs, but rather than being listened to, I was taunted and mocked and called a crazy lady. But one day there was a new guard at the palace gates and I approached him thinking, "He's the one who will let me in." I bowed, slightly, told him my story and showed him the seal around my neck, but instead of becoming my hero he shouted out to the passersby, "This nutcase thinks that she's Serach, and even claims to have proof of it, on an old piece of string hanging around her neck." Well, Goddess works in strange ways, because an old gentleman just happened to be walking by who had served in Assyria in the diplomatic corps. He came up to me, asked to see the seal, which he rolled in his hands and read—in cuneiform—then turned to the guard and said to the him, "I myself will escort her in to see His Majesty," or the ancient equivalent, showing the guard his own signet ring as proof of his noble identity.

The palace was larger than it had been under Solomon, but the ornately redecorated throne room was in the same place, where that kind old man—(and isn't it odd to call someone who was in his fifties "old" when I was over seven hundred years old myself?)—that kind old man named Eliezer introduced me to the king, who asked me for many corroborating details about myself and about things that he knew as sovereign, about the ark and the tent in the storeroom that had belong to my mother Arsiyah. He asked me questions about our ancestors, about the palace, the walls, hidden passageways, things that I had learned from Solomon, and then, with tears in his eyes he came down from his throne, bowed to me, took my hands in his hands, said that he had heard rumors of my continued life, and invited me to move into the palace with him.

I was upset by the rumors, which I'd never heard about, accepted his offer, and told him why I had come. To my delight then and shame for long centuries later on, Josiah thought that my idea was brilliant, and by the end of the week he had established a room off the outer courtyard of the temple where priests from the north and priests from the south sat with their two variant collections of stories, their two proto-Torahs, reading them one after the other and, from time to time continuing to shout at each other, as they slowly weaved their two different texts into one new text.

I turned down the king's invitation to live in the palace but accepted his offer to find me lodgings—a comfortable room near the north gate of the city. He also understood why I wanted to keep my identity a secret, as did

Eliezer, so I was able to wander about unknown, although the guard continued to taunt me each time he was on duty and I went to visit the king. As the supervisor of the Torah-making project I did my best to keep the rival priests calm and focused, which was such a distraction that I often lost sight of the text itself. In the end it took more than three years to craft that new text, a text that was then copied by multiple scribes and sent out to priests all over Judah and to the surviving scattered priests in the ruins of the north. It was a text that didn't always make sense, I realized as I listened to it, but when read publicly for the first time in the outer courtyard of the temple it left everyone in silence—for the parts that everyone from the south and from the north knew . . . were there!—sometimes garbled and often flowing elegantly one into the other. And that's how the very first version of something that you would totally recognize as the Torah was created, in the spirit of unity that Bast's and my son Moses had brought to our people in the wilderness. It was and remains a flawed text, but while my own first version did not make Moses the central character, there is something appropriate about the way in which his capacity to bring us together ripples through that composite text that took an entire year of Shabbats to read. Flawed, at times overly xenophobic, with so much missing from it, it's guided us for all this time although it sometimes trapped us in narrow ways of thinking, and my hope is that this new book of mine will be my way of making amends and restitution for all the troubles that it's caused over the millennia, and as a way of honoring Bast's and my beloved Hapmose, without whom we would all have died eons ago in that horrid workers city—all died perhaps except me.

Chapter Sixteen

Here your weary guide continues her adventures,

and shares with you a few favorite stories

YOU MAY THINK IT odd that a woman my age had never traveled anywhere but to Egypt and back, then up and down Canaan for several hundred years—but even when I was in hiding I felt a responsibility for our people, felt I had to be near them as our eldest elder, even if I was living a stealth existence. Had things been different then, Bast and I might have traveled a bit as she was a woman of means, but Moses had other ideas for us and as you say—the rest is history. But with that book done, that core Torah, even if it troubled me then and has continued to trouble me over the ages, I felt that our people had no more need of me—and for the first time in my life I felt like a free woman, totally free, as Josiah had paid me just as had Solomon before him, in gold and precious stones that I could trade as I needed to.

Egypt had been my second home, I'd often thought of it with a mixture of happy and sad memories, and I went back down there with one of our caravans, carrying a letter of passage from King Josiah, who was sadly killed a few years later in a battle with the Egyptians, which made me regret my decision to return. However, I hadn't been back since we left with Moses, and the changes were even more amazing than what had happened to Jerusalem. Our old workers city had become a huge metropolis, sprawling over both banks of the Nile. There were large temples and palaces and I could barely recognize anything of our old little ghetto in the fancy up-scale neighborhood that I discovered, with its trendy shops and a large wide-open plaza where our mud-brick homes once stood.

I thought I'd be happy there but Egypt was jarring. I'd forgotten the noise, the intensity, the hundreds of deities and their crowded temples. Yes, slowly over time, along with the rest of our people, I'd become a kind of monotheist, and even if God still privately remained Goddess for me—and there on the banks of the Nile, whose god our son Moses was named for, Hapmose, I felt not comfort but heightened loss. One day I was wandering by the river in our old quarter, and I came upon a Judahite merchant named Reuben, who I recognized by his garb as he recognized mine. We got to talking and he told me that he was heading down to Kush, which is now called Ethiopia, and was looking for a cook. Well if you've lived for almost eight hundred years you've done a lot of cooking, and if you've lived for almost eight hundred years you'll have found yourself getting sick to death of the same meals and developed an enormous mental file of recipes. So I took the job, we traveled south by riverboat with a crew of ten—and what a joy it was to be out on the water, leaving everything behind and almost starting over.

Kush and Egypt had a strange relationship, not unlike that of Judah and Israel, related and yet warring sometimes, taking turns invading each other. As luck would have it, we arrived in a time of peace and after a year, when Reuben was ready to head back, I chose to stay. I loved the land, so very different from Egypt and Canaan, and I got a job working by the river in a little marketplace selling Egyptian fabric for a man who Reuben knew. One day a handsome older woman approached my stall. She was lovely, and from a tilt of the head, a look in her eyes, the way that people recognize each other who are what we now call Queer, we connected. I was struggling to learn the local language. She knew some Egyptian and while mine was rusty we managed to communicate well enough so that I could sell her some dyed Egyptian cloth. She came back a few days later and you can imagine the conflict I felt.

How would you feel if you hadn't made love with anyone in several hundred years? My skin was screaming out for touch, the doors of my heart were about to swing open, but I'd also been hiding the truth about myself for hundreds of years. The conversation I dreaded having with her was my version of the one that my gay friends have about their HIV status, and other friends of mine have with new partners about their cancer treatments and prognosis. I was glad that another customer approached my little stall and relieved when she left. But she came back later and gave me a penetrating look that said, "Girl, I know you better than you know yourself." I was powerless and ended up following her home.

The first kiss, so sweet, long and lingering. Yehadana ran her fingers over my face, tracing the lines of it. The way she pulled out the seal on its string from around my neck, smiled at me and said, "You are one of us." I thought she meant that I was a woman-loving-woman just like she was till she added, "The moment I saw you in the marketplace I knew. You're how old now? Twenty generations, thirty, forty?" I was stunned. How had she known? She took my face in her hands, kissed me deeply and said, "Darling, I am the same. I have lived through at least fifty generations." I pulled away. Stepped back. Looked at her, deeply, not seeing in her yet what she was seeing in me. She gave words to it. "The look in your eyes, both utterly world-weary and so very full of life. That odd combination other people do not have, who either know they are going to die soon, or don't know that of course they will."

She held out her hand to me and I took it. She led me to her bed and we spent the rest of the night there. There was no hurry. We entered a version of forever, and left her bed only as light returned to the sky. She led me to a nearby hill with a little shrine to a local goddess at its summit. There, holding hands, we prayed and watched the fiery orb rise high above us, a sun that in her language was female and not male. Day by day I learned to see and feel in her what she felt in me—a version of immortality. I still had my old copper mirror from Dinah, but for the very first time in my entire life I had a living mirror to reflect me back to me. And even more wonderful, Yehadana knew another person like us, an even older man who lived much further down the Nile, and not long after I moved in with her we went to visit him. His name was Asumma, and in like fashion he was the one who had first recognized Yehadana, also in a marketplace. I praise again and again the many-named goddess who presides over them for all the ways that she has blessed me in my life.

Imagine it—on my way to being one thousand and sitting for the very first time with two other people like me. We told our stories, asked each other questions, and what a joy it was also for the first time since I was a young woman to sit with elders again and become a child. Unlike Yehadana and I, who were used to hiding, needing to hide, needing to keep on the move, Assuma was revered in his village, a village he had never left. He was revered as a god, and it seems to me now that the various cultures around the world that tell stories about gods walking the earth are probably telling stories about the few other people who are genetic anomalies, not divine, but rare, just like the three of us were.

I thought I would stay with Yehadana for a long long time, loving, laughing, and learning new songs on whole new stringed instruments, but two things happened. Just as is beginning to happen to me, within ten years of my arriving in her village Yehadana's aging process began to speed up. She said she was relieved to finally be going, heartbroken to know that I would have to bury another beloved one, and felt that in a way she had held on for so long in order to meet me, to pass on her legacy to me. She died peacefully, and not very long after that my friend Reuben returned to the village with more items to trade, and informed me that the situation had deteriorated back in Judah, so I decided to return with him

It took us longer to return than we expected, and it was strange so many hundreds of years later to make parts of the same journey that we had made with Moses. Reuben took me to see King Zedekiah, one of Josiah's sons, who the Babylonians had placed upon the throne. I should have known better but I learn slowly and I foolishly told him who I was, a mistake I only made one more time with a ruler. Zedekiah was making everything worse in his relationship with Babylonia and refused to listen to anything that I had to say, or to the men who were his advisors, like the prophet Jeremiah, or to the immensely wise woman whose counsel he and Josiah sought frequently, the prophetess Huldah. (Pardon me for using gendered language, which is out of favor in this time, but I am old and while I favor gender-neutral words in some instances, I miss words like actress, poetess, sculptress, prophetess, and even Jewess—for I am proud of Huldah's womanness and want to acclaim her.)

Tempting fate, Zedekiah made an alliance with Egypt, which brought down the wrath of Babylon, and I remained there during their long siege, attack, and was there when they began the destruction of the city, from the walls to the palaces and homes, then to the temple on its height, on that hill where once the lovely farm of Araunah sat, with its vines and its olive trees, that beautiful farm where once hundreds of years ago I had married Anat and David and later given my first and only concert. Whatever my ambivalent feelings were about that temple, it housed objects that brought me back to my childhood, my early years, the years when Bast and I were raising Moses and then wandering with our people in the desert. Most painful of all to me when they set fire to the temple was that the ark and the cherubim that were once *teraphim* went up in flames. Zedekiah tried to escape and was captured. However foolish he was, he didn't deserve to be forced to watch his sons be killed in front of him, then be blinded and dragged in chains to Babylon, where he remained a prisoner for the rest of his life.

Good at hiding, I could have escaped from the city, but when most of our people, including all of the ruling class were taken off to Babylon— I went with them, for even in hiding I came to believe that my curious survival and my mission ought to be dedicated to our people. It was the policy of the time to weaken an enemy's power by breaking their ties to their homeland, to its soil, so the carting away of people was common, having been done earlier by the Assyrians when they destroyed Samaria. In our exhausting journey by foot to Babylon we came upon some of our long-exiled and long-lost relations from the north, and to this day there are people who are descended from us and them who live in the Middle East, Central Asia,

South Asia and the Far East. We are everywhere, and in my long life I have tried to be as well. Having revisited Egypt there was something powerful for me about our long march north and then east, and then our resettlement in Babylon, for it took us through the ancestral land of our ancestors, Sarah and Abraham.

I remember the first time I saw Ur, their home town, with its a mud-brick and occasional stone homes and temples that looked so familiar to me because I'd grown up hearing stories about them, about Sarah's mother and father Ataah and Haddah, and Abraham's mother Kaivah and her husband Terah. And while I knew that almost a thousand years later I was probably looking at nothing that was there in their time, the town 'felt' familiar to me, if that makes sense, it 'felt' like home in an unexpected way that I'd never experienced before. And truth be told, as I've said before, we didn't think about time in the way that people do today. We didn't have clocks or anything but the most basic calendars, which were really only lists of the names of the months. We lived by sunset and sunrise, by moonrise and moonset, we lived by seasons and if we counted at all it was by the years of the reign of a king, and each time one died and another ascended the throne we started counting all over again with Year One. About a decade ago I went with a neighbor in San Francisco to a mindfulness meditation workshop. The "goalless goal," our instructor told us, was to come to live more fully in the moment. She had everyone take off their watches and put away their mobile phones. I had and have neither. As we sat and walked and slowed down over the course of the weekend I thought—this is exactly how I lived for more than two thousand years.

That period, called the Babylonian Exile or Babylonian Captivity, was not an easy time for our people, but if you live long enough you will discover how often history repeats itself, and you will see that history is almost always moved ahead by one single thing—that some man in power will do something foolish (if we're lucky) or stupid or dangerous or destructive or evil—and everyone else will have to deal with the consequences. So the Assyrians conquered the northern tribes, but not long after that the Babylonians conquered the Assyrians and then the people living in Judah. Then we were carted off to the north, to the land of our ancient ancestors, where we were exposed to new religions and religious practices, which would divide us in whole new ways, some of which we still struggle with. For example, we're still grappling the tension between following our conscience, an ancient Hebrew notion—and following The Law, which came to us from the regimes of Egypt and Mesopotamia; and grappling with the tension between the narrow-minded clannishness that came from our own people and the more expansive cosmopolitanism that came to us from Mesopotamia and Egypt.

In saying this I don't want you to think that I was miserable in exile. Up in the north, where my true identity was unknown to everyone, I grew more and more happy, so happy that when the Persians conquered the Babylonians and their king, a rare visionary MAN named Cyrus, allowed all of the captive peoples who'd been carted away to go back to their own homelands, most of them and most of us—remained where we'd settled. For if you live long enough you will discover how often history repeats itself, and I was reminded of that time in our history when I first came to the United States. Not that our people were bought here as captives like the millions of Africans who were so cruelly dragged away from their homes and families—but once we got here this became a new kind of Promised Land, and while one might have expected after the foundation of the State of Israel that American Jews would all go back there, few did. America became Home. And for me, living in the Persian Empire felt just like that.

Here is another way in which history repeats itself. When you read the Torah you find stories about Moses being adopted by Pharaoh's daughter and growing up in her palace. But just as I've told you before—there was no palace and no Pharaoh, just Bast and me in our little workers city that shall remain nameless forever. And much later in the Hebrew Bible you will come upon another story that gives a woman a kind of a central role, which also includes a palace and an important king. I am talking about the book of *Esther*. Much as I dreaded telling you the story about my earlier writings, this is a story that I have been looking forward to telling you.

I'd settled in Ur and had been living there for some time. In addition to cooking and amassing a vast library of recipes, among the many things I'd learned down through the centuries was how to work with herbal remedies, so I opened a small apothecary shop near the center of town, across from a larger old home that I used to pretend to myself was the ancestral home of Sarah, Sarah whose name I would eventually adopt as my own. After the Persians conquered the Babylonians, King Cyrus sent a man named Adurnarseh to be the mayor of Ur and he ended up living in that large stone house across the street from my shop. He was a tall burly man who reminded me of my only child (not that I'm talking reincarnation here)—who I probably would never have gotten to know, but as often happens to people who come to new places—he got sick. Very sick. You know what I'm talking about, one of those traveler's bugs where your body is exploding from both ends at the same time. One of his guards, a very serious man named Marduniya, knew about my practice and came to see me. I gave him an herbal remedy for his boss that worked in a matter of days, a combination of myrtle and other local leaves and roots, and a week later Adurnarseh came across the street himself to thank me personally.

He was charming, not handsome but with a winning smile, and soon he was coming over every few days. Both of us were strangers in a strange land, and both of us were hungry for friendship. Adurnarseh was one of those big burly hairy men of power we now call bears who have another side, many but not all of whom are gay. At night he liked nothing better than dressing up in women's clothing, and having been a fabric seller for many years, I began to hunt for cloth and old garments for him that I would turn into fabulous outfits. Several nights a week we would get together to party behind locked doors so that his guards never knew what was going on. We'd drink and laugh and I'd sing for him and gradually, as sometimes happens, two people who might have thought of themselves otherwise, find that they are drawn together physically, as were the two of us.

I never told Adurnarseh the truth about who I really am. I still looked like I was in my thirties when we met, and that was his actual age. For that era he was bordering on being old, but I found him engaging and delightful and we had some wonderful times together. Neither of us had ever been sexual with someone of the other gender before, so you can imagine the bumbling adventures we had the first few times we tried to make love. "Really. You want to put that where?" "You want me to do what?" "How did my face get there?" Sometimes I would be laughing so hard I nearly had to piss, wanting to tell him, "Darling, I'm almost one thousand years old and I've never done this before," but I doubted he'd believe me and I don't regret not telling him. It was odd to get older but not look older and it was sad to watch him age, grow frail, then slowly begin to fade away.

This is something that I don't believe I've ever said before, and I won't say it again. I was a beauty, a great beauty. A bit on the short side, as were many of our people, but, frankly, to use the word that my friend Estelle used to describe me when I showed her pictures of me from the 1930s—"You were ravishing!" she said, "and you're even more gorgeous now." (She always liked older women.) So word got out about the two of us, the mayor and his ravishing Hebrew wife, for we did actually get married, by a lovely priestess of the goddess Ishtar whose temple was one of the oldest in the city, a temple where I used to imagine that Sarah and Abraham once worshipped. And you know this from your own time. You're standing in a long line in the supermarket, and you can't help but look at the tabloids to see which famous person is leaving which other famous person, being cheated on, going into rehab—again—or about to have more cosmetic surgery. There may not have been tabloids then but people did the same thing, and word got out about us in Ur, about the big old Persian man and his hot young Hebrew wife. Then, as stories do, everything got all jumbled together, with elements of truth and fantasy woven together. But let me sort it out for you.

There was no king, and there was no palace. There was no earlier wife and there was no threat against the Jews. All of that was added later. But here are a few wonderful details that should amuse you as much as they amuse me to this very day. The main ingredient of the remedy I gave to Adurnarseh was myrtle, which is good for many things including diarrhea. Now what was Esther's birth name in the book that you have? Hadassah—which means myrtle. And where did we get married? In the temple of Ishtar. Think hard here. What does Esther sound like? You got it! Ishtar. And if one child in a classroom is playing telephone with the truth and turns Ishtar into something that sounds more Hebrew, more Jewish, then someone else is bound to rename Marduniya, the charming guard who I gave the remedy to—into Mordechai, another Hebrew name, which sounds so much like the Babylonian god Marduk. Then Adurnarseh becomes Ahasuerus, the Hebrew equivalent of the name of several kings of Persia—and you have the outline of a great story.

It used to amuse Adurnarseh to hear the permutations of our story as they spread through the Persian Empire and came back to us. When he died I had him buried in a gorgeous dress that I sewed for him myself. A few weeks after the funeral Adurnarseh's successor arrived and I went to the barracks where he was staying to welcome him to Ur. A nasty scrawny bigoted Mede who'd heard about the two of us, he shouted at me the equivalent of, "You stupid Jewish slut, get the hell out of here. We should have wiped out all of you lousy people a long long time ago!" which provided the last little element to what became a marvelous story—when gossip morphed him into a character named Haman, which comes from the root of an ancient word that means—"Noise."

Chapter Seventeen

Travel with the author and share a few more adventures,
one or two of which may be surprising, or not

After Adurnarseh died I intended to go back to Canaan, but before I had a chance to do that an old childhood friend of his named Farhad came to visit, at the end of a long trading expedition. He was sad about his friend's passing and grateful when I invited him to stay with me. Over a hot brewed beverage one evening, tracing our ancestry, it turned out that his family used to trade with ours, they from Haran and we from Canaan, but later they shifted their work to the East, to India, on boats going down the Persian Gulf into the Arabian Sea to India, while, coincidentally, ships of ours going back to the days of Solomon were sailing down the Red Sea to the Arabian Sea to India.

After Adurnarseh died, I decided two things—I'll never fall in love again—(When I came to this part of my story, Estelle pulled out an old record and played me Dionne Warwick singing a song of that title, which I'd never heard before.) I also decided that I wanted to see parts of the world that I'd never seen before, other places that our people had traveled to. Having told him a bit about my life, with all the dates compressed, when Farhad invited me to join him as a cook and healer on his next expedition to India I said yes—a yes that I've never regretted. It was a very long journey, more than a year as we stopped along the way to do our trading, but by foot, camel, donkey, raft, foot, boat and raft again, we finally arrived on the western coast of India, docking at a tiny village named Suvah, where just as Farhad promised me there were resident Hebrew traders and merchants. Their routes had been interrupted by the Babylonian destruction of Judah and had never quite returned after the Persians allowed our people to go back to

Canaan. Restored Judah was a tiny struggling province in those days, but I had some news of it that they were glad to hear.

Manasseh, the elder of that community, turned out to be a direct descendant of my Moses through his older son Gershom and served as the priest of the Hebrews of that region. He was a man of great spiritual insight and interest and was friends with the priestesses and priests in all the temples in the area. (To call them Hindu would be an anachronism.) He was well-versed in their teachings, shared them with me, and we spent many wonderful hours teaching each other the differing songs of our people that we each knew.

Comfortably settled in his village, I learned the local herbs and their healing properties by working for Manasseh's recently widowed neighbor Gad as a cook. (I don't think that I believe in fate or in our being watched over, but somehow details like this have always been taken care of in my life.) A few years later Gad's older son Ananiah, a kind of a proto-hippie who I was fond of for more reasons than just his name, decided that he wanted to go up north to study with a new teacher he'd heard about who had gained quite a reputation—and wanting another new adventure, I decided to go with him. The trip was long, and how thrilling it was to be walking through dense jungles, then coming upon hills and then mountains larger than anything I'd ever seen before or ever imagined—after almost a thousand years of living in and on the edge of deserts. Eventually we arrived at a little village that is now called Varanasi, and thus it was that I sat on the edge of a clearing of trees with Ananiah—listening to the Buddha teaching his students.

After several weeks of learning I felt both changed and excluded, as a woman. Ananiah and I discussed it and he decided to stay and I decided to travel on, but I'm grateful for my time with that wise elegant older man. While I'm not sure that I believe in reincarnation or karma, one of my favorite contemporary American Buddhist teachers (who like almost all of them comes from a Jewish background) very much reminds me of Ananiah. (I did a weekend workshop with her when I lived in San Francisco) so I'm not surprised that there continues to be a connection between our two peoples. As in this book I am sure to have offended many Jews and Christians by my statements about the ways in which our most sacred texts were repeatedly edited, the same could be said about the texts of every tradition on this planet including Buddhism, whose scriptures were written down from oral accounts several hundred years after the Buddha's death. So lovely Ananiah chose to remain with the Buddha, who renamed him Ananda, which means Bliss, and over time, to obscure his foreign origins, Ananda was turned into a native, and then gradually became—the Buddha's first cousin! You heard

it here for the first time in more than two thousand years—that wise and enlightened Ananda was by birth what we might today call A Nice Jewish Boy.

One of the Buddha's followers, a nun named Sitah, told me that a few
years before, in her quest for wisdom, she'd heard about but never visited
an immortal teacher living in the mountains of what today is Afghanistan.
Remembering that our family had sent traders there over the centuries to
obtain the lapis lazuli that was so popular in Egypt, Canaan, and Mesopotamia, and that others had gone there after the Assyrians carted many of us
away—that became my next destination. Saying good-bye to Ananiah, I left
India and traveled north and west by foot, going deep into territory that was
constantly at war, with local, nomadic, and other powers battling for territory and control, including the descendants of Greeks who first went there
with Alexander the Great.

I sometime traveled alone, sometimes with traders, and other times
with fleeing refugees. For safety I sometimes disguised myself as a man, an
annoying practice as I am rather large in the chest and binders always pain
me. But the world since my childhood had grown increasingly patriarchal,
and even that region, with its long rich tradition of worshipping goddesses
(as human beings did for at least a hundred thousand years) wasn't always
a safe place to travel as a woman. Millennia later I thought about that time
in my life when I saw the musical *West Side Story*, which in early drafts
was about a conflict between an Irish Catholic and a Jewish family living
on the Lower East Side. In the retelling *East* became *West* and a character
named Anybodys—was she a tomboy, a lesbian, or trans?—reminded me of
myself during that time in my life, so often the only 'woman' in the company
of men.

O the joy of climbing those mountains, towering like one might think
of when they think of Sinai, but so very different from little Dusty/Desolate.
In the wonderful way that travelers have, with hand gestures and facial expressions, again and again I met people with whom I shared no common
language, who guided me north and then west to a village that Sitah had told
me was called something like Samrah.

Finally a mountain trader knew, by vigorous head shakes and strange
words, exactly where I wanted to go and took me there. The moment I came
before the teacher is sealed in my mind forever—or some neuro-enduring
version of it. It was a perfect summer day, warm, windy, and clear, as I approached. One of *my* days, a Serach day. He was seated on the ground on
an old woven mat, sitting in silence in a circle of about fifteen students in
the middle of a cluster of buildings that today we might call an ashram. He
looked up as I approached and our eyes met, dark eyes and dark eyes, in
dark skin and dark skin. Familiar. He nodded and smiled and rose, and I

could feel the shock among his students as he came toward me, hands outstretched. All of them were men, young men, and one of them was a local prince, but never before had their teacher, their master, approached him or anyone else like that, particularly not a ragged dusty woman!

We stood holding hands for the longest time, staring into each other's eyes. With Yehadana and Asumma I didn't know what to see or feel or recognize, but when I met that man I *knew*, just as he did. Then he smiled and said to me in a curious but comprehensible Hebrew, "Welcome. You must be Serach. My grandmother told me all about you." Stunned, still holding hands, I said yes and he introduced himself. "I am Yuzif, Joseph, of the tribe of Asher, brought here as a little boy from Samaria with my family, all of us in flight."

Tears came to my eyes. A kinsman, who knows me, here at the top of the world! His eyes began to well up too, as he recited his lineage, the early members of which I knew, going all the way back to my baby brother Beriah. Not as old as I, but still centuries old, we stood there gazing into each other, falling into each other, smiling and crying at the same time. Then, still holding onto one of my hands, he turned and led me toward his mat. "This is my dear beloved aunt," he said to his stunned disciples. "Serach. And now she has come home to us."

I thought I was going to a strange land, to learn from a stranger, but instead I found another immoral, a kinsman, speaking a version of the language of my birth. And to this day there are stories told in those mountains, including one about a man given various names including Avaghana, who was said to have been a grandson of our good and troubled ruler Saul—by one of the many peoples of that region, the Pashtuns, one of what we call The Lost Ten Tribes, descended from our own people in exile, descended from Yuzif's students. Yes, our kinfolk!

In those mountains where so many tribes and peoples have met, a different culture emerged than in Canaan. Near to India and Tibet, with their many different traditions, Yuzif had long been recognized as an immortal teacher and like Assuma had never had to hide, which shaped him in such a different way than I had been shaped. Every afternoon, following his teaching-time—and some of his teachings would make sense to you if you've ever studied Kabbalah—Yuzif would spend time with me. Given his different history he was grounded in his immortality in ways that I had not experienced, younger than me in centuries but so much older than me in wisdom, and he helped me understand and accept myself as a genetic anomaly—which prepared me for the rest of my life, right up to the very present.

When I met Clara in Berlin in 1929 she was reading Hindu texts and doing yoga and meditating, which you may not have realized Germans were doing in the years of the Weimar Republic. She introduced me to books I'd never heard of, to deities and saints and gurus I'd never heard of, including Sri Aurobindo and his companion Mirra Richard, called The Mother, who had a Turkish Jewish father and an Egyptian Jewish mother. When I learned about them I thought—"That was Yuzif and me." For over two hundred years the two of us sat side by side and taught whoever came up that mountain to learn—all in Hebrew! Yuzif's primary work was doing what we now call "energy healing" and mine (to my great delight) brought me back to my first great love. With his guidance, while I never gave a concert there, I learned to play what today would be called Fusion Music, mixing together songs and chants and prayers from every tradition I'd ever encountered. He helped me understand that my job there was to give out energy though sound, vibration. So that became my new vocation, to help retune people and move them closer to the Oneness I eventually grew comfortable calling Yahweh.

Yuzif and I were never lovers, nor did he have any. He was however the best friend that I've ever had, or ever had—so far. And I've had many, some of whom you'll meet in later chapters. Many of our students had what we now call spiritual experiences, and it often troubled me that I never did. When I asked Yuzif about it he said, "At your age, Auntie, such things are not needed. You are a powerful sound healer, and you are awake by virtue of your experience." I never quite believed him and often felt like a fraud, sitting beside him, humming and singing, but those two hundred years in his little village of Samrah, his Samaria in exile, were among the happiest years of my long long life. Not that there weren't wars up in those magnificent mountains, but Canaan and its bloody soil were blessedly far away.

One morning I was squatting by a fire in the courtyard of our compound. The sun had not yet risen up from behind the mountains, but the sky had grown light. There was an iron pot hanging over that fire, filled with tea about to come to a boil. I was holding a clay tea cup in my hand, about to fill it up and bring it to Yuzif, when he came out of his cell, walked over to me, bowed and said, "I had a dream. You must go home now, Auntie." I paused, dumbstruck, and he continued. "You are needed."

Chapter Eighteen

In which your guide through history
tells you a few more stories about war,
and texts, and rival sects

I LEFT A MIDDLE Eastern city in flames and came back centuries later to something I didn't have words for yet– a Hellenistic metropolis. I'd never seen a Doric, Ionic, or Corinthian column before, and they were every-where as I entered the city through one of the southern gates and began to wander. The walls of this new Jerusalem were vast, the buildings were enormous compared to what I remembered, and the second temple—was shiny of marble and wasn't (don't tell anyone this) in the exact same place as Solomon's temple had been. It was pushed back on the site and much taller, which was obvious when seen against the Mount of Olives behind it and from the large outer courtyard, its arguing priests from north and south long forgotten.

There were soldiers everywhere, and smoke blowing down from the temple, and people wearing kinds of clothing I'd never seen before. It had taken me a year to get back from Afghanistan to Canaan, then called Judea, a journey in stages that I financed with a large pouch of lapis lazuli chunks that Yuzif and his students had gifted me with. Along the way I'd stopped in every community where our people were living, never of course reveal-ing who I was, and everywhere I went I made music, usually sitting in the corner of a market, a small cup in front of me for donations.

During my travels I'd heard more than fifty different languages, only a few of which I understood, and in the Jerusalem I returned to the lan-guages I heard were also strange. Many people were speaking Aramaic, but in a strange and whiny dialect. Others were speaking Greek, which I'd only heard a few times before. Only a very few were speaking Hebrew, a Hebrew spiced with words I didn't understand at all.

Toward sunset, after having wandered through the city all day, I stopped an old man in a priest's robe who was wearing strange leather boxes on his forehead and left arm. (Later I learned what they were—*tefillin*. In my youth the "signs" that some of us wore on our foreheads and the back of both of our hands were tattoos rather like some Bedouins wear to this very day—and the English-speaking me delights in the sound coincidence of *tattoo* and the Hebrew word for those signs, *tottafot*.) I asked the old man in Hebrew if he could recommend a place to stay. From his furrowed brow I could tell he was wondering about my accent, but being a gentleman he didn't comment on it and suggested a little inn hugging the north wall of the city where I was able to rent a tiny attic room for myself.

I collapsed upon a hard narrow bed, weary and confused. In all of my years of wandering there were only two possessions that I'd managed to hold onto, Sarah's seal and Dinah's mirror. They'd survived raider attacks and brigands and shipwrecks and other disasters that I don't want to talk about. When I left Samrah, as a parting gift, I gave the mirror to Yuzif, but I remember sitting on that narrow little bed in that tiny room lit with a single oil lamp flickering, rolling the small carved seal hanging around my neck on a new green silk cord, thinking—"Serach, what are you doing here? Why did Yuzif send you back?" In a state of utter exhaustion, I fell into a deep sleep and dreamed that Grandfather Jacob came and stood at the foot of my bed, looking just as he looked when he was still alive. And he said to me words that were the bookend (not that books had been invented yet. All there were were scrolls) of what Yuzif said to me: "You must go home now, Auntie. You are needed." What Grandpa Jacob stood at the foot of my bed said to me in the Hebrew of my childhood was—"Sit in the marketplace every day, my child. You are needed."

Some of our people, Azibah for example (whose story I so foolishly misappropriated when I spliced it into Joseph's) understood what other people's dreams meant and received information from God in their dreams. I never had that gift. But my dream was so clear that I woke up knowing my next steps and went downstairs to greet Tamar, the woman who owned the inn. We got to talking, in Aramaic, and it turned out that her sister Shulamit was a baker with a little stall at the bottom of the northern stairs to the temple where she sold offering loaves to pilgrims, those stairs named for the wise old prophetess Huldah. Shulamit needed an assistant and Tamar took me to meet her. It was always jarring, and still is, to be with someone who looks so much older than I do but who is so very very much younger. Forty at most, Shulamit looked like a woman in her late seventies would look today. She hired me on the spot and was the perfect boss. We sat there six days a week selling flatbread to Jews from all over the world, and because her late husband had been from Alexandria—she also taught me Greek.

While we were sitting there I would hum and quietly sing songs and soon people were coming to us to buy their sacrificial bread because they'd heard about my singing, and because of that, Shulamit's business grew. As the political situation deteriorated I expanded my repertoire, adding songs in many different languages.

This may not make sense to you who may think of the Jerusalem I returned to as an ancient, holy city that you would love to have seen. But looking back on it—that Jerusalem of the second century BCE was utterly Modern—by which I mean that it was smelly, dirty, noisy, crowded—and the conversations I heard were exactly the same ones we're having now: about politics, the end of the world, taxes, sex, and religion, none of which we talked about when I was growing up. Everything was different from what I remembered. The Jerusalemites were divided into more sects than I could ever have imagined, and people were constantly yelling at each other, in the equivalent of cafes, walking on the street, and sitting with their families over meals, just as people do today: "I can't believe that you really think . . . !" And by Modern what I also mean is that everyone there was crazy in exactly the same way that people are crazy now.

In addition to fights over the beliefs of the various sects, there were endless fights about practice. Men were wearing all different kinds of tefillin, none of them tattoos, and they were fighting about who was wearing the right kind, the right size, with the right texts in them. When I'd last been there we had a kind of early Torah, but when I came back there was a very clear version of it, nearly identical to the one that we have today—filled with all sorts of rules I'd never heard about before. The second section of the *Tanach* was nearly canonized—filled with all the male prophets we have today—but not a single book by Noadiah, Ozeret, Simchah, Orah, or even Huldah! If you'd asked me what our spiritual and religious practices were in the last days of the first temple I would have told you that there were very few. We were *us* because we said so and not because of what we did. So while we all agreed to not work on the seventh day, to never ever ever eat a calf cooked in its mother's milk—even though no one any longer remembered why not to but me. We had our holidays and new moons and our rituals in the temple—but things were so much simpler back then. The minutia that people argued about when I returned amazed and saddened me. "Hey relax," I wanted to say, "and let me sing you a song that Miriam wrote." Of course I never said that—but I often sang her songs.

Shulamit became a good friend, and in addition to employing me her great gift was teaching me Greek. Among the many things I've never talked about here, and probably won't, was what it was like to have been born into a world where women were not entirely chattel, but to have lived long enough to see that happen—and then slowly, many centuries later, begin to change back again. But learning Greek, reading the works of Sappho—all of them!—was a kind of healing for me. Since I'd last been there coins had caught on in a big way, and the coins with which Shulamit paid me and the tips I was receiving for my music (which were sometimes larger than my salary) went toward rent, buying food, and with what was left—buying scrolls. (I love that people now say "I was scrolling through a play by Euripides on my tablet," unconsciously referring back to the word-technologies of the second temple era and the clay texts that existed before there were parchment scrolls.) I fell in love with Sappho, Heraclitus, Plato, Aeschylus, and a long forgotten woman playwright named Kore of Sparta. I wished I'd read Homer before I wrote my old long saga, and was also glad to be able to understand what the Greek-speaking soldiers were saying who filled the city.

It was from that vantage point that I watched the soldiers of nasty King Antiochus storm into the temple and desecrate it, and from that vantage point that I watched Judean leaders start to fight back. There were times when Shulamit and I could not do our work, and there were days when we watched men, always men, marching about with their spears and swords, some of them men who would be remembered by history. I remember Judah the Maccabee, a brusque, efficient, arrogant man, and as some historians can now see, the war between us and them was really more a war between us and us, between the traditionalists among us who, to use modern language, called their opponents "assimiliationists" and those same people who thought of themselves as "modernists" and who called their opponents "reactionaries"—all of them Judeans, all of them Jews.

There was a joy about having stepped back from center stage. My days were spent selling bread and singing, selling bread when we could and singing subtle resistance songs, songs meant to invite all the factions to resist their own dogmatic inclinations, although they rarely succeeded. Together my dear friend and I lived through the desecration of the temple and then its cleansing and rededication—with absolutely no miracle concerning sacred oil. You don't celebrate Hanukkah because a jar of olive oil burned for eight nights, you celebrate it because we missed the major Jewish holiday of that time, not Rosh Hashanah or Passover but the eight day festival of Sukkot, so the way that some of you hold a Christmas in July party, we held Sukkot a season too late—and our doing that caught on.

I love the word "Novel," love that an entire genre of books is labeled "New." And I love the way that literary critics have dissected the novel, stating that some narrators are to be trusted and others are not. This book is not a novel, although much of the information contained within its pages may be New to you, and while your narrator can state emphatically that she is reliable when it comes to everything that she's written down, she can also state that she hasn't mentioned Everything, for a variety of reasons, some of which she is about to enunciate, all of which render her unreliable.

From what I haven't said, you may imagine that I began this book recently, but in fact I started making notes for it in 1995, while Clara was dying. It was her idea. "Darling, some day you must write down everything that you remember." I made my first notes in a little notebook with a black and white speckled cover, the kind of notebook elementary school students used to use in that era. And of course there are so many stories that I left out. (Lucky for you or this would be a massive work.) And having gotten this far—after twenty-two years of writing, I am grateful that I've finally come to the end of my tale, even though I have two thousand and more years to go until I get to the present. But while I have often had to tell you my own stories to tell you yours—this is not strictly an autobiography but a work of restorative history. So pardon me while I sit on the edge of things, relating what I saw from a distance, trusting that if you come away from reading this memoir with one insight only—that the changing narrators of our most sacred texts are unreliable—I will not have written this book in vain.

Now back to my story. It was shocking to be in Greco-Judean Jerusalem, looking at a Torah that was a strange composite text, listening to priests declaim words that were strange to me, and longing for the past or for a future that I could only half-imagine. Here is one single example of what I'm talking about, which I haven't mentioned before. No, two of them. For two millennia our people have called ourselves (note I include myself in that pronoun) *Bnei Yisrael,* literally "The Sons of Israel," or by extension, "The Children of Israel." Your Torah makes it sound like that was what we named ourselves in Egypt and ever after, but please recall that throughout our time in Egypt, the period in the wilderness, the time of Joshua, the judges, and during the years of the first temple, what we called ourselves most often was—*Beit Sarah,* The House of Sarah. Remember, Sarah was both princess and priestess, and our roots were in a time when we were still matrilineal, tracing our spiritual descent through our mothers not our fathers, a custom which we abandoned and then much later came back to. And, my second example. I cannot tell you how many times since I've been in America I've heard rabbis invite us to recite "The watchwords of our faith," the Shema. But those words—"Listen Israel, the Lord our God (today, the Eternal our

God) the Lord is one"—were a deliberate revision of the words our ancestors said for at least twenty generations as our most central prayer, given
our lineage as the heirs of a priestess who worshipped Asherah, when we
recited these ancient words—"*Shema beit Sarah, Asherah imoteinu, Asherah
echat*"—Listen, House of Sarah, Asherah is our mother, Asherah is one."

All of that was completely forgotten in those days, and there was no
way that I was going to tell anyone. I enjoyed stepping back, and I have for
two thousand years. So while my story so far has focused on our history and
on restoring the truth whenever I was a firsthand witness to it, now I will
relate only those moments where I was a witness, so that while it's taken me
about a thousand years to get here, I will travel on in just a few more chapters. (That last sentence is in part a lie. I could give a more detailed account,
but after working on this book for more than twenty years, I am exhausted
and want to be done.) And as I've said before—over the years since Joshua
I have told seventeen people the truth about who I am. Some have believed
me, some have not, but without exception, what all of them wanted to know
was what I already told you.

So, wars and more wars. Kings and more kings. Every now and then
a queen. I saw them all come and go. But imagine it yourself—you are fifty
and look fifty. No problem there. But long before Botox and plastic surgery,
imagine that you are three hundred and fifty and look fifty, that you are one
thousand and fifty and look fifty. I have no idea why my body continued to
age till fifty and then stopped aging for a very long time, but it did. Alas, I
watched my friend Shulamit grow old and frail and I stayed by her side till
she died—but a woman who does not grow older will over time draw attention to herself, particularly in millennia and centuries when the average
lifespan was less than half of what it is today—so I took off again, spending two decades in Alexandria, working at a stall in a vegetable market in
the Jewish quarter by day, humming and singing and perfecting my Greek,
which was the only language the Jews of Egypt spoke in that time. Of course
no one knew me, which was lovely, and I would have stayed there forever—
but Grandpa Jacob came back to me in a dream, stood at the food of my bed,
and said, "Child, it's time to go back to Jerusalem."

More noise. More people. More walls. Herod enlarging the temple.
More chaos, more sects, more craziness. Herod was a madman, but in brief
I can assure you—he never ordered any possible Davidic inheritors to be
killed in Bethlehem—but anyone could tell that things were heading in the
wrong direction. The little kingdom established by the descendants of the
Maccabees had been taken over by him, and things were getting worse and
worse. I set myself up in a corner of a large new market at the base of the
western steps to the temple, where both pilgrims and laborers at work on its

expansion would pass me. All day long, I sang songs about peace, healing, and community, feeling that they were doing no good at all, but one night Grandpa came to me in a dream and said, simply, "You cannot know what comes from what you do. You can only do it." So I did. I sang as Herod got madder and madder, killed family members, and finally died himself. I watched the city fill with Roman soldiers, many of whom spoke Latin, and I took lessons in it from an old Jewish man who had lived in Rome, in exchange for cooking for him. So odd, as he was so much younger than I.

And yes, I did meet Jesus, although I always think of him as Joshua or Yeshua, the name by which he was called. I heard him speak a few times, which was always moving. Looking back over all of our history, he's filed away in my brain with two other of our men who went on to become famous—Joseph and David, all three of them short and charismatic. Did he claim to be the messiah? Never. His concerns were other. He was not a revolutionary either, rather a man who was interested in helping people cultivate their spiritual lives. His death was horrific. I watched him suffer, he and the two other spiritual teachers he was killed with by the Romans, ostensibly for stirring up people's discontent. But this is what is still distressing to me— the Romans targeted those three wise, lovely, powerless men (two of whom were later turned into thieves by the first Gospel writers, to distinguish them from their own chosen teacher)—because they were afraid to go after the real troublemakers, afraid that their deaths would turn them into martyrs and attract more followers to their various causes. No. Instead of targeting the political leaders with large followings who thought of themselves as neo-Maccabees and were calling for armed resistance against the largest empire in the world at that time, the Roman authorities tortured and killed three innocent men to intimidate the others, and when they were dead they threw their bodies into a guarded pit outside the city walls and covered them with garbage.

One of those men was from a monastic sect related to the Essenes. His name was Nachum, while the other man, Naphtali, came from a group whose members took vows of silence. Rather than speak in public as Joshua and Nachum did, Naphtali would stand in the market place in utter silence, wearing a long robe onto the front and back of which he'd sewn in blue letters these words from Psalm 65—"For You, silence is praise." Neither of them had many followers and they were soon forgotten. Joshua saw himself as a teacher and over time his disciples and others did what human beings so often do, tell and retell stories until they become something new, novel.

After his death Joshua's mother Miriam remained in Jerusalem, and I often saw her on her way to the temple with a younger woman who was also named Miriam, and from time to time with other of his followers. Deep in mourning, when I saw them I would shift my songs to those of comfort, and they would sometimes stop to listen. I would have long ago forgotten them if not for what history did with Joshua, and I remember that they were particularly fond of a song that I'd brought back from India. The song came from a lost epic about one of their gods and his son by a mortal woman. After that son was attacked by his father's sons by his goddess wives, he ran to his father for comfort, and it's from that part of the story that the song emerged. I leave it to you to wonder if that song might have anything to do with how Joshua's life was later recalled.

> *He lifted him into his loving arms.*
> *Bruised and afraid, meek and small.*
> *His father comforted and rocked him.*
> *He blessed him and said to him—*
> *"You will inherit the earth,*
> *for you are the son of my body."*
> *And so he comforts us all*
> *and rocks us in his loving arms,*
> *our heavenly father.*

Chapter Nineteen

Race through history with your narrator
from the destruction of the second temple
almost until the present moment

IN THOSE DAYS WIDOWS wore shawls of a certain shade of dark red, and as widows were allowed more freedom than both married and unmarried women, that's how I dressed. With my shawl pulled over my face, people ignored me as I left Jerusalem heading north, wanting to see Endor again. A small town had grown up there so I didn't stay. Instead, knowing that there was a large community of Jews living in Rome and curious to see a whole new place, I headed to the coast, booked passage on a ship, and headed west for the very first time. I found myself in the capital of a vast empire that others have spoken of far better than I could, whose size made Herod's Jerusalem look like a hick town. But the Jewish community there was large and lively and I found a little corner in the Jewish market where I could sing. One day the leader of the main synagogue in the city happened to walk by, a woman named Julia, who hired me on the spot to be a soloist in their services. This kind of egalitarianism has been lost from our history, but in the days of the second temple, many many synagogues were headed by women, something which would continue for more than three hundred years after it was gone. In fact, let me take this opportunity to say a few things about the origins of the synagogue that have been lost in time.

Up and down Canaan in the period of the judges our people created little shrines to worship in. Given that we mostly still called ourselves *Beit Sarah* after our priestess ancestress, and given that she was a priestess of Asherah, most of the shrines we established for ourselves were dedicated to that goddess. Each one had its own beautiful tree, and there we prayed.

Recently I read a book about trees that stated that walking among them will lower your blood pressure. We knew that, somehow, but once our people started building temples and then created a main central one, and as Yahweh went from being one of many to the One and only, those shrines became suspect and then forbidden. Many of them were destroyed by zealous priests and prophets but they were never forgotten by the local people, and in almost every place in Canaan where there was once a little goddess shrine—a synagogue later popped up! And then those community gathering places spread—from China all the way to Los Angeles.

Now back to Rome. I liked Rome, loved the people, the culture, the food, and got to be fluent in Latin—one of those little pleasures immortal creatures find comfort in. I might have stayed for a long time, but once again foolish men were doing foolish things and Yuzif came to me again in a dream and told me it was time to return to Jerusalem. Enough time had passed and I knew no one would recognize me, so I went back—just before the Great Revolt began. The city was even bigger. There were more soldiers than ever. Herod's vast temple had been recently completed by his foolish sons, although his kingdom had been divided up among them by the Romans. It was clear where things were headed and having seen one temple destroyed already and knowing the chaos that followed, while I continued to sing in the same marketplace I sang in before I went to Rome, I was keeping my eyes out for people who I thought would carry on our legacy.

One day I was finishing up a song I'd learned from Yuzif when a young woman came down the temple stairs, heading toward me. For a moment our eyes caught, then she looked away, but in that instant my heart leaped up in my chest, and I knew, in every cell of my body—that she was an immortal! Yes. I saw in her exactly what Yehadana had seen in me all those years before—"The look in your eyes, both utterly world-weary and so very full of life. That odd combination other people do not have, who either know they are going to die soon, or don't know that of course they will."

I continued to look at her as I sang, willing her to not turn away, and soon she came toward me, stopped at the edge of the circle of people listening to me, and waited. I was shaking, thrilled, afraid, and for a moment didn't know what to sing. I wanted everyone to go away but her, was terrified that she would go and I would never see her again, so slim and dark and beautiful, like the woman in *Song of Songs*, the version back then somewhat longer than yours. But she waited. Lingered. Listened. And when I took my break and everyone else wandered off, she stayed. I stood, went up to her, bowed, and introduced myself. "Sarah bat Asher." She smiled, awkwardly, bowed herself, and said, "Rebecca bat Simeon." Then she turned, looked back at me, said, "I will return tomorrow."

I hardly slept. Went through all the songs I knew, looking for the ones that would speak to her most clearly. She very much reminded me of Shalomeh, and while at my advanced age I was usually poised if not reticent with others, I felt like a young woman of her apparent age—early twenties— and couldn't wait for her to return, which she briefly did every afternoon for four days. On the fourth day she arrived . . . and remained. At twilight when I stopped singing, she approached and asked if she could talk with me. I offered to walk her home, she insisted on walking *me* home, and in my tiny little room with its view of the Mount of Olives through a single narrow window, we told each other the truth of who we were—a truth which she had suspected, with profound hope and expectation. She was born in the time of the Maccabees and remembered being in her mother's arms at the rededication of the temple, which made her more than two hundred years old—but she had never yet met anyone else like her!

Having not made love for hundreds of years, I was hoping that she might be interested in me, but the moment I revealed myself to her I became her mentor, my feelings blessedly shifted, so I didn't have to enter into what today we call a dual relationship. I did however tell her everything that I've told you, and so much more. Like Shalomeh she was a remarkable student with a brain like a vast computer. She could memorize a story as I was telling it to her, and her questions to me were deep and directed. As a young girl she had always wanted to be a priest, just like her father had been, and was delighted by my stories about Asherah and Sarah and the priestesses of my childhood. In fact, I told her everything I knew and had experienced, and she told me all of her stories as well.

In the months of our getting to know each other the situation continued to deteriorate, both with the Romans and between our own pro-war and anti-war parties. Men, always men, would take up speaking posts on the steps to the temple, yelling out their positions, and some days they were so noisy that I couldn't even sing. Rebecca and I knew that war was inevitable, agreed that it made sense for one of us to try to survive, and agreed that given my age it made more sense for her to leave Judea. Her father had been from Jerusalem, her mother from Babylon, and when she realized that she wasn't going to get older or die she made the decision to go back and forth between the two places. She left for Babylon about three months before the war broke out, carrying with her all of her own stories—and all of mine. Those stories, written down, would have created a book eight or ten times larger than this one. And while she didn't write that book, I don't want you to forget her, for she has some bearing on our history.

Shortly after Rebecca left I was singing in the market one day when I heard a new voice among the men shouting about politics, a tall scrawny man shouting about peace. I couldn't hear most of what he was saying because another man was standing across from him, shouting about war. Of course I was reminded of those days during the first temple when there were rival priests shouting out verses from their different Torahs, one from the north and one from the south, and ironically the tall scrawny man had a northern accent. He came every day, I grew more and more impressed with him, and would sometimes stop singing and go listen to him. One day he came to listen to me, and a few days later he appeared as I was packing up to go home. He was a sage and proto-rabbi named Johannan ben Zakkai and as the situation deteriorated he came down to Jerusalem to confer with the elders of our people, the priests and the leaders, none of whom would meet with him, so he began speaking in the marketplace instead, wanting—no, needing—to share his message. It turned out that he was a recent widower, saw me in my widow's garb, and may have been attracted to me. He never said so and I never asked, but we'd take turns listening to each other and I began to sing songs that I thought would speak to him—which they did. Given the tiny bit of freedom I was allowed by dressing as a widow, as a woman who did not belong to any man, toward the end of the day he would sometimes talk with me, and one evening he offered to walk me back to my quarter.

Partway there I stopped to rest by one of the ablution fountains near the temple, because it was closed for the night so one else was there. I took a risk, pulled out Sarah's bead, and told him who I was. He asked me many questions, rather as King Josiah had done all those years before, and I answered them, watching the look on his face change from scorn to doubt to puzzlement and then wonder. There were still rumors about me floating around the Jewish world and he knew them. Today he might have pulled out his cell phone and called to have me taken away for a psychiatric evaluation, but in the world of the first century CE my story made far more sense than it does now. We sat there talking all night. He wanted to know everything about our past and I told him some of what I told you and Rebecca, leaving out my writing project, leaving out Asherah, the evolution of the Torah, and trusting in my gut that what was needed in that moment wasn't historical accuracy—but spiritual truth—something that I'd learned from Yuzif.

Johannan's one burning question was—"What did the parting of the sea look like?" Not wanting to break his heart and tell him what I told you—"There was no sea, no parting, no miracles at all"—I sat there quietly, my brain racing for what to tell him. To fill the awkward silence he told me that his teacher, the great Hillel, who I never met, taught his students that the parting waters looked like two great lattices rising up toward the sky. When he said that I flashed on Dinah's old mirror, the one I'd given to Yuzif, and said to him, "Actually it looked like two great mirrors rising up on either side of us," an image he loved and passed on to his own students, and a version of this story made its way into the Talmud.

Now it doesn't take a clairvoyant to know where we were headed, and I suggested that he leave as soon as possible, taking with him those scholars and priests he trusted to carry on the core of our people's wisdom, along with all the old scrolls that they could get their hands on, which is exactly what he did. Oh, there's a lovely little twist to the story. Johannan's late wife Naomi came from a town near the coast called Jamnia or Yavneh. Her family were coffin makers. So yes, you guessed it! Another case of playing telephone. A story that began: "Before its destruction, Johannan ben Zakkai carried out of the city many of our most sacred scrolls and brought them to the village where his in-laws lived, who were coffin makers" turned into: "Johannan ben Zakkai was carried out of the city in a coffin and went to the city of Jamnia where he established the small rabbinic community that preserved our sacred traditions." He never met with the future emperor of Rome, a marvelous touch in the story that you know, but he and his followers were stopped by a group of Roman soldiers along the way, and bribed them with some of my remaining lapis, which I'd given to him for just such moments. Oh, and one more lovely little detail. Do you remember the King and the Giant and their famous song competition, old David and Goliath? The annual music festival they competed in was held—right outside of the town that was later called Jamnia, Yavneh.

Rebecca and Johannan left. I stayed. Things got worse and worse. Please allow me to quote the words of the immortal Yogi Berra: "It's like déjà vu over again." Having seen one Jerusalem burn, watching a replay was horrible, but I had to stay, had to watch, had to witness, from a hidden perch on the Mount of Olives, huddled in the door of an old tomb, wishing that it were mine.

The year—and you know how rarely I mention them, but this one is certifiable—was 70 CE—and it was horrible. War always is. The Romans were far more brutal than the Babylonians had been, but don't allow me to digress here on the medical treatment we desperately need for disorders of the Y chromosome. Others may write about war. Photographers in your time have captured images that ought to turn all decent people against it forever. I could say something about our still-evolving primate brains with their 'us versus them' hardwiring, or conjure up for you in words the images that are the most evocative to me of that which we must outgrow, and wish I could send back to 70 CE—the series of prints known as "The Disasters of War" done by the Spanish artist Francisco Goya, and Pablo Picasso's painting "Guernica." I used to visit it in the years when it hung in the Museum of Modern Art in New York, sitting on a bench across from it, deep in meditation on man's inhumanity to man—and I'm not using that word in an gender-inclusive way. But because teleporting images backwards in time hasn't been invited yet, all that I will say now is—I watched, I heard, I smelled, I wept.

I hid.

I went back to Babylon and spent some time with Rebecca, who was teaching women in the main synagogue in the city, right where she told me I would be able to find her. But weary, as might anyone be after so long and after all that I'd been through, knowing that she was fine, I went back to Afghanistan and spent a year with Yuzif. It was a wonderful year but at the end of it he sent me back. I spent more time with Rebecca, whose teaching was so powerful that men were starting to sit in in her classes. Then I returned to Galilee where I found an inn near an old synagogue. A large tree was growing up beside it, and there I lived for several months. Eventually I made my way to Jamnia and lived there for several years, my true identity known only to the now-elderly Johannan, but through him many of my teachings made their way to the first generation of sages who gathered there, men we now think of as rabbis. Then, to stay safe, I went back to Babylon, where I caught up with Rebecca again.

Unlike me, who a neighbor on Long Island once called "a practical gal," Rebecca was what we'd call today a mystic. She had visions, heard voices, and had profound dreams—which is why she was able to recognize me as an immortal from the very first time that we saw each other and was also able to send out what I might call "strong telepathic waves of connection" so that we could find each other again and again, in Canaan and in Babylon, as if by chance. Just the other day I heard a neighbor tell the story of being in Costa Rica and walking on the beach and running into the woman who runs the health food store around the corner from us. It was like that with Rebecca and me, having "chance" encounters over time and space, and in addition to being a mystic she was a poet of great talent, and although it no longer exists, during that period in her life Rebecca bat Simeon wrote a small book that she called, "The Tree of Life," which to the best of my knowledge was the very first text ever written about practical Jewish mysticism. It circulated underground for hundreds of years among our people and I'll come back to later, in addition to telling you a few other stories about her.

After Johannan's death I settled for a short time in a little village in Galilee where I set up a stall in the marketplace and sold herbal remedies. One day a young shepherd approached me whose small son was ailing. I gave him a remedy, which worked. His name was Akiva and, because he was a poor shepherd he had to come back several times to pay me, and each time he came, we talked. I could see who he could become, offered to teach him to read, and watched his learning grow in leaps and bounds. Stories told much later about his wife are not true, nor that he was forty when he started to learn. He reminded me of Joshua from the past, and of Barak Obama in the present. Akiva was a gem in the rough, not likely to be polished in the days before scholarships, so I did something I've only done on one or two other occasions—I gave him the last remaining lapis that I'd held onto, which paid for his rabbinic training.

All right, there is the problem of his later support of Bar Kochba. It came when he was much older and as an occasional practitioner of medicine I would say that he was suffering from Early Onset Alzheimer's and was swayed by our people's desperation and the intense charisma of the man he claimed was the messiah. Even I, as you know, who am not in general a great fan of most men, found Bar Kochba compelling. I almost revealed myself to the two of them, hoping to sway them in a different direction. But I knew that no woman, however ancient, could at that moment in time make them believe that it was the huge mistake it turned out to be to go against the Roman Empire—again!! Poor Akiva. When I think of his horrible death I sometimes wish that I'd left him tending his flocks of sheep, not students.

When you dear reader get up in the morning, if you are older and perhaps retired, you may ask yourself as you stretch and get out of bed, "What shall I do today?" But the question you ask yourself when you are fifteen hundred years old is—"What won't I do today?" And your answers— "Don't walk down Melech Street. The guard in front of the temple has been eyeing you, wondering why you look the same as you did the day he first whistled at you, but he's an old man now. Don't go to the bath house again. The woman attendant there is also getting suspicious. In fact Serach, now Sarah, don't go out at all. Start to pack up your few belongings and hit the road—again."

After the war ended I went back to Egypt for a while and worked as a cook for a woman in Alexandria named Beatrice who headed the synagogue there, one so large that in the years before microphones or printed prayer books the worshippers had to watch men waving little red flags from the bimah to know when to say "Amen." The city was so different, I can't say that I liked it, so after ten or so years I returned to Canaan with a glowing letter of recommendation from Beatrice, which got me a wonderful job cooking for the great Rabbi Judah the Prince. He was an insomniac and would often stagger into the kitchen in the middle of the night, waking me in my tiny adjacent room. I would mix him up some herbs in hot water, tell him a few stories, give him some oblique guidance, and send him back to bed. I watched his compilation, the *Mishnah*, grow up in the few years I worked for him, glad for the subtle ways that I could help him shape it for our people.

For three hundred years Rebecca and I did the same thing over and over. Like those rich families that dedicate things in synagogues and museums, whose names are engraved on little plaques on walls and doors and pews that read "Milton and Sylvia Feinberg of New York City and Palm Beach, Florida," we became women who lived their lives back and forth between Canaan and Babylonia, although both of them went through many name changes, various dynasties, droughts, floods, famines, religious conflicts, and endless wars. During that time when rabbinic academies were springing up in Babylonia I took Rebecca with me and we went off to visit Yuzif. The mountains and his company should have been a balm to our souls, but in spite of the thrill for her of being with *two* other immortals, the political situation in that part of the world was changing. There were constant invasions and vast cultural changes that made Yuzif's presence for the first time as unsafe as ours had long been and he decided it was time for him to leave, so many centuries after he'd arrived there. The three of us headed west, he so afraid and so amazed by the changed world we encountered. But I taught him all of my stealth-tricks, he and Rebecca bonded over their own common interests, she and I felt so much safer traveling with a man in that world, and after spending some time in the city of Sura, where a great Talmudic academy had sprung up, it became clear to us that whatever reason there was for our existences, we could best fulfill them for our people by living in separate places.

Yuzif decided to do something radical for a man who had lived for so many many centuries in one place—he decided to go as far west as he could go, intending to live among the Jews of Spain, who had first settled there in the time of Solomon. Rebecca gave him a copy of her book and he and I set off for Canaan, where he took passage on a ship heading east, while I chose to remain there. But we three had agreed to keep in touch with each other, not through mail which was limited to royalty in those days, but through dreaming, the art of which they were masters of. We agreed that we would meet up each month in a beautiful garden that they had conjured, on the nights of the new moon. They never failed to appear there and I, by far the oldest but not wisest, appeared whenever my dreaming self allowed it, sometimes with months between appearances, although I could often feel the two of them trying to help me get there during the months in between.

Over the years in our separate spheres we three channeled our creativity into finding the right Jewish homes to work in, serving elders and rabbis, patriarchs and exilarchs, always doing our best to steer them in directions that we thought reasonable for insuring our longevity as a people. And thus, from our work, over the centuries, we watched two *Talmuds* grow up around Judah's *Mishnah*, one in Canaan and one in Babylonia, and under Yuzif's guidance, having brought Rebecca's wonderful book on the Tree of Life with him, we watched the deep seeds of Jewish mysticism begin to grow strong in Spain, seeds that would sprout, grow, and blossom there several centuries later.

During one night visit when I did appear (and I've long suspected that the inventors of the telephone secretly had this skill and wanted to share it with others like me) Rebecca told us that she was working in what today is Turkey as a tutor for the children of a rabbi. One night over dinner he and another rabbi were discussing the descendants of Abraham's children with Hagar and Keturah, and that inspired her to travel south for a change, to see the lands where they had settled. She ended up in Mecca, which had an old settled Jewish community. There was no synagogue there to teach in, and needing to support herself she began to look for the kind of work I'd been doing and met an older woman who was taking care of her orphaned grandson, a bright little boy named Muhammad. Just as I may have perhaps offended others by my tales, Jews, Buddhists, and Christians, it's now my opportunity to offend Muslims as well. Rebecca loved the little boy as her own, for he was something of a storyteller and a dreamer himself, which she understood, and she told him endless stories from her life and her stud-ies and her travels, stories which he delighted in. Years later some of those stories found their way into his recitations. One example only will suffice. It says in the Mishnah and, if memory serves me, in both *Talmuds*: "Whoever destroys a soul, it is as if he had destroyed an entire world, and whoever saves a life, it is as if he had saved an entire world." In Sura 5:32 in the *Qur'an* you can read almost exactly the same words.

So it was that the three of us continued to do our work, watching each other from a distance. I did get better at appearing in the garden, and given that we weren't living that far apart, Rebecca and I decided to have a reunion in the flesh and agreed—in our shared dreams—to meet up in the city of Ur where our ancestors came from. I had to wait for three weeks for her to ap-pear, but what's three weeks when you're as old as we were? She who always traveled in male grab, passing herself off as this or that youth, found me at the inn where I was staying, right as Shabbat was approaching. We lit our traveling oil lamps, said our prayers, ate and went to sit out under a spray of infinite stars, stars that often make mortals feel tiny and make immortals feel normal.

We sat in the darkness, silent, side by side on the earth. Then a single shooting star arced its way across the sky and I turned to her and said that there was something I wanted to talk about with her. She cut me off to say that there was something she wanted to talk about with *me*—and with words pouring out, after hundreds of years, each of us confessed to the other her attraction. What joy! What bliss! Oh, the nights that we spent together in a small inn on the edge of the city. She at the time looked like a woman in her late twenties and I looked like a woman in her late thirties but for the first time in almost two thousand years I thought that I had finally found not just my soul mate, as I'd felt with Dinah and Bast, but a whole new kind of marriage, the chance to share my life—with another immortal!

I said this before, that I wouldn't talk about all the times that I was attacked by brigands and thieves, by soldiers and mercenaries, all of them, always, men.

I buried Rebecca outside of a small town that today is called Pir Bakran, about 30 kilometers from Isfahan, in Iran. Later generations said the tomb was mine.

I was old. I was tired. It was the lowest point of my entire life.

I hid.

I was tired. I was tired of hiding, tired of moving. Bereft, in despair and filled with rage against that which had come to be called God, I made a radical choice that I'd never made before. It was late in the 7th century and there were several synagogues in nearby Isfahan. I went there to speak with the rabbi of the largest and oldest one. A serving woman who was around the same age that I appeared to be, led me to the courtyard of his home, with the women's quarters in the back. The rabbi was already seated there and invited me to join him. The servant sat at a distance shelling beans in a large glazed bowl. The light of afternoon was soft, a gentle breeze was blowing, as I pulled out the seal around my neck and told him who I was. And he, good wise and gentle Rafael ben Judah—after asking me the kinds of questions that Josiah and Johannan and anyone else might ask of a person like me, said exactly what I was hoping he would say—"Stay here with us. We will take care of you." Then he bowed, slipped to the floor on his knees, and pressed his forehead to my feet.

Chapter Twenty

Three and more thousand years later,
your weary narrator completes her saga,
bringing you right up to the present moment
(more or less)

A FEW SHORT YEARS ago a man in London, England (where I spent a long weekend in 1929 with Clara) started something that he called a Death Café, inviting people to sit over cake and coffee and talk about the last great taboo—and now they've spread around the world. There were no Death Cafés back then, and I could have used one. But Rav Rafael offered me something else—the comfort of a home that I'd never thought possible.

I've never seen a ghost, nor do I believe in them. If someone was going to see a ghost you'd think it would be me, but what I know is that each death that we experience is connected to all the deaths that went before it. So I won't say that my wonderful room in the back of Rafael and his wife Sheva's home was haunted by Rebecca and everyone I'd ever loved and lost going all the way back to Bast and Dinah. No, I *myself* was haunted, haunted by their memories, in a bodily way that I am sure you can understand if ever you've lost someone you loved. And what made my grieving worse was that without Rebecca's extra pull in dreamtime, I found myself less connected to Yuzif as well.

I've watched people whose partners died soon wither and die themselves, and I've envied them. But just as I lost one miracle—I was granted another one—an entire community of people who all agreed to take me in, protect me, honor me, and never let anyone outside their community ever know who I was. This week I read that today there are over sixty-five million refugees in the world and that the crisis of people seeking safe homes is greater than at any time since the Second World War. As a refugee for more than two thousand years, finding sanctuary in that large sunny back room in Sheva and Rafael's home, with fragrant vines growing up over the windows and adjacent to the synagogue that was later named for me, was something that I never dreamed of.

For several hundred years I lived freely in Isfahan, walking about in my widow's garb in every season, reveling in each day. And as an honored elder who looked like a forty-something woman, I taught and was granted privileges that few, in fact, no other women were granted. I wasn't the first woman rabbi. No one ordained me. But there in Isfahan I taught, sang, led services, gave sermons, married couples, weaving together in ways that no one quite understood (because I never told them) all that I had been taught as a priestess with all that I had learned over the centuries from and about our people. Books and stories, legends and truths, were my domain to share, and I was happy in Isfahan in a way that I hadn't known since childhood. Not that there weren't wars, persecutions, famines, plagues, and the like, and not that like Bar Kochba before him I didn't watch another young man named Abu 'Isa be proclaimed the messiah by his followers. Oh, I tried to calm them down, but even *I* could not do that. And I saw the rise into prominence in that region of another branch on our Jewish tree, that of the Karaites, with their roots going back to the days of the temple, who flourish now in only two places that I know of, in Israel and in a little town near San Francisco whose name I've forgotten. Oh, yes. Daly City.

People talk about how beautiful Paris is, and I agree. But the most beautiful city I've ever seen is Isfahan. There's a column in the *New York Times* that I read sometimes, called "Modern Love." I've thought about writing something for it myself, not about falling in love with another human being but about falling in love with a city. In that city of broad plazas and pools and fountains and magnificent mosques I grew and thrived, and while I never took another human lover in the time I lived there, my love affair with Isfahan went on for centuries.

Free to be myself for the first time ever, I was able to do what all immortals ought to be able to do—watch one generation be born, grow up and have children, raise them, age, and slowly die as the next generation rises up to replace them, over and over again. As over and over again I led the Mourners' Kaddish for people who as babies I had named in our synagogue. I watched noses appear and change and disappear and return again in certain families. I was able to tell one young woman—"You have exactly your great, great grandmother Lilah's laugh"—and tell another young man—"Your great, great uncle Issachar had the very same gift for dancing that has come to you." I saw traits appear and change and watched lineages weave together and strengthen or weaken, and had I been a creature with a scientific mind I might have caught on to the workings of our genes, but I'm not a scientist or an historian, so that opportunity passed me by. But I was a human parent to a family of cats for at least one hundred generations, those cats among the very ancestors of the Persian cats we know today. I could tell you much about them and about the shifting patterns of colors, fur length, noses, and personality traits, some annoying and others delightful.

From time to time on a new moon night I would encounter Yuzif, and am so proud to tell you that in our Golden Age in Spain he was teaching students from Rebecca's wonderful book "The Tree of Life," which still existed. Then he served for a time as the mentor for that moody marvelous poet Solomon ibn Gabirol. Soon after that he crossed the Pyrenees into France where he was the tutor for young Rashi, and a bit later he was living in North Africa where he taught the great Maimonides both Midrash and *Talmud*. Imagine what our history would be like if not for Yuzif's deep influence on the three of them and on several other of our important masters, to all of whom he told our secret stories, without every revealing the secret story of his own ancient Israelite self.

Trading habits, he traveled the world as I had done for centuries while I remained in beautiful Isfahan. I arrived there soon after Islam had, which came to a land that had long been home to Zoroastrians, Christians, and Jews, which land took a bit of time to weave into its life, not always with ease, yet another faith. Thirty years ago almost no one knew about me, certainly not in the Ashkenazi world where I'd been almost entirely forgotten, which was a kind of a blessing when I began to travel there. But in the world of the east I continued to be remembered, with people debating whether or not I'd died in a great fire in the synagogue, or been carried off to heaven in a fiery chariot like Elijah, or whether I was still alive, an immortal.

There *was* a fire in the 12th century in that synagogue, and while the embers were still glowing, my old beloved home beside it still standing, with everything reeking of smoke—which triggered what today we would call PTSD, remembering all the places I'd seen burned to the ground—the miracle I'd been hoping for finally happened—and you know that I don't believe in miracles! Rebecca came to me in a dream and said, "Darling, it's time for you to move on again. I know it will be hard to leave after hundreds of years, but I suggest you head east to China, where our traders have been journeying for centuries." So I did.

If you are, say, Jewish, or a lesbian, or a member of any other outsider group, you should be able to relate to how I felt when I crossed over into western China with a caravan and found myself mysteriously drawn to a little mountain town where a woman in the marketplace—please note that recurring detail—invited me to a little party where I met nine—count them—nine—other immortals—all delightful and all younger than I. It was heaven on earth, and I don't believe in heaven either! But I do want to make a comment about Jews and Chinese food. Even in the 12th century Jews would talk about it, those many Persian Jewish traders who found themselves there. The spices, the way that food was prepared, was actually—and you're hearing it here for the very first time—so very like the food that we ate when I was a little girl, that even though I didn't discover DNA I can assure you that a love of Chinese food is encoded in our genes. And, given that there were ten of us at that gathering of immortals, I suppose we were a sort of a *minyan* too.

China was so very different from Persia, women repressed there in different ways that I as a foreigner was somewhat less restricted by. I loved the culture, the music, the clothing—silk was expensive everywhere else I'd lived before. And having met the Buddha when I was on the road all of those years before, it was amazing to me to see the way that versions of his teachings had spread north from India to every part of China, for over the years that I was there I traveled extensively. Today people seem to know about the Jews of the city of Kaifeng, but when I arrived there were Jews living in many other cities, and in what today is called Guangzhou I met a rabbi who told me that his ancestors had come there soon after the destruction of the second temple. He had a document that listed their names going all the way back, written gorgeously in Hebrew with a brush and not a pen, and at the very beginning of his list I found the name of someone I once knew, Manasseh ben Yoram, a trader whose route in the time of Herod and his horrible descendants went back and forth from Judea to Persia. So you see, not just a love of Chinese food but our very deepest roots as a nation of traders are encoded in our genes.

I went underground again in China, and remained that way except for the times I spent in the mountains of western China with my immortal friends, where I could be out again. In China Jews and Muslims were often confused, especially as we often came from the same places, and I must say that I liked that and it prepared me for my life in the west, where the same thing often happens to me to this very day, as a dark-skinned Middle Eastern-looking woman. And there was a joy in my body at standing on the opposite end of the continent I was born on, something that I did not understand until I saw the first accurate maps of Asia in China and began to comprehend what the physical world is really like. It was also in China that I woke one night in terror from the worst nightmare I've ever had.

Broad daylight. A hot spring day. Men on foot and on horseback are storming the gates of the Jewish quarter, screaming for the blood of the

Christ- killers. Dragging Jews who've taken refuge in their homes out into the street where they slash at them with swords, slit their throats, their mad horses trampling them. Then storming the old synagogue where hundreds of our people have taken refuge.

I knew that thousands of Jews had died that day, among them—and there are tear in my eyes as I type (which has happened before but I didn't mention it)—my oldest and most beloved friend Yuzif. Later I came to understand that he had died in what today we call a pogrom. It was the 14th century of the calendar that most of the world uses today, a calendar grounded in the Christian tradition, and all I can say at this point is that poor Joshua, Yeshua, must be horrified by acts like that that have been done in his name.

Soon after that dream I left China, where I had planned to say for the rest of my life, in the circle of my wonderful friends. By the time I left I was quite fluent in three different Chinese languages, had learned a host of new recipes, but I also felt two things—that the center of the Jewish world was shifting westward to Europe, and that I wanted and needed to find the place where Yuzif had been killed and say Kaddish for him there, not the Kaddish that you all know but a far more ancient version of it.

When you think of an immortal you might think of an elder or a sage, but in my long life I have often felt more kinship with smugglers and thieves and others living on the fringes than I have with anyone wise, and so it was that I worked my way west with a band of drug dealers who my immortal friends knew, serving as their cook and herbalist. Like Anybodys in *West Side Story* I was their butch sidekick, and in a very different way than I was in Isfahan, they watched over me and kept me safe as we headed west. When you mention drugs and China in the same sentence people always think: opium. But what I learned six hundred years and more ago is that cannabis plants evolved on the steppes of what today is called Mongolia, and were being cultivated for their medicinal properties more than ten thousand years ago. From there cannabis spread to the rest of the world, and because of its ancient lineage Chinese cannabis resins were considered the very best in the world. That's what my guardians were transporting from western China to their many different markets on the Mediterranean.

It was strange to go back to places I'd been in hundreds and even thousands of years before. Some, like Ur, were almost the same, and others were radically different, in ruin, or so vastly changed that I could hardly recognize them. I traveled with my companions (who were also by the way descendants of the so-called Lost Ten Tribes) for more than three years, going from city to city and selling their wares, to doctors and healers and herbalists who knew of their product's various healing properties. It's been interesting in the last few decades to see a resurgence in the use of cannabis and to watch the legal fights around its use. It says in *Ecclesiastes*, which of course was not written by King Solomon but by an old friend of mine, Shallum ben Azariah—"There is nothing new under the sun."

It was good to wander, good to remember, good to forget. Whoever said "Time heals all wounds" was wrong—but a bit of hashish in a carved jade pipe, and a whole lot of time, can soften their edges. Eventually I knew that it was time for me to set off on my own again. One might think that longevity was a source of intelligence but there are times when I've thought that living so long has actually slowed down my mental development in the same way as my physical development. Even as a little girl Shalomeh trusted her instincts, her intuitions, but it took me a thousand and more years, to do the same. When I said goodbye to my traveling companions at the port of Jaffa, passage booked on a small ship heading toward the Greek isles, I knew that I was going to find the city of my nightmare, knew that I would be led to it so that I could say Kaddish for Yuzif.

I wanted to go to Lesbos, and I did, rich with the money I was paid by the men I had cooked for and tended. It was a thrill to walk streets that Sappho may or may not have ever walked, reciting to myself long lines of verses that are long lost, verses that I had learned "by heart"—that lovely lovely expression! Then I went to Athens and spent time with the Jewish community there, old and well-established, where I met a merchant, of course—marketplaces and merchants are part of my karma—who of course was heading north and who offered to take me along. Chaim was a lovely gay man who wanted to use me as his cover, and I was happy to comply. (This has happened to me many many times over the years. Not so very long ago a charming closeted gay former mayor of the city of New York, Clara's and my downstairs neighbor, invited me to go to a fundraiser as his date. I stayed home. She went instead.)

I won't tell you each step along the way that took me to my destination. But the merchant passed me on to a rabbi cousin who was traveling north, who . . . until I ended up exactly where I needed to be. Some years ago, back in New York, I met a lovely woman named Barbara Shor who died much too soon of a rare disease, to whom things like this were always happening, that dream and reality were intertwined—but they do not happen to me. Only, there I was, walking the streets of a strange city, a city I've heard is most beautiful—but all that I could see was blood and all that I could smell was fire, and the nightmare pulled me into it and drew me to the exact quarter of Prague where so many of our people had been massacred, including the best friend I've ever had, so far.

What I learned while we were there is that Yuzif died during the Easter Massacre of 1389, instigated by the city's clergy who accused the local Jews of having desecrated the host, an act for which they should be killed. As I walked those streets, many buildings still in ruins I heard the screaming mobs and saw as an overlay exactly what I'd seen in my dream. Weeping, glad I was with a tall broad rabbi and his two tall sons, I said the Kaddish that Yuzif and I said in our younger years, and I wept and I wept and I wept as I'd never wept before, wishing that I had been there with him, wishing that as with Rebecca I had been able to bury him myself, the act of shoveling dirt into a beloved one's grave the best form of therapy for easing the bodily pangs of grief that I've ever yet come upon. Thinking with anger about their deaths and my continued existence, which you might or might not call "a life."

From Prague with its later tales of golems I wandered across Europe in a strange kind of pilgrimage, needing to see everywhere that my friend had lived. I went to Rome, where he'd spent time, which was both unrecognizable and familiar, so many old buildings I remembered in ruins, and so much that was new. I went to Troyes in France and walked streets that were vaguely familiar, seen in the background of the dreams with Yuzif that I occasionally appeared in, thinking of Yuzif and Rashi walking them together, sometimes with Rashi's daughters, to whom he served as an occasional tutor. Then I slowly headed further west to Spain, skirting petty wars and feuds, not always dressing as a woman and not always dressing as a Jew, doing whatever I felt guided to do in order to get to my destination. I loved the landscape of Spain and Portugal, both soft and rugged, and loved wandering from place to place picking up traces of Yuzif—and Rebecca—for he had brought her "Tree of Life" there and I could hear in conversations and see in new texts its lasting influence, particularly in the work of Moses de Leon that later became the core of the great *Zohar*.

Claiming that my father was a Palestinian rabbi, I passed myself off as Sarah bat Asher and sat with rabbis' wives and every once in a while with rabbis themselves, and I prayed in elaborate synagogues and very plain ones, in those years when Muslim Spain was giving way to Catholic Spain. I went to North Africa for a time to visit Fez in Morocco, where Yuzif had spent time with Maimonides, and then I went back to Spain, which I grew to love more and more. It was there that I formally adopted the name that I have kept until this very day, a Portuguese Jewish family name whose roots will make sense to you. I became Sarah Da Silva—Da Silva chosen because "silva" in Latin means "Of the wood, From the trees," the perfect stealth-name for I knew that the Tree I was named for belonged to our family's ancient goddess Asherah—but no one else did.

I wandered in Portugal and Spain observing what I'd observed be-fore—the deterioration of human decency, almost always inspired by hu-man beings with Y chromosomes but occasionally supported by their angry wounded manipulative mothers, sisters, and wives. I watched ethnic and religious differences be fanned into hatred and watched the crazy notion "Peoplehood = Territory" turn into slaughter once again. And as things got worse and worse I did something that I'd promised myself that I would never do again. In fact—unreliable narrator—I may have told you that I never did. But I came out to occasional people in their various synagogues, telling them the truth about who I was, showing them our ancestor Sarah's little carved carnelian bead with its tree on it, explaining what it meant, singing our songs and reminding people that our history is encoded in our bodies—that we are Hebrews, the people from the other side of the river, originally the Euphrates, but then, and now—any river.

I knew what was coming, a waking nightmare. I didn't know what form it would take—but when it came, I was there. I went to the court and tried with no success to meet with the king and queen, Ferdinand and Isabella, both of whom had Jewish ancestors. Through trading contacts I was able to meet Christopher Columbus, who also had Jewish ancestors, but there was nothing that I or anyone else could do, and in the summer of 1492, as you know, our people were given the choice—convert to Catholicism or leave! Some converted, including many of wealth in positions of power, but most of our people chose to leave.

If I give few details here, please pardon me, but I am weary from this task, so much of this can be better read in history books, and for me it was what happened yesterday, not old news at all. Scholars estimate that more than 80,000 of our people left Spain, and I left with them, singing our old songs and doing my best to inspire our people. The legends about my going out of Spain with them are true. Forgotten is that for several generations I wandered from community to community, from North Africa to Turkey—where we were welcomed, to Italy and Greece and other safe havens, offer-ing comfort to our people, in the way of songs, stories, and healing herbs.

Sitting on the dock before we left Spain, I found myself next to an interesting man named Joseph Caro, who was heading off to Turkey where I believe he had family. Some years later he moved again, to Safed, where he set up a yeshiva and where I soon joined him. Much has been written about him and he left behind so many teachings. I told him the truth of my identity and told him parts of what I've been telling you, and he often took dictation from me. What he told others was that he was listening to the voice of his maggid, his spirit teacher, but he told them that to protect my identity. Thank you Joseph. All through my life Josephs have helped me out and I am grateful to them all.

While I was in Safed I did one other thing. I started an underground school of Jewish women mystics, sharing with all of them my beloved Rebecca's book. A few of their names have survived, including Francesa Sarah, Rachel Aberlin, her student Leah Shira Anav, all of them teaching in stealth, their words of wisdom spreading out from there to all parts of the Jewish world, from my beloved Afghanistan to North Africa, from Europe to Ethiopia. It was while I was living in Safed that I heard about another group of fools, centered around an otherwise delightful man named Nathan of Gaza who had proclaimed to be the messiah a charmingly imbalanced man named Shabbetai Zevi, another of those bi-polar characters in our history, like but not as extreme as my dear old friend Saul. I went to talk to both of them, revealed myself, got a marriage offer from Zevi, and knew once again that we were in big trouble.

The rest is history.

Tired of drama, a sullen but helpful merchant in Jaffa suggested that I go to Amsterdam, the safest place he knew of in the world for Jews to live in. I went, and through the Jewish community there I heard about a man named Baruch Spinoza, a bachelor from a merchant family (I won't comment any further on this) who had been excommunicated by the Jewish authorities. Although no one was allowed to have any contact with him, his family and friends kept an eye on him, and it was through one of them that I found out that he was in need of an occasional cook and cleaning woman. At the time he was working as a lens grinder, a very new profession, and his work was known to be outstanding. All of this is history, so I won't go into it. What I will say is that one of the things that got him in trouble before his excommunication was that he had fallen in love with a Christian young man who loved him in return, whose father reported Spinoza for immorality. I thought of this some years later when Oscar Wilde was on trial. The difference in Spinoza's case is that all of this was entirely kept hidden because the Jewish community elders secretly paid off the Dutch authorities. I adored Spinoza, made him some of my favorite Afghani and Chinese Jewish dishes, usually having to substitute local ingredients for the actual ones—and of the many many the people I've met in my three thousand years he was one of the most brilliant. A bit awkward socially, we would ask ourselves today if he had some kind of spectrum disorder. I never told him who I was—he had enough problems without having to digest that—but we had some amazing conversations over the time that I worked for him, some of which seem to have rippled out into his surviving writings, with a bit more in the ones that he destroyed.

My job, Yuzif had helped me to understand, was to support our people from a distance, energetically, you might say. So I wandered on from Amsterdam to other parts of Europe, watching the rise of Ashkenazi Jews, watching them assimilate, watching some of them almost be able to conjure up from their genes lost aspects of who we are—a people who share, a people who move, a people who fully include women in every part of our communal lives. I lived for a while in what today is Germany, went further east into Poland where I met the Baal Shem Tov and had a delightful conversation with his wife Chana, who I told a few stories about our Jewish women mystics. I wonder what happened to them. I wandered into Russia, washing dishes and cooking, getting letters of recommendation from one rabbi that I would take to the rabbi of the next place that I went to.

Let me say that there are things about Orthodox Jewish practice that don't resonate with me. Oppression has made some of us fussy and neurotic, going back to the time of the Assyrians. But our roots are not obsessive or compulsive. We were a people of joy and music and freedom. So I don't keep kosher, although I have not once cooked a calf in its mother's milk in over three thousand years, and I seldom eat pork, except on the anniversary of Spinoza's excommunication. (I will not tell you if he liked it or not. That's his business.) I turn lights on and off on Shabbat, and so I think would Moses have done if someone had invented electricity a bit sooner. And I sing any and all songs that our people sing, from every and all cultures that we come from.

It's odd after so long to have people be telling stories about me once again. Scholars and seekers are reading through all the Talmudic and midrashic stories and I am sometimes included in Passover Seders and occasionally sung about during Havdallah, along with Elijah the Prophet, that strict and passionate man. (Another homosexual. Go back and read into the story with Elisha what was really going on.) And it seems to me both right and proper to keep hiding and allow myself to be recreated by others in an image that they need. And yet. And yet. After so long, and after resisting this project for so long, as you can tell—I do have a few more things to say.

Let's start with Israel. You must be wondering why I'm not living there, in the land of our ancestors, the land of my birth. That I've lived away from it for far far longer than I ever lived there has something to do with my living here, in America, by the Pacific Ocean. Pacific, Peaceful, it was called. Yes, I live in Los Angeles, that sprawl of a city, unlike anything that's ever gone before it, the opposite of the Tower of Babel—a flat city strewn across the landscape. And yet, perhaps for that very reason—I love it.

But why do I live in this horizontal Babel? Israel, if you ask me, is an historical mistake, a wrong turn, the end-result of a set of faulty assumptions.

People lived there. Our own distant kin. How could so many of us have forgotten that? What did they think the people of Palestine would do when we arrived? Be standing at the docks with long lists of all of our ancient clans, checking people off and sending them on their way home again, back to their ancestral property? Oh, but they didn't think, not enough of them, and didn't realize that our people would be trading in ten thousand little ghettoes for one long skinny one. They were unconscious. And how could they not be, so many of them, of us, after so many centuries of persecution? But don't for a moment imagine that I'm forgetting the Holocaust. Yes, Clara and I got out, but we could have been killed, like *all* of her family, *all* of our friends. I don't believe in God or angels. If I did I might say that there was or has been some higher purpose in keeping me alive, if only to tell these stories. But in the absence of belief there is something else—the accident of fate that the few other un-dying folk I've met along the way all share. None of us say that we are immortal. All that we say is, "I'm not dead yet."

Outside my window as I write a tiny little yellow bird is sitting on a palm frond. I don't know what kind of bird it is, but it's darting from frond to frond and soon it will dart off. It has! That bird, that bird is our people, in movement, in motion, always. When the messiah comes, she can decide what we should do, where we should live. But for now, I live in Babel by the Sea, not Spring Hill, Tel Aviv. No, I live here, on land stolen from others long before I arrived, and it's here that I shall remain. As long as I remain. Or until it's time for me to dart off again, my little yellow wings unfolded.

So here I am, sitting at the desk I bought in a yard sale, remembering that there are a few other things that I haven't told you yet. Some I withheld because they're long forgotten and I don't want to shame anyone from the past. This isn't quite avoiding *lahson ha'ra,* for as you can see a fear of that hasn't held me back so far. No, rather, it's a bit like that expression—"Let sleeping dogs lie." What I told you is what I thought was essential, which I've been thinking about for a very long time. And there are other things I left out, thinking they would be selling points if I ever decide to write another book. "The oldest woman in the world tells more!" Not likely, but you never know.

In the very beginning of this book I said that I would address three important questions:

"Why should we believe anything this old woman is telling us?"

"Why is she writing her memoir now?"

"Why has she lived this long?"

After recently coming out to someone new and showing her everything that I've written so far, she suggested that there's another question I ought to address:

"What is it like to have lived for so long?"

Initially I was not just reluctant to address that question. I was resistant to it. But with the gentle delicate hand-holding of that new friend, Estelle, I've decided to approach it. She's been trying to get me to spit into a little vial and have my DNA tested. Thus far—would you call me stubborn, as she does?—I've refused. She's tried with flowers and delicious dinners to blackmail me into feeling that my refusal is denying access to others of the medical knowledge on health and longevity that will be learned through studying my genes. This, I have recently decided, is an invitation for me to discard the theory that I am a genetic anomaly and return to the old old old story of my fate—that I am an entirely ordinary woman with perfectly ordinary genes, whose great longevity is entirely due to the power of her grandfather Jacob's blessing upon her, that the angel of death never come to pay her a visit.

Now, back to my dear friend's question. "What is it like to have lived for so long?" I ask myself this every day, looking in the mirror. It's that face, that old familiar somewhat lopsided face, one eye and one eyebrow higher than the other, that has stared back at me since I got my very first mirror, that small disc of polished brass with a handle carved of ebony that Dinah gave me, sometime around the year 1382 BCE, which I gave to Yuzif many years later. I have no idea what happened to it. Perhaps one of the people who slaughtered him and those three thousand others found it in his pack and took it home and kept it and now it's sitting in an old moldy wooden trunk in an attic in Prague, waiting for someone to take it out and polish it up again. Because time, as we know, is relative.

Am I as young as I look? As old as I feel? In the last years of the 19th century I was living in Munich and working as a cook, again, for a family named Einstein, who had another of the precocious sons who have again and again wandered into my life. (He reminded me a bit of our little Moses.) Young Albert was awkward, shy, but would often sit with me in the kitchen while I was making dinner. Of course I never told him who I was, but I told him all kinds of "strange and funny stories" as he called them, stories about times past and time present—and who knows what kind of an influence those stories might have had.

So many others have written about this period far better than I ever could (and of the nightmare that followed) but there is one other notable person I met in Germany who I want to mention. I saw Regina Jonas for the first time at a party hosted by mutual friends, in the days before she was studying for the rabbinate. From across a crowded drawing room she stood out—striking, brooding, brilliant, and so very like our ancient judge Shalomeh in stature and presence. Of course I went up to her, and while I never told her who I was (or talked about reincarnation) I told her I'd done a great deal of traveling and told her many of our stories, that night and several times later, over tea. We talked about the notable women of our past, our prophetesses and leaders, and it still breaks my heart that when the war was over the male rabbis who knew Rabbiner Jonas and her work, after her ordination and then in the camps, "forgot" to mention her, our first officially ordained woman rabbi. Their names I shall not mention, but I mention her now in pride and sorrow, in despair and celebration, for she opened a door for our people that had been closed for centuries, and each year on her birthday—the 3rd of August—I make a pot of hot black tea in celebration, and say my old favorite form of Kaddish, because we don't know the exact date of her death in Auschwitz.

Given that this book is littered with the names of famous people, including Napoleon's mother Letizia, for whom I worked for a time, a recluse and chronically depressed—let me say that there are many many famous people I wish that I had met, in no particular order—Sappho of course, Cleopatra, Joan of Arc, our ancestor Sarah the priestess, Artemisia, Hypatia, definitely Lady Murasaki Shikibu—I've read her stories about Genji in multiple versions and translations since Clara first introduced me to her in Berlin—Queen Rudrama Devi of India, Wu Zetian the unofficial ruler of China in the 8th century, who spread the Buddha's teachings throughout her realm, and Dahiah the Berber Jewish queen of North Africa. Oh, and definitely Virginia Woolf: I wish I could say that I met her at a dinner party the only time I was ever in London, with my dear wonderful Clara. We didn't, but I love her work more than any other modern writer, in the original and also in Portuguese translations where a certain music emerges that reminds me of my underground Jewish mystical woman friends in Portugal before the Expulsion.

I met Clara while shopping in Berlin—hail the goddess of the marketplace! I was carrying under my arm a book of Woolf's that had been published the year before, *Orlando,* the half-revealed cover of which she recognized and a copy of which she pulled out of her purse. We went out for coffee, talked for hours about Woolf—Clara was working on her doctorate in English literature, a language I'd been studying in my spare time, with the fantasy of one day going to America, and over the next three months she slowly courted me and became the first person I'd made love with in more than a thousand years, since Rebecca. (My very brief stint as an Essene, a story I seem to have skipped over, and my time with the Buddha, which I did discuss, both helped to sustain me.)

In the beginning of this book, which I've been struggling with for over two decades, I mentioned my favorite inventions of all times: hot running water, the printing press, and the camera. Looking back on human history, while it isn't my favorite invention, I do want to say what I think the most important human invention has been in terms of social evolution. In fact, my upstairs neighbor Margo, a grad student in sociology at UCLA, has been encouraging me to think about going to school—for the very first time in my entire life! I did recently meet a charming man named Steven, not at a cocktail party but at the memorial service for a mutual LA friend. He teaches at Stanford, and I suppose I could talk with him about this. In fact I've already chosen the topic of my dissertation:

The Roll of Toilet Paper in the Transformation
of the Bicameral Brain

For most of human history the majority of we semi-sentient animals all around the world have been right-handed, often enforcing that trait among lefties, and we've created binary judgments based upon the hand we ate with: Right: good, clean, male. Left: dirty, bad, female. For eons we've used grass and twigs and moss and sand and husks to wipe ourselves, and when available we used rags and sponges, or rubbed our LEFT hands in dirt and washed them in water, if there was any nearby. But it was only in China around two thousand years ago that someone invented toilet paper, a Buddhist monk actually, and from there it very slowly spread around the world, not reaching Europe till around the time of the Renaissance. (Many of the greatest of human inventions come from China, including the compass, the kite, and my favorite—the printing press.) As toilet paper became more and more available, for the first time in human history (I do not know anything about how or if our primate kin wipe themselves) our left hands were freed up to be the equal of our right hands—which began all kinds of shifts in our brains that influenced cultures all around the world and that have helped to break down the long lists of binaries that have been such a part of human history. And that, that is the gist of my dissertation. Thank you for listening.

Pause here.

Yesterday I was walking on the beach with Estelle, my new friend, my new... partner? That sounds like a business arrangement. Girlfriend? She's sixty-nine. Wife? Perhaps in the future. What I go back to is the true simple elegant word we used in the 1970s.

Yesterday I was walking on the beach with my new lover. It's 2017 now, and in spite of the fact that there's a proto-fascist regime in power in Washington, this is still for the moment California—where two older women who met standing on line in our local health food store, started chatting, became friends, and have recently become lovers, can walk safely on the beach at Santa Monica holding hands. We were walking past muscle men with bodies swollen up like nothing I've ever seen before, anywhere in the world, and wild young women on roller blades wearing what to me still looks like underwear, zipping by, their blond hair streaming out behind them, with little babies in strollers gliding in front of them, looking round and about with curious or startled eyes that often say, "Where am I?" And, "How did I get here?"

I never expected to be in love again, not after Clara and not at what seems so late in my life. As we were leaving the health food store Estelle asked for my number. I told her the truth—"I don't have a mobile phone"— and gave her my landline number. She called a few days later. We met for lunch in Santa Monica, at a café near the beach, sitting outside under palm trees, their fronds clattering in the breeze. She drove. I walked, having never learned to drive.

A week later we went to the movies. *The Danish Girl,* which she liked more than I did. Had dinner a week after that, slowly getting to know each other. I put off anything more than kissing her for three months, wanting to be sure of our feelings and knowing that I would need to tell her the truth before we spent the night together. Her first reaction, as a person *and* a psychotherapist, was to give me such a marvelous look of horror and dismay, a look which I read (correctly, she later told me) as—"Oh my God. This woman is completely out of her mind! And given my age—*and* my vocation—I should have known this from our very first conversation!" But because all along she could feel that I was withholding something, she was also relieved to discover that I didn't have a husband or a wife, or both, and by the end of that very very long evening, although it took her a few more weeks and a lot more stories for everything to sink in, she more or less believed me. (Showing her my bead and a book on Middle Eastern archaeology that had similar objects in it also helped.) And that was our first night together, six months ago, followed by the first of what became our regular Friday morning beach walks, Friday her day off, those walks the perfect beginning of our shared Shabbat.

We were walking. We were talking. We were barefoot. She was lathered in sunblock and I, counting on my Middle Eastern coloring and at my age unafraid of skin cancer, was breathing in the salt air, captivated by the sparkling highlights on the incoming waves. My aging dog Malkah, who would have once been dragging me along the sand, was ambling beside us, stopping, sniffing, sometimes looking up at birds with an indifference to her former passion that she was finding curious, and I was telling Estelle about this book (again) and my struggle in writing it, my fear of being attacked or ridiculed for its contents, for my inadequate writing skills, and my deeper fears about betraying some of the people I'd known, distorting some, and leaving others out.

Then Estelle, shaking out her long thick beautiful gray hair—I keep mine short—was about to say something—when a family of six dolphins shot up from the depths and began to follow us in the water as we headed south on the sand, swimming about twenty feet out and leaping, soaring, diving, descending, gliding below the surface and then rising up again—so very beautiful!!! And while in my heart of hearts I have always remained what I was at the beginning of my life—a goddess worshipper—I seldom pray or feel Her presence in any clear and direct way. But Estelle and I were walking on the beach, Malkah's leash in my left hand and her warm oiled left hand in my right, and the smell of the sea, the dolphins rising and falling and rising again from the diamond-bright waves—shifted something in me—and I felt my mother Arsiyah, Grandpa Jacob, and Dinah and Bast and Hapmose and Yuzif and Rebecca and Clara. I felt our mother Sarah and all of our people there, walking with us there—as if it were the fulfillment of a forgotten promise. And everywhere, in the sand, the sky, the waves, the light, I felt the presence of Asherah whose priestess I am. And I brought our joined hands up to my chest so that I could feel that ancient bead with Her tree on it, that ancient red carved carnelian bead hanging there under my blouse. And I thought—"It's okay, Serach. It's really okay. You can let go. Relax. You can forgive yourself your failings. You can forgive all those countless other ones theirs. And now, and now, at long last—you can finish telling your story."

The End !!!!

In the writing process, the more a story cooks, the better.

Doris Lessing

It is the responsibility of writers to listen to gossip and pass it on.
It's the way story tellers learn about life.

Grace Paley

There's the story, then there's the real story,

then there's the story of how the story came to be told.

Then there's what you leave out of the story.

Which is part of the story too.

Margaret Atwood

Afterword

Voice. Memory. Silence. History.

When I was four my grandmother took me on her lap and told me this story: "When I was exactly your age men on horseback came riding into our village to kill all the Jews. Our good Christian neighbors hid me in their coal bin. If they hadn't, I wouldn't be here, your mother wouldn't be here, and you wouldn't be here either." My grandmother's voice is in this book, as is the story behind the silence of the rabbi who trained me for my bar mitzvah, who had a row of numbers tattooed on his forearm. My mother looked away when I asked her why and said, "Terrible things happened to him," things I knew that I must never ask him about.

Our history is long and many of its chapters are painful. Others are solemn, some are delicious, some are comical, and this book contains elements of them all. I first read about Serach more than a dozen years ago in Howard Schwartz's anthology *Gabriel's Palace: Jewish Mystical Tales*. I learned that she's mentioned by name three times in the Bible and that there are stories about her in the Talmud and in folk legends like the one Schwartz collected from Persia. The rabbis of old claimed that she was one of only nine people bodily taken up into heaven, and as far as I know she's the only woman in the Talmud to tell a rabbi to his face that he's wrong, while he's teaching in the house of study—that's Johanan ben Zakkai talking about the parting of the Sea of Reeds, but describing it wrong.

A few years after I first read about Serach, I wrote an eight page, first-person narrative about her early life. When I showed the story to friends they all said, "What a great character. You should write more about her." But on my desk sat a novel that I'd been working on for more than twenty-five years, a four-generation saga of a suburban Jewish family in New York. Not to say that I wasn't interested in the subject of immortality: Over the years I've written several stories for a website called "Doorknobs and BodyPaint" about Feigelman, a Jewish vampire.

Flaubert wrote that he was Madame Bovary, I eventually finished my novel, but instead of continuing to write about an ageless Jewish man I found a long difficult story telling itself through me in the voice of an ageless Jewish woman whose name is usually spelled Serah in English—but I've chosen to spell it Serach so that you know the last sound is a guttural CH, and so that you don't confuse her name with that of her great-great-grandmother, the matriarch Sarah.

We mark the beginning of Shabbat with candles, wine, and bread, and mark the end of the Sabbath with Havdallah, my favorite Jewish ritual. I love the braided candle, the cup of water I substitute for wine, the container of fragrant spices, and the melodies which end with an invocation of Elijah the Prophet and the coming of the messiah the son of David. For several decades now a wonderful verse in honor of Miriam has been sung in feminist circles, but after learning about Serach (who I think of as our female analog to Elijah, rather than Miriam) I composed the following verse, which first appeared in the prayer book of Congregation Sha'ar Zahav in San Francisco. In addition to singing about Serach you will also find a reference to the messiah, the daughter of David—may she come soon! You can sing this verse to the same melody you use for "Eliyahu Ha'navi."

Serach Ha-Tzah-di-kah	*Serach the Righteous*
bat Ah-sher	*Daughter of Asher*
Nech-dat Zil-pah	*Zilpah's granddaughter*
Serach Serach	*Serach Serach*
Serach Ha-Chah-chah-mah	*Serach the Wise*
Bim-hey-rah v'yah-mey-nu	*Soon in our days*
Tah-avoh ey-ley-nu	*Come to us*
Eem meh-she-chah	*With the messiah*
bat Dah-veed	*David's daughter*
Eem meh-she-chah	*With the messiah*
bat Dah-veed	*David's daughter*

Books by Andrew Ramer

also from Wipf and Stock:
Torah Told Different
Revelations for a New Millennium
The Spiritual Dimensions of Healing Addictions &
Further Dimensions of Healing Addictions— *with Donna Cunningham*

and:
Queering the Text
Angel Answers
Two Flutes Playing
little pictures

with Alma Daniel and Timothy Wyllie
Ask Your Angels

Acknowledgments

ONLY IN VERY RECENT times have children been born with genetic material from more than two parents—but stories have had multiple parents since our earliest ancestors first started telling them around a crackling fire, beneath the stars. My deep gratitude to this book's many co-parents who are gone from the world and deathless in my heart—my ancestors, Alexander, Beata, Gitel, Shabbetai. My great grandmother, Dora. My grandparents, Carla, Lester, Max, Nan, Rose. My parents, Gerry, Irmgard, Jack, Merl. My aunts and uncles, Bob, Helen, Henry, Jack, Luba, Manny, Manny, Mina, Myra, Rachel. My cousins, Annice, Michael, Sue, Traci. Benjamin, always. And my teachers, Mrs. Countryman, Miss O'Brien, Mrs. Roth, Mrs. Winetsky. My friends, Donna Cunningham, Erick Faigin, Janet Fine, John Fletcher Harris, Mark Honaker, Richard Krawetz, Tony Losi, Joseph McKay, Gerard Rizza, Mary Ann Scofield, Barbara Shor, Fred Stahl, John Stowe, King Thackston, Gregory Tomestic, Raven Wolfdancer.

Among the living, my family of origin and choice, who are the tent pegs that hold me to this windy wobbly world—deep thanks to Alma, Alyson, Andréa, Andrew, Aysha, Bert, Bonnie, Carol, Cheryl, Chris, Dale, Darren, David-Michael, Dev, Don, Eileen, Eileen, Ellen, Ewen, Gary, Harvey, Heidi, Irene, Isaac, Jackie, Jasminder, Jayne, Jeremy, Jeremy, Jesse, Jim, John, Jonathan, Joy, Joy, Kate, Katherine, Kevin, Kinari, Laura, Laurie, Leo, Levi, Linda, Linda, Lolly, Lynne, Lyssa, Marc, Mark, Martha, Mary Jane, Maxine, Michael, Michael, Michele, Monica, Patanjali, Penina, Randy, Randy, Richard, Rose Anne, Rob, Ruth, Sara, Sara, Sara, Sarah, Sheri, Shoshana, Steve, Sue, Sue, Suzanne, Tamara, Wendy, Zoë. And Jill, Janice, Helen, Gary, Eva, who tend to the fabric of the tent.

Amichai Lau-Lavie for your wonderful opening blessing. Kevin Johnson for your listening eye turned toward an unfolding saga. Maurice Harris for a close reading of the text and for helping to organize its multiple limbs into a dancing singing body.

The painting on the front cover, "Threshold," was done by San Francisco artist and gallery owner Anne Marguerite Herbst.—www.anneherbst.com.

The author's picture on the back cover was taken by Oakland documentary photographer Janet Sheard—https://janetsheard.photoshelter.com/

This book was designed and typeset in Minion, created by Robert Slimbach for Adobe Systems in 1990, inspired by the elegant typefaces of the late Renaissance.

With deep thanks to everyone at Wipf and Stock who worked on this book:

Jim Tedrick	Managing Editor
Matt Wimer	Assistant Managing Editor
RaeAnne Harris	Editorial Administrative Assistant
Daniel Lanning	Typesetter
Ian Creeger	Proofer
Shannon Carter	Cover Design
Dan Crawford	Production
Neil DeBerry	Production
Joshua Sumantri	Production
Ryan McGill	Production
Dustin Minder	Production
Nathaniel Stock	Production
Trevor Stock	Production

www.ingramcontent.com/pod-product-compliance
Lightning Source LLC
Chambersburg PA
CBHW072354030726
47505CB00014B/1830